THE METEOR EXPERIMENT

Clark raced into the lab.

The room was filled with a fine, green glow...and he was feeling the effects. Immediately, he gasped in intense pain. He could barely move, barely breathe. Clark crawled to Dr. Brucker and picked her up in his arms. Then, with supreme effort, he struggled to his feet. As quickly as he could...which was not quickly at all...he lurched to the door. Sweat poured down Clark's face. Lex appeared and took Dr. Brucker, shouting, "Medic on the double!"

Relieved of his burden, Clark stumbled back against the wall.

"I'll be okay," he told Lex. "I'll be fine." But the pain and weakness stayed with him. Even after Lex made him sit in a wheelchair and got him back outside, it stayed.

What if I've been permanently injured? Clark, alarmed, wondered. *What if I've been exposed enough times that I'm not going to come back?*

OTHER BOOKS IN THE SERIES

SMALLVILLE

HAUNTINGS

NANCY HOLDER

**Superman created by
Jerry Siegel and Joe Shuster**

ASPECT®

WARNER BOOKS

An AOL Time Warner Company

WARNER BOOKS EDITION

Copyright © 2003 by DC Comics
All rights reserved under international copyright conventions. No part of this book may be reproduced in any form or by any electronic or mechanical means, including information storage and retrieval systems, without permission in writing from DC Comics, except by a reviewer who may quote brief passages in a review. Inquiries should be addressed to DC Comics, 1700 Broadway, New York, New York 10019.

Cover design by Don Puckey
Book design by L&G McRee

Warner Books, Inc.
1271 Avenue of the Americas
New York, NY 10020

Visit our Web site at
www.twbookmark.com.

Visit DC Comics on-line at keyword DCComics on America Online or at http://www.dccomics.com.

 An AOL Time Warner Company

Printed in the United States of America

First Printing: January 2003

10 9 8 7 6 5 4 3 2 1

This book is for Dal Perry . . . of course.

This is how history is made, Janice Brucker thought. She was so nervous that she could not take a deep breath.

Deep within the bowels of their Metropolis lab, Janice and her husband, George, watched eagerly, hands clammy, hearts pounding, as the particle accelerators did their work: Fame and fortune were waiting.

To all appearances nothing exciting was happening. The big accelerators were fairly quiet; the only noise came from the fans, water pipes and cryogenic equipment used to support the devices.

An array of ion implant accelerators, cyclotrons, betatrons, and electron linear accelerators all pointed toward a specialized beamstop that she and George had constructed; it was an elliptical reflector, with a small container at one of the foci. The reflector was made out of graphite and aluminum, with thin tubes of liquid helium running through it to keep the heat of the dispersed particles at acceptable levels.

The lab setup *looked* . . . interesting, but as George liked to say, it lacked flair. There were no Frankenstein-style sparks and crackling sounds, no wild stormy nights, or chichi lab coats. George, who had once thought about becoming an actor, had confessed while they were dating that the labs from some of the old monster movies had inspired him to go into nuclear physics.

"It was either the Nobel prize or the Oscar," he'd said, laughing.

He'd wanted to install a Jacob's ladder—the zizzing, zapping electrical towers in *The Bride of Frankenstein*, but

Janice had vetoed the idea; the last thing she and her husband needed was to be *thought* of as mad scientists.

What they were *doing* was mad enough.

The Bruckers were trying to create a man-made element.

That in itself was not new. Most laypeople didn't give it much thought, but after element number 92 on the periodic table of elements, everything up to 120 was man-made. Little gems like Americium-241, atomic number 95 on the table—a commercial success—which created ionized radiation used for smoke detectors, was man-made. As was Californium, atomic number 98—an excellent portable source of neutrons for activation analysis of gold or silver.

Much of what had been discovered between elements 93 and 120 was useless—of no scientific or commercial value. And it had all been discovered in a haphazard manner. One isotope was bombarded with ions and neutrons, and the scientists all watched to see what happened, like kids who'd just set off a cherry bomb.

They'd run tests, announce a discovery, then the arguments over the name would begin.

Not so Janice and George.

The element they were aiming to create was interesting in a minor way—a relatively stable, heavy element that they would sign over to LuthorCorp, where it could be used as a source of ionizing radiation for pesticide research.

But it was the process—the calculated design of a new element and the production of *exactly* that element—that was the big win. Janice had worked out a carefully theorized protocol of adding neutrons, electrons, and ions that worked like completing a Rubik's cube. The process of adjusting the atomic weight was kind of a two-step-forward, one-step-back game, through careful orchestration of a series of particle accelerators.

But once they got it right, their careers, their footsteps in the sands of time were assured.

The pair stood near a workstation in the lead-lined control area. The accelerators produced several kinds of radiation, ranging from magnetic to X rays, many of which could kill a human being if he or she were exposed to them directly. Careful scientists that they were, the two made sure to stay out of harm's way.

"Liftoff," George whispered, and she nodded.

A light fluttery feeling ran through Janice as she tapped the computer keyboard to start the final sequence. Faster than she could think, silicon circuitry switched their array of particle accelerators, blasting their crucible with a variety of charged particles.

Another display showed incident radiation from the crucible, alongside a graph of temperature. A third display showed the atomic weight of the element they were working on, carefully calculated with a computer algorithm and a series of reception plates, as passive as she could make it.

Everything was going perfectly.

George looked over at her and grinned.

"How's it feel to master nature?"

Janice's anxiety was beginning to show as she smiled tightly back.

"I'll tell you when it's finished."

He chuckled. "We've got it, honey, you and me. We always have. Atomic love, pure and simple."

She smiled back, responding to him this time. George provided the foundation on which she built her theories. He was a master tinkerer, and more important, a genius with people. It had been he who had arranged the funding from LuthorCorp, after getting a meeting with Lionel Luthor himself.

Janice had played it quiet during the interview. Something

about the billionaire had disturbed her. He'd given off a steady undercurrent of intense alpha-male energy, a riff that said, "Don't mess with me."

George had carefully maneuvered the negotiations toward his and his wife's true goal by obscuring it. He'd pressed for half the mineral rights of the new element they were designing, providing focus on the end, and not the means. He hadn't expected or even planned for them to retain any rights, and had gradually let himself be won over by Luthor's counteroffer: a higher rate of pay, and all publishing rights.

Apparently it hadn't occurred to Luthor that someone might want to keep the method instead of the product. A rare oversight, given the man's reputation for hard bargaining and shrewd investing, but there it was.

And now the product was nearly ready.

Janice checked the readouts: Only a few seconds to go.

Silently, she and George counted the seconds together, holding hands and squeezing each other's fingers as each number ticked off the digital readout.

A computerized beep announced that the program was complete, and Janice checked the incident readouts.

Atomic weight: 275. Relatively high ionizing radiation emitting, isotope stability: Good.

We did it!

They let out a cheer, and kissed, hugging each other before exiting the control room and moving closer to the crucible. They had to *see* it. They neared the new isotope and looked at the mirror they'd placed near the beamstop. The reflection within showed the isotope; a grayish white metallic that they'd *made*.

Aside from her wedding day, and the day their daughter Ginger was born, Janice could think of no more important moment in her life.

With an eager grace in his movements, George moved closer.

She took a breath. "Honey, be careful." The only danger now was from the isotope they'd created; now that the machines were off, none of their surfaces was activated. They were not emitting radiation.

He gave a her a little wave-off and grinned at her. They'd been married for sixteen years, and still the grin on that handsome chiseled face could create a brand-new universe inside her heart. God, she loved him. He was so amazing. *The two of us are so amazing.*

"Stop worrying, gorgeous. I just want to see how *heavy* it is."

George swooped toward their brand-new creation and grasped the crucible with a pair of tongs. He lifted it, making a show of seeming puzzled. "Seems kind of light to me." It was a joke, of course. Atomic weight was not the same as standard weight.

"We'll call it Janisium Sweet 16," he told her, radiant with love for her.

"After Ginger," she shot back. It was an old script, an old tease, for of course it was for her, too. Tears of joy welled, and she began to cry.

History books, she told herself again. *We did it.*

And then everything went to pieces.

The incident alarm sounded a vocal alert. "Warning; instability detected—fission/gamma in 1.2."

George looked at her in shock. Eyes huge, she stared back. *Wrong*, she thought wildly. *The computer is wrong. There should be a mild beta decay. If we have gamma rays and spontaneous fission, we'll go up—*

George looked at her. "Run."

Without hesitation, he grabbed the crucible with his bare hands and rolled to the floor in a fetal position around it.

In that moment, he had killed himself. Even if the computer was wrong, the radiation from the isotope was fatal. And if the computer was right, he had bought her a fistful of seconds at best.

All this occurred to her in a blur of thought, honed to clarity by the nightmare shaking around her; she was a scientist, she could think her way through anything, out of anything—

—*not this time*—

Shrieking, Janice dived for the protection of the control room. Fission occurred in 1.2. George had time to scream, once.

And Janice went somewhere else, physically and mentally, for a long, long time.

As the lovely woman across the table from Clark Kent smiled, a few pale lines fanned the corners of her eyes in an otherwise evenly tanned face. Her hair was loose, and she was glowing with happiness. She lifted her coffee cup to her lips and said, "This is the perfect ending to a perfect evening."

Martha Kent's adopted son smiled at her, then glanced over at his dad. It was Mother's Day, and the two Kent men had taken Martha out for dinner at the Smallville Steak House, then brought her back to the Talon for dessert and coffee. All that was left of their special celebration was the present the two of them had purchased for her, which Clark's father, Jonathan, was cradling on his lap. They had worked long and hard on what to get her for a gift. She did so much for them; what could they possibly give her in return?

"Hi. Need a top-off?" Lana Lang asked, gliding over with a coffeepot in hand. She looked wistful as she viewed the trio at the table. *Mother's Day is hard on Lana,* Clark realized. Her own mother had died in the meteor crash that had brought Clark to Earth years ago. That moment had been frozen forever, with little Lana's tear-streaked, terrorized face splashed across the cover of *Time* magazine after the meteor shower.

Now Lana lived with her aunt Nell, whom she loved very much. But Clark knew that it wasn't the same as growing up with her mother. Like Lana, Clark had always known he was adopted—Jonathan and Martha Kent had made him understand that at an early age. But unlike Lana, he had no idea who his birth parents were. Without the Kents' revelation that he had come from outer space, coupled with the proof of the rocket ship they had hidden on their property, Clark would have assumed that the meteor rocks had given him his superstrength and X-ray vision.

Lana caught his eye and gazed at him for a beat, almost as if she could read his mind. With her enormous eyes and luminescent skin, she was the most beautiful girl in Smallville. Which meant of course, that she was the girlfriend of Smallville High's star quarterback, Whitney Fordman. *Some clichés are clichés because they're always true . . .*

"Thanks. I'd love some more coffee," Martha said to Lana. "It's so good. You must have a secret."

Lana dimpled. "I do." She hesitated. "But if I told you . . ."

"It wouldn't be a secret," Martha finished for her. "You're a good businesswoman, Lana."

Lana blushed, and said, "I'll be sure to write that down on my monthly report to Lex . . . um, my business partner," she fumbled. She knew Clark's parents didn't like Lex—*Correction, my father doesn't like Lex,* Clark thought—and in her typically thoughtful way, Lana took pains not to mention his name around Jonathan Kent.

Then Lana leaned over, and murmured softly to Clark's

mom, "I put a teaspoon of cinnamon in every pot. And I keep the pot very, very clean."

"Thanks." Martha's eyes shone. It was obvious that she really liked Lana, and that made Clark very happy. His mind skipped ahead to an imagined meal at the farm, Lana by his side, his mom making cinnamon-spiced coffee for the four of them, then he snapped out of it. Most likely that kind of evening would come true for Whitney Fordman, not him.

Lana smiled again at the three and glided away. The chime on the front door tinkled, and Lana's aunt Nell came in with two other women, all wearing baby rose wrist corsages and fanning themselves with theater programs. One of them waved at Martha, who waved back.

"We've been to Metropolis. To the ballet!" the woman called across the room.

Then Lex walked in. He had taken them to the ballet, Clark realized. *For Mother's Day.* Like his and Lana's, Lex's own mother was dead.

The quartet sat at a table by a window, and Lana hurried over. Her aunt smiled at her, and they began chatting eagerly, the group picking up menus and discussing what to order.

"I think it's time we got home," Jonathan said a bit abruptly.

"Dad, the present," Clark whispered.

Jonathan Kent looked abashed. He took a small breath and nodded at his son. "Of course." He lifted the gift-wrapped box from his lap and handed it to his wife. "Happy Mother's Day, Martha."

"Happy Mother's Day, Mom," Clark added.

Martha's eyes widened with pleased surprise. Clark couldn't count the times he'd seen that expression on her face. He'd seen it, cherished it, all his life. She'd given him that same smile each time he came home from elementary

school with one of his innumerable handmade projects—a
bird feeder made out of glue-encrusted coffee stirrers, a lopsided bowl made out of clay. When he'd landed the pivotal
role of the Bean Seller in his third-grade class's production
of *Jack and the Beanstalk*, it was there.

It was a timeless, wholehearted look that said, *I love
being your mom, and I will love you forever, even when I'm
not here.*

Eagerly she opened the box. She raised a dainty silver
bracelet out of the wrappings. On it were silver charms of
gardening implements—a tiny spade, a shovel, some deli-
cate pruning shears that really opened and closed. And there
was a red-enameled rose dotted with a diamond chip—more
of a speck, really.

"We know you like practical things," Clark said before
she had a chance to speak. Jonathan nodded along. "But we
wanted to get you something, you know, not practical, just
for you—"

"It's perfect. I can't imagine a better Mother's Day present," she cut in, smiling first at her son, then at his father.
"Thank you both."

She held out her strong sun-bronzed arm for Clark to help
her put the bracelet on. Then she said, "And speaking of
practical, we should get the check, Jonathan. We've still got
to go out to Linda's to check on her animals. And there'll be
chores tomorrow morning no matter what day this is."

With a half-lifted finger, Jonathan called Lana over, who
had their bill all ready. Then Clark quickly got up and pulled
out his mother's chair, a gesture duly noted by the three
women at Lex's table, and the Kents left the restaurant.

They got into their truck and headed out toward Linda
Anderson's house. She was in Kansas City visiting her
mother for a week, and Martha had promised to look after
her five cats.

His father drove, his mom crammed in the center, and Clark rode shotgun beside the passenger door. As he gazed up at the stars, wondering which one he had come from, his parents began to speak of farm matters. Rows of corn rushed by as they bumped along past the fields. Clark was half-listening . . . *pick up the fertilizer, get another estimate on the chipper repair* . . . when suddenly a flash of white darted from the corn rows and raced toward the center of the road . . . directly into the path of their truck.

"Dad!" Clark shouted.

Jonathan gave a yell of surprise while Clark opened the door and dived out of the truck.

"Clark!" his mother cried.

Moving at superspeed, he put a hand on the bumper, slowing the vehicle, while at the same time grabbing the moving figure around the waist and hauling him out of the way. The two rolled to the side of the road. The guy was shouting and fighting against Clark, who quickly released him. As the tall, thin man scrabbled away and tried to stand up, Clark took quick inventory. He was still learning how to use his powers, and he wanted to make sure he hadn't hurt him—or himself.

"I'm out!" the guy screamed. Clark recognized him; he was Joel Beck, from school. And he was terrified.

"Hey," Clark said, holding out a steadying hand.

Joel wheeled around and faced the cornfield. Then he froze, shaking, and moved his head back and forth. "It worked! I can't believe it worked!" he shouted. "I have to tell Holly."

He sank to his knees and buried his face in his hands.

"Is he all right?" Clark's father shouted behind him.

Then Clark's parents hurried up on either side of him, Martha racing past to crouch at the side of the stricken boy.

"Are you hurt?" she asked in a firm, calm voice. "Do you need to go to a hospital?"

Joel's shoulders heaved. Then he inhaled slowly and dropped his hands from his face. He said to Martha Kent, "No. I need to go to an insane asylum." He looked at the three Kents. "I've been to hell, and now I'm back."

Through the rearview mirror, Jonathan glanced at the two boys seated in the flatbed as he pulled up to the Beck house. Joel climbed out very slowly, gesturing for Clark to stay put.

Jonathan said to Martha, "Stay here, okay?"

Then he joined Joel on the cracked, weed-strewn path that led to his front door.

The door burst open. A man stood on the porch in a pair of Dockers and a chambray shirt, looking for all the world like a college professor.

A very drunk college professor, Jonathan thought disapprovingly.

He said, "Good evening, Mr. Beck. I'm—"

"Where the hell have you been?" Joel's father bellowed. He was swaying. He reeked of alcohol.

As Joel drew closer, the man lurched forward and smacked him on the forehead.

" 'S drugs, isn't it?" he demanded. "You've been out loading up on something!" He narrowed his eyes at Jonathan. "You from juvenile authority?"

"No, sir," Jonathan said, fighting to keep his temper. "Joel's a friend of my son's. We just gave him a lift home."

Joel flashed a grateful look at Jonathan.

Beck snorted. "Kid skipped fourth grade. My *genius*. Now he's flunking out."

"Mr. Beck," Jonathan began, but Joel made a warning gesture with his hand.

"It's okay, Mr. Kent," Joel said miserably.

"It's okay? Nothing about you is okay!" Beck slurred. "Now get in here!"

As Jonathan watched angrily, the man grabbed his son's wrist, yanked him across the threshold, and slammed the door in Jonathan's face.

"You good-for-nothing loser! Don't you *ever* humiliate me like this again!" Beck bellowed through the front door.

Seething, Jonathan moved away and stomped back to his truck.

Clark was climbing out of the bed, and as they met up beside the truck, Clark said, "We can't leave him here, Dad."

Jonathan shook his head in helpless frustration.

"We have to, Clark."

Clark sighed. "No wonder he ran away."

"He'll do it again, too," Jonathan muttered. "Let's go home."

"I killed him. I killed him," Janice Brucker muttered in her sleep. "George, let me go. Let me go."

I hate this, Ginger thought, as she padded down the hall to the master bedroom. At least three nights a week, and sometimes every single night, her mother tossed and turned in her sleep, tormented by nightmares. She always wept and cried out that she had killed her husband.

What happened in the lab, Mom? Ginger wanted to ask. *How did Daddy die? Did you really have something to do with it?*

But these were questions she wouldn't ask her mother. Would never ask her mother.

"Mom," Ginger whispered, shaking her mother's shoulder. "Mom, wake up."

She watched as her mother opened her eyes and took in her surroundings. They were in their high-rise apartment in Metropolis, in the room Ginger's parents had shared before her father's death. Now Janice slept alone as the nightmare of the accident replayed in her mind over and over, nearly every night. Ginger had gotten used to waking her up. Neither had had a decent night's sleep in months.

"Thanks," Janice said wearily, distantly. She wiped her face; her fingertips came away streaked with tears. "I'm sorry."

"It's okay." It was what they always said to each other, night after night. But tonight Ginger said something new. "I think . . . Mom, I think we should move to Smallville after all. I think you should take that job." She gestured to her mom's bedroom. Janice had not changed a thing since her husband's death. His belongings were still everywhere—books, his watch on the bureau, his shoes lined up in the closet. "I think we should go through . . . through his things and try to move on . . ."

Ginger's throat caught, and she began to sob. Maybe another girl's mother would gather her stricken daughter in her arms and rock her like a baby. But Ginger's mother did not. She had always been a little standoffish, but since Ginger's father's death, she had grown more so. And it was killing Ginger, who so needed comfort, and contact, and hope . . .

"All right," Janice said halfheartedly. "It's all right, Ginger. Everything is going to be all right."

No, it's not, Ginger thought brokenly. *It's never going to be all right again.*

But aloud, to her mother, she said, "I know."

And as with many other nights in the Brucker apartment, the pain and the night seemed to drag on forever.

Back in Smallville, two figures, a boy and a girl, stood at the edge of the cornfield across the street from the old Welles place. The boy held open their Book of Spells. They chanted, and burned candles, and a piece of forever wobbled and glowed. The large meteor nearby kept it stable, contained and perpetuated it. And inside that piece of forever, a little boy screamed . . . and screamed . . .

. . . screamed loudly enough to wake the dead. . . .

. . . and the girl whispered to the boy, "I feel it. It's getting stronger."

CHAPTER ONE

By the time the Kents got home, Clark was too overloaded to think about history papers—and wished he'd started work on it after school on Friday, the way his mom had suggested—and he barely slept all night.

School the next day was pretty much a disaster. He looked for Joel, who was absent, and Chloe and Peter were on a field trip to some kind of political rally. The few times Clark spotted Lana, she was with Whitney, and they were lost in each other's eyes.

Then . . . no history paper. His teacher, Mr. Cox was pissed off at him for it, gave him one more day "to earn a B at best," and told him that for each day he was late, he would knock him down one letter grade.

After the last bell, Clark decided to cut through the cornfields rather than take the bus, maybe find out what had scared Joel so badly . . . and then he heard someone calling him. He was walking past the Talon's plate-glass windows, trying as casually as he could to see if Lana had arrived to take over the afternoon shift, when he heard his name.

"Hey, Clark."

Lex stood in front of one of his many Porsches, this one a dark graphite that made Clark think of charcoal.

Lex was the penultimate poor little rich guy—lots of toys, no love. His father hadn't endeared himself to the people of Smallville when he'd built the fertilizer plant in the mideighties, buying up farm after farm. The sins of the father had been attributed to the son when Lex had been sent to run the plant about a year ago.

True, Lex *was* kind of secretive—whether it was a natural

product of having been raised by Lionel Luthor, or the result of years of management training, Clark didn't know.

But he could hardly point fingers at Lex for keeping secrets when he had so many himself. What was the saying? "When you point at someone else, three of your fingers are still pointing at you."

Clark hadn't realized that he would gain a friend when he saved Lex from drowning the previous year. At first he'd thought that Lex had just been feeling guilty, trying to make up for his driving too fast down Carlin Road before crashing through the railings on the Old Mill Bridge. To be sure, it had been a freak accident: His car's tires were ripped out by barbed wire. But the speeding hadn't helped.

After a while, though, Clark had realized that Lex actually liked hanging out with him. There was something else there, intangible—almost a sense of balance when they were together. Lex envied Clark's close family ties, and frankly, the Kents could use some of the gobs of money Lex threw away on wicked-slick cars, clothes, and fencing lessons. Despite their hard work, it was tough to make a financial go of farm life these days.

Now, on the street, Lex was wearing a white silk shirt and a light gray coat that looked like they'd been pressed only moments ago, immaculate and refined, as always, the epitome of fashion. His bald head gleamed in the Smallville afternoon sun.

"Got a minute?" Lex asked.

History paper, Clark reminded himself. *Chores*.

I've got some time. After all, I've got superspeed. It's not every farm boy who can feed the chickens, buck the hay, and water the cows in just a few seconds.

He wondered not for the first time what it would be like to be an ordinary teenager on a farm. The chores he did in a few minutes would be stretched out over hours, the labor would be backbreaking, and he'd probably be far too tired to search the skies with a telescope after it got dark.

There were certainly advantages to having his gifts.

"Sure, what's up?" he asked his friend.

Clark glanced casually at the Talon's front door, trying one last time to see if he could spot Lana inside. Lex shook his head, smiling.

"She's not there, Clark. Nell told me she was staying late at school to work on some project for the *Torch*."

Clark frowned, then looked at Lex, his eyebrows raised. "Taking up mind reading, Lex?"

The younger Luthor smiled, this one making its way to his eyes. "No, just reading my friends." He paused. "But it would be a good skill to have sometimes at board meetings—particularly with my dad." A ghost of a frown, the tiniest crease in his forehead, flashed across Lex's face like frost on a hot day.

Clark kept smiling, keeping his thoughts to himself. He was definitely glad he had such a good relationship with his dad. Then he thought about Joel Beck. He was about to tell Lex about the weirdness of last night, when Lex spoke again.

"I've got an appointment in a few minutes with a new employee. She's just moved into Smallville with her daughter, and she's setting up at a house out toward your place. It's the old Welles house. Did you know it?"

Clark nodded. "Sure."

The house was a huge old thing, as big as a barn. He'd gone by there a few times on hikes, and when he and Pete had been ten, they'd tried to sneak inside. Pete had said the house was haunted.

"You want to come along?" Lex paused, letting the offer sink in, then set the hook. "I'll let you drive."

Chores, he reminded himself. *Homework.*

Still, the thought of trying out Lex's latest car was attractive. He gave the car a once-over, remembering the truck Lex had tried to give him for saving his life, which Jonathan had made Clark return.

Without another word, Lex flipped the keys toward Clark, his toss a little fast and his aim off. The keys sailed through the air, just outside Clark's reach.

So he compensated. When he focused, things around him seemed to move slower. The keys arced in the sunlight, glittering, spinning, end over end. He'd heard that many people could make a perceptual shift—but with his abilities, he could see things in slow motion and still move at full speed.

It was an effort to make it look normal speed, but he reached past the keys, turning his torso for extra reach, stretching his shoulder out, catching them with his fingers just as they were passing.

Lex raised his brows. "Nice catch. I'm still surprised you didn't suit up again." Clark had had a brief career on the football team, but with his strength, team sports had always been a tricky—if not downright dangerous—proposition.

There were disadvantages to having his abilities, too.

The two made their way over to Lex's car, a Porsche, but not one Clark had seen before. Lex had more cars than some people had dishes or silverware. From up close, the exterior of the car looked Japanese, low and windswept. The contours were far more streamlined than some of Lex's other cars. The headlights didn't jut out, but were enclosed in plastic, attached turn signal indicators making the round lights, which resembled eyes, appear as if tears were coming out of them. Even sitting there next to the curb, the car looked like a study in extreme curve-hugging motion. The dark paint had metallic flecks in it, and the seats were a deep gray leather.

Nice.

As they got into the car, Clark sliding behind the wheel, Lex mentioned a few of the features.

"It's supposed to hit close to 190 miles an hour." He grinned at Clark. "But with my driving record, I haven't taken it above 150."

Clark shook his head, both in amazement at the vehicle and in mild exasperation at the chances his friend took with his life.

"It's got a six-speed, so watch the shift pattern."

Clark nodded. He took a quick breath and turned the key in the ignition; the engine caught, and the deep throaty purr had not a single hint of disharmony in it. It sounded like the platonic ideal of a sports car, a contented cheetah.

Wow.

Carefully, Clark pulled out from in front of the Talon. Lex chuckled.

"Speed limit's twenty-five, Clark. You're only doing fifteen."

Clark felt himself turn red as he trundled down Maple Street, heading for Carlin Road. Once he was out of the city he'd push it a little harder.

He was almost dazzled enough not to ask about the people they were going to meet, or why Lex wanted him to come along, but he had enough of his dad in him that he could look beyond the glitter. Not that driving Lex's car had a downside. He appreciated Lex's offer, but as good friends as they were, the younger Luthor rarely did anything nice without making sure there was something in it for himself.

"So why'd you want me to come along, Lex?"

Clark enjoyed the view from the cockpit—certainly in a car like this it wouldn't be called anything less—as he waited for Lex to answer. The wide-open sky of Kansas was a deep blue today, with white fluffy clouds scattered across it like cotton balls. The fields of winter wheat were still

green, and the wind stirred their stalks, sending ripples as far
as the eye could see, the effect like watching water swirl.

Eyes on the road.

Clark focused his attention on driving. It wouldn't do to
have an accident with Lex in the car. Clark knew *he*
wouldn't be hurt, but it might be hard to explain. Lex already had enough questions from the day he'd had *his* accident. The widely spaced fence posts along Carlin Road
flashed by, making the normally open lane seem like it was
bordered by a picket fence.

Clark had never been able to clock himself at full speed
when he was using his powers, but if the speedometer was
any indication, he could easily move much faster than the
seventy he was approaching.

Cool.

Lex looked a little hurt when Clark glanced over at him,
waiting for the answer to his question.

"What's the matter, Clark? Can't I just invite you out for
a ride?"

So Lex didn't want to say. No problem. He'd find out
soon enough.

"Sure, Lex. Whatever."

The younger Luthor sighed, conceding the point.

"Let's just say that the family we're going to see has had
some hard times. I thought a friendly face might make them
feel welcome. And if there's anything you are Clark, it's
friendly."

Clark grinned. Up ahead was the turnoff toward the
Welles place. They'd be there soon.

I think I blew it. Big-time.

Ginger Brucker stared out at the green fields surrounding
the huge house that they were going to move into. It was
creepy. She kept expecting someone named Jebediah or

something to come walking out of the green rows carrying a scythe—*Children of the Corn* in the extreme.

Of course since the plants—they looked a little like wheat, only *green*—were only about two feet high, it wouldn't be a very large man.

She giggled despite everything.

Babies of the Wheat.

It had a certain ring to it. Probably nothing Stephen King would be writing anytime soon, but if he came out here and took a look, he'd at least feel the inspiration.

Mom was still talking to the real-estate lady, a nice-looking middle-aged woman named Robin.

Would the house even have cable? She didn't think she could survive without cable.

The lady didn't know it yet, but Mom was already sold. Ginger knew her mother's moods and moves. When she started tapping her chin with her finger like that, it meant her mind was made up and she was just working out the details.

Ginger shuddered. *This place is gross. And these farm kids . . . I thought Smallville would be a new start, not a dead end . . . .*

Oh, Daddy, if you hadn't died . . . if only it could all be the way it was before . . .

She sniffed a bit, biting back a sob. It didn't help her throat any; it was already feeling clogged. Where was that tissue? She rummaged through her bag until she found it, and blew her nose.

Memories washed over her as she looked out over the field. She'd been at school when she'd gotten the news about her father. It had been a great day; she'd gotten an "A" on her portrait project, and Mrs. High, the art teacher, had complimented her on her latest series of charcoal sketches.

Then Mr. Dellafaire, the vice principal, had come to the classroom and leaned in, calling Mrs. High over. Oblivious,

Ginger had stood there, smiling, enjoying her great grade, her praise in front of the other students.

And her dad was already dead by then. Later on, even now, it seemed so *wrong* to have been enjoying that moment. She should have *known*.

Mrs. High had come back with a look on her face—Ginger hadn't ever seen a look like that on anyone before, and she'd studied dozens of faces in her art classes. It had been sort of resigned—sad, and sort of *weary*.

Of course now Ginger saw that look every day. Anytime she looked in the mirror.

Ginger had followed Mr. Dellafaire to the principal's office. Mrs. Regan had handed her the phone. Her mother was on the other end.

Mom had started off in business mode, crisp and precise.

"Ginger? I have something to tell you."

And then, the scariest part of all: Her mother had completely crumbled.

"It's your father. Oh, my God, there was an accident, oh, what are we going to do? He's . . . he's gone. Oh, Ginger . . . I did it . . ."

Ginger vagued out for a few moments, trying to understand what was happening. Her mother couldn't be crying. Mom never cried. Daddy was the emotional one. Hey, he still cried during *Bambi*.

So if Mom was crying . . . if Mom was falling apart . . .

My father is dead.

Hearing her mother cry had made it all true. Something horrible had happened; her life as she'd known it was over.

And now she was *here,* standing out in front of a crummy-looking farmhouse, waiting for her mom to close the deal with the realtor. Exile to a strange land, all in the name of "starting over," and she, Ginger, was the one who had suggested it.

Now Ginger saw how foolish that was. She and her mom should be near their friends, near all the old, familiar places, where Daddy would still be with them, in a way . . .

He wouldn't have brought her out here.

And as she thought it, it was as though a little part of her dad spoke to her, piping up in the back of her mind.

Come on, spice girl, she could hear him saying. *It'll be fine. Sometimes you've got to take the lemons life gives you and squish the heck out of 'em. You say it'll make lemonade? Really? Bonus!*

She smiled at the thought, the memory of his endearing corny optimism so crystal clear in her mind, and dabbed at her eyes with the tissue she'd found. She walked back toward her mom and the real-estate lady.

He's always with me, she thought hopefully. *As long as I remember him, keep him alive in my mind . . .*

She felt better. Maybe the real-estate lady had a daughter, someone who might know what there was to *do* in this town.

As she neared the two older women, she heard the sound of a car in the distance. No ordinary car, either. The engine had that kind of throaty growl that screamed sports car.

Ginger looked out toward the road. A dark, low-slung blur swooped along the country road, streamlined to the max.

Well, well, maybe it's not so boring out here in Smallville after all.

The car came straight on for them, slowing as it neared, the driver taking care not to cause a dust cloud as he pulled off the road and came to a stop. Ginger composed a sketch in her head—bright sunny day, light flaring on the metallic gray paint of the car, dark-haired guy driving within.

The doors opened, and out stepped two young men. One was older, probably in his early twenties, although it was hard to tell, because he had no hair. He was well dressed, and had attractive enough features, although he had a wariness to his smile that detracted from the overall picture.

The other guy . . . he looked like he was about her age, and the word *hottie* came straight to mind. He had rich black hair, under which were high cheekbones and yowser green eyes. Or were they blue? It was hard to tell in this light. Without thinking, Ginger stepped closer to look.

The face continued its beauty as her eyes moved down it. A strong but not overbearing nose, and rich-looking lips rose over a straight jaw and firm-looking body.

If this is how they grow them out in Smallville . . .

The bald one walked straight over to her mother with his hand extended.

"What do you think?"

"It's nice, Mr. Luthor," Mom replied.

It broke the spell.

Lex Luthor? Here? Her mom had said she was going to be working for him, but the idea of meeting a billionaire's son was kind of intimidating. She was glad she'd wiped her nose.

"Ginger?" her mother said. "This is my new employer."

Ginger came forward and shook Lex's hand as her mother introduced them.

Mr. Luthor said, "And this is Clark Kent. He lives on a farm nearby, and wanted to come out and welcome you to the neighborhood."

Clark—his name was Clark!— looked over at Lex, catching the man's eye. Some male thing passed between them, then Clark was looking at her.

"Hi," he said, shaking her hand, a friendly and guileless look on his face.

"Hello," she replied, trying not to stare.

"I wanted to talk to your mom about a few business things," Mr. Luthor told Ginger. "Would you mind if Clark showed you around?" Before she could reply, Mr. Luthor said, "That okay with you, Clark?"

Clark nodded. "Sure, Lex." He paused, then added with some emphasis, "Shall I take the car?"

The younger Luthor leaned over to her mom. "He drives like a Boy Scout, don't worry. I practically fell asleep on the way out here."

Clark flushed a little, and Ginger was fascinated to note the play of color on his skin. *Maybe he'll let me paint him*, she thought, then realized she was getting way, way ahead of herself here. *He's probably got a girlfriend.*

They headed for the car, leaving her mom and Lex to talk business.

Smallville was looking up.

Janice Brucker watched her daughter get into the car with the young man. Clark. That was it.

He certainly seemed harmless enough. Janice had spent enough time gauging men to be able to tell the difference between dangerous and defanged. And *fang-free*. Clark looked like what Lex had said: A Boy Scout. That meant careful. That meant good driver.

She could almost hear her husband chuckling, teasing her about running her life by if-then statements.

God, she missed him.

Waves of guilt threatened to overwhelm her.

If only I had it to do over. The accident was all my fault.

When Lex Luthor had called and offered her a chance to work at his fertilizer facility in Smallville, she'd jumped at it. LuthorCorp had funded their Metropolis lab, and after the investigation into the accident—no conclusions about fault drawn, and there had been some serious financial compensation for her anyway—she'd been sure she'd never hear from them again. Most companies their size stayed as far away as possible from anyone associated with destroyed labs and dead scientists. And she and George had kept their private research just that . . . very private. No one else knew what they had nearly achieved.

Tired and grief-stricken, she had just wanted to quit.

She mourned for six months, then she got restless. Her accountant warned her to put the rest of the accident settlement away, or she would end up giving it to the government in taxes. Ginger had a great college savings plan in place now, enough to go on to graduate school once she had her bachelor's. And it had been Ginger who seemed most interested in moving to Smallville, although now, looking around, Janice wondered why. It was a hick town. Nice, but definitely not the kind of place she would have thought Ginger would want to live.

"Okay," Lex said, turning to her. Privately she thought of him as Lex. She was old enough to be his mother—*okay, if I had had him really young*.

The woman nodded, and Lex gestured for Janice to accompany him into the house.

Robin said, "I'll go back to the office now." She smiled at Janice. "Please let me know . . ."

"We'll take it," Janice said, and she realized that until that very moment, she hadn't really made the decision to move here.

"Wonderful" The woman broke into a pleased smile. "I'll get all the documents in order. I'll give you a call." She smiled at Lex. "Thanks."

He only smiled. The woman got into her Toyota Camry, a cloud of dust following her exit.

Lex stood beside Janice for a moment, watching the Camry. Then he turned to her. "So far so good?" he asked in a friendly way.

"Yes," she said.

They were only going to be renting for a while until she could find a better—or at least more modern—place, but it would do for now. It had come furnished, which had been the deal maker. In addition, he had offered to continue to pay on her Metropolis apartment while she sorted out her life. She didn't have time to move everything immediately. At least, that's what she told herself. The truth was, she couldn't deal with it. After almost a year, she still hadn't gone through George's things.

They walked through the large front hallway, floorboards creaking, footsteps echoing. The house looked like something that could have been used in the making of *The Addams Family*, only much less dusty.

She considered Lionel Luthor's son as they walked. Having now worked for Luthor senior, she had been intrigued that his son had been the one to hire her. She assured herself that he had no clue about her research, but of course she had her suspicions. Besides that, he had a certain reputation that she'd ignored when she took his offer. No one would say anything bad about him, but the word was out among her peers that he went after unorthodox results, in unorthodox ways. She'd pressed a few of her colleagues on the matter, and the most she'd gotten anyone to say was that Lex took "shortcuts" to get results. But not in safety, not in personnel. No one would say what these shortcuts were.

If she really was going to work on fertilizers, such comments weren't worrying. But if Lex was going to offer her more challenging work—if he knew that she and George had been on the brink of a history-making accomplishment—they might be.

They reached what must have been a sitting room. There was a huge sofa covered by a white sheet. Janice pulled the sheet off, and they sat down.

"Thanks for taking the time to speak with me, Dr.

Brucker. I really appreciate it." There was nothing wrong with his words, they were smooth, courteous. But underneath, she sensed a strong desire to get . . . what?

"Do you know much about Smallville?"

"Please, Lex, just call me Janice. I feel like I'm your professor every time you say 'Dr. Brucker.' "

Lex smiled, and waited, his question asked, but not yet answered. Again she could feel the impatience beneath his calm manner.

"Meteors," she said leadingly, and sensed immediately that she'd hit the mark.

Lex nodded. "Clearly, you've read up."

"I'm a scientist," she replied.

Lex continued. "Thirteen years ago, Smallville was hit by a series of meteors. Part of the town was destroyed. There were two deaths."

"Yes."

Lex reached into his coat pocket and pulled out a small box. Within was a crystal with a slight green tinge so vivid it appeared to be glowing.

"This is one of the pieces of meteor rock that touched down that day. I've been studying the effects of the rocks on people since the meteors hit." He gave her a look. "Because there *are* effects. A lot of them."

She was interested. "But you would only have been . . ."

"Nine, actually." He gave her a little shrug. "And I started studying myself first." He touched his bald head. "I used to have more red hair than Carrot Top. And I'm seldom, if ever, sick."

"The meteor fragments . . ."

"Radiation," he replied. At her instantaneous pulling away, he added, "In most cases it takes prolonged exposure for anything to happen."

The two were silent for a moment, he as if out of respect for the dead.

"You could do a lot of good," he said.

She swallowed. "How?"

"I want you to find a way to artificially re-create the radiation given off by the meteors." He cocked his head. "It's close to what you were trying to do for my father."

Aha!

She took a breath, wondering how much he really knew. "So the fertilizer research, it's . . ."

"A cover." He said the words as if there was absolutely nothing wrong with it. "You'd be in the facility's research lab. It's just outside the main building. Your salary would be doubled, of course, and I would pay the increase out of pocket."

No way to trace it.

"Your husband died a horrible death," he conceded, "but it was doing something he believed in. That makes it a little better, doesn't it?" He stared hard at her, as if willing her to come along with him on a journey. "He wouldn't want you to give up your dreams, Janice. The dreams you shared together. That's what science is all about. Discovery."

Saying nothing, the tears welling, she inclined her head. *George would know what to do,* she thought, *but I don't. I'm awash here.*

"Ask for R&D when you get to the plant tomorrow," he told her. "They'll escort you to your 'real' lab. I'll leave word that it's all right."

The two of them stood and shook hands, closing the deal. *Did I just sell my soul?* she wondered.

They strolled toward the front of the house. As if on cue, Janice could hear the sound of Lex's car in the distance.

"Sounds like Clark is back. Great timing."

He turned to face her, smiling again.

"Welcome to Smallville, Janice, and welcome to the team."

Janice smiled uncertainly back at Lex, and they left the house together.

Behind them, in the house, the door to the grandfather clock that stood in the front hallway opened, and both clock weights—the one for chimes, and the one for the escapement—wound upward, rising to their top positions. The pendulum in the clock, set with a large golden medallion, moved to the left, and started its swing arc, the escapement of the mechanism clicking and clacking.

Tick-tock-tick-tock.

The face of the clock opened and the hands wound round to set the time. As they crossed the half hour and the hour marks, chimes pealed out over the empty house.

The clock had sat in the farmhouse for decades. Seeing it when she inspected the property, Robin the realtor had thought it lent a homey touch and had had it cleaned and oiled. She had no idea that ghostly hands had wound it every day, faithfully, for sixty years.

The time was set, and the house waited for its new residents to return home, the last echoes of the ringing chimes fading away in the growing darkness.

In the fields, the wheat rustled.

CHAPTER TWO

Ginger walked the halls of Smallville High, the first-day-at-school feeling in her stomach making her queasy. The place was fairly modern for such a small town. She'd expected old woodwork and aging photos of farm kids gone by. Instead she'd found a model school, halls lined with lockers, everything well kept up and maintained, the floors gleaming with institutional freshness. The only odd thing was the number of posters promoting sporting events. "Go Crows!" "The Crows will Fly on Saturday!" and "See the Crows Devour the Griffins on Saturday!" were only a few of the ones she saw as she walked from the bathroom to the water fountain.

Either there was a lot of spirit at the school, or there really was nothing else to do in this town.

All the usual questions ran through her head: Would she fit in? Would she make a good first impression? Would she be *liked*?

She'd been the new girl a couple of times before, but only at the beginning of the school year. Joining near the very end made it worse, putting a spotlight on her, making people wonder *why*. What was *her* story?

And that was something she didn't want to tell anyone.

She'd had to discuss it with Principal Kwan. He'd gone over her transcripts, nodded sympathetically about her situation, and proceeded to enroll her in a number of classes.

There had been both good and bad surprises during the transcript conversion process. All of the art classes had made it. There was only one painting course offered, so she'd taken it. There were more languages offered, which was a surprise: Her old high school, Northridge, a triple-A school where she'd been one of five hundred students in her class, only offered French, German, and Spanish. Here, where she was one of maybe two hundred, they offered French, German, Spanish, Latin, and—of all things—Greek. She'd opted to continue her French, in case she ever made it to Paris to see the big art museums as she'd once planned, but next year she might consider Latin.

The biggest bummer had been the keyboarding class. Here it was still called typing, and they didn't accept a half-year course as a transfer. If she wanted the credit, she'd have to finish the year.

It was stupid, but she needed the credit, so she'd taken it.

It was almost time for first bell. *Showtime.*

Nervously she made her way back to her locker to see if she'd remembered the combination: 36 then right to 42, then left to 16 . . .

She lifted up on the handle, but it didn't move.

Darn it! I know that's the right combination!

"If you hit it, it'll go. Here, I'll show you."

Ginger looked up and saw that the speaker was a girl about her own age, with long dark hair and a high forehead. Her mouth was wide and expressive, and it looked like she smiled a lot from the dimples on each cheek. Her lips were full, and tastefully done in a light, warm lipstick.

Apparently Smallville was full of beautiful people.

As she did with most girls her own age, Ginger compared herself to the competition. Unaware, the girl took the heel of her hand and rapped it sharply against the metal of the locker, just above the lock mechanism. She tugged it, and the bolt popped loose without any further struggle.

"I had this locker last year," the girl said warmly. "I'm Lana Lang."

"Ginger Brucker. Nice to meet you."

It took a few seconds for the name to register, and then

she had it. She'd done some web research on Smallville before they'd left Metropolis. *She watched both of her parents die that day, the only people who died in the meteor shower.*

This couldn't be a coincidence.

Did Kwan sic her on me?

"Thanks," she said tightly, turning to look in her locker.

But Lana didn't leave.

"I'm sorry—did I say something wrong?"

Ginger looked back at her and saw that she really seemed surprised.

"Principal Kwan didn't send you over to talk to me?"

Lana shook her head, "Should he?" Her voice was musical and light.

Ginger flushed. The last thing she needed to do was insult people with her insecurities.

"No. I'm the one who should be sorry. I jumped to the wrong conclusion." She sighed, realizing that now she had to go into it, talk about it, bring it out in the open, when she could have stayed under the radar about it at this new school if she'd just kept her mouth shut. "My mom and I just moved here from Metropolis—my dad, he uh—"

She couldn't say it.

"My dad was in an . . ."

She tried to go on, but she couldn't. Her throat closed up, and the tears tried to come.

But Lana Lang got it.

"You've read the news stories about me," the other girl said, "and the meteor shower."

Ginger nodded, grateful not to be talking.

"You thought because *my* parents had died, and—*your* dad had—that Kwan had asked me to talk to you?"

The artist nodded, miserable. She stared into the back of her locker; someone had scratched it at some point, the mark going from the upper left of the shelf area toward the lower right. She stared at the scratch, wishing she could climb inside the locker and shut the door behind her.

"Hey Ginger, it's okay," Lana said softly. "I still get times when I can't stop thinking about it, and it was thirteen years ago for me."

Lana paused for a moment.

"Sometimes I feel guilty, like when I'm having a good time."

Ginger nodded. Exactly how she felt sometimes.

"And sometimes I get worried that . . . that I'll *forget*."

Ginger turned back to face Lana looking right at her. She saw it then, the expression she'd seen on Mrs. High, the weariness, the sadness. The fear.

And she knew that Lana could see it on her.

"But I don't. Forget. I try really hard not to. Because I don't have that many memories of them to start with . . ."

"You were so young," Ginger said.

They had a moment then, the two of them, and Ginger could almost feel the ghosts of their three dead parents around her.

Then, spell broken, the bell rang. As they began to move off, Ginger heard footfalls behind her and turned to look. Lana, facing her, had already seen who it was—and she was glowing.

"Hey, Clark, come meet Ginger," she urged.

It was car boy, dashing toward them, a little disheveled and out of breath. Ginger felt a little thrill run up her, and lit up with a much brighter smile than she'd been capable of a few minutes ago. There he was, still looking as innocent as a deer.

"Late as usual," Lana teased him. "Ginger, Clark is—"

"We met yesterday," Ginger said. She heard the possessiveness in her own voice, and she was embarrassed by it.

"Hi. Again," Clark said to her. Then he added, "Her

mom's working for Lex," as if they would explain how they knew each other.

Ginger thought she registered some shock on Lana's part. *Oh-oh, is she his girlfriend?*

Then another guy came walking up, a blond in a letter jacket, and he slid his arm around Lana. Clark slowed his step, allowing Lana and the other guy to move slightly ahead of him in the crowd. His eyes were still on Lana, though, and his sweet smile faded. Ginger understood his body language—triangle city, and Clark was the pointy top—not the boyfriend. Hence, fair game.

At least, by Metropolis rules.

And those are my rules, for now.

Clark looked at Whitney Fordman and Lana, wishing he was somewhere else. It wasn't *fair*. Whitney got to be himself, to push as hard as he wanted to, to go after what he wanted without having to hold back.

Clark, on the other hand, had to keep it all in, lest he risk hurting someone with his abilities. So he toed the line, kept his talents hidden, and sat back and watched Lana Lang, the girl he'd wanted his entire life, get charmed and dazzled and impressed by Whitney Fordman, captain of the football team.

Not fair at all.

Fare's what you pay the bus driver, son.

His dad had said that to him so often that when he remembered the phrase it was always in the elder Kent's voice.

Trying to look cool, unfazed, unaching, he rested his gaze anywhere else . . . which meant the new girl, Ginger. She smiled brightly at him, and he felt strangely comforted.

Whitney looked at Ginger, too, and Lana spoke up.

"Ginger, this is Whitney Fordman. My boyfriend." To Whitney, she added, "This is Ginger's first day."

"I'm from Metropolis," Ginger offered.

"What'd you do wrong?" Whitney asked, and everyone chuckled grimly.

"Her mom works for Lex," Clark offered, and the others looked politely interested.

"Lots of parents do," Whitney said. "Well, I've got to go." He gave Lana a quick kiss before disappearing down the hall.

Clark shot a look toward the nearest classroom, using his X-ray vision to see the clock. As usual, he had pushed it getting to school, missing the bus and then racing through the fields to beat the tardy bell. It was a small miracle that he had actually arrived on time.

"Clark, Lana! And who's this?"

It was Pete, charming as usual. Clark did the introductions.

"Ginger Brucker, this is Pete Ross. Pete, Ginger."

"Hey," Pete said, smiling appreciatively. Ginger looked flattered. "Lana," he added, "I've got something I want to ask you—"

But before he could, Chloe showed up.

"I see an impromptu meeting of the *Torch* has convened in the hallway," she announced. "Which is good, because I have a great story."

Pete nodded. Then he said, "Chloe, this is Ginger. She's new."

"Hi." Chloe's grin was warm and genuine. "You'll hate it here." To the others, she added, "I have stuff to tell you at lunch." She waggled her brows. "Stay tuned."

"Chloe is the editor of the school paper," Lana said to Ginger.

"Yeah, she's always looking for a great story," Pete

added. "Which means we've got the inside track on all the weirdness that is Smallville."

"Do you think you might let me interview you?" Chloe asked Ginger. She laughed. "Not that I think you're weird. But I do think it would be enlightening to share an outsider's view of Smallville with our readers."

Ginger caught Clark's eye and raised an eyebrow.

Yes?

Clark shook his head and made a face.

No.

The new girl giggled, and Chloe looked around.

"Interfering with the press, Clark?"

This time Lana and Pete laughed.

"What's your first class?" Chloe asked Ginger.

"Portraiture," Ginger replied. She fumbled for the print-out of her schedule that Principal Kwan had given her.

Chloe took it from her. "Room 210." She pointed to a door a little way up the corridor. "That's your stop."

"Oh. Thanks." Ginger smiled shyly at her.

"Cafeteria," Chloe said warmly. "Lunch. Juicy Smallville weirdness."

"Okay," Ginger said, trying not to sound pathetically grateful. Then she joined the crush of students hurrying into their classrooms before the tardy bell rang.

"Wow, she's a hottie," she heard Pete say.

She flushed, grinning from ear to ear.

I wonder if Clark agrees with him?

Lunch.

Since Lana had been working at the Talon, she looked at things differently. Preparing the business plan she'd used to sell Lex on the idea of renovating the old theater had given her a better understanding of the hard realities of hangouts.

Take the cafeteria. It was jammed full of students, a

guaranteed market, some of whom had probably skipped breakfast and might be pretty darn hungry by now. But very few of them were lining up to purchase the day's special, which was creamed chicken, rice, and canned green beans. Most of them would probably buy nachos or just get something from a vending machine.

They really need to do something about the food, she thought. *Sure, it's hard to cook for this many people, but I've found some great websites with terrific recipes for institutions. We could have things like stir-fry, maybe even a burger bar.*

She briefly considered making a suggestion to Principal Kwan, but vetoed the idea before it even had a chance to get scheduled.

I just don't have the time. With the Talon, Whitney, and her schoolwork, free time was very dear indeed. Which was why she gave Whitney a lot of slack about his own overloaded life. He spent time with her when he could. Let others judge; she and her boyfriend had *lives*.

And maybe I'm just a little bit too defensive about that, she thought, stealing a glance at Clark.

"So do you think you might be interested in working on the *Torch*?" Chloe asked Ginger, as everyone took a seat.

"Maybe," said Ginger. "Do you ever need illustrations?" Shyly, she added, "I'm an artist—I don't mess with writing much. Back home . . . I mean, in Metropolis, I illustrated the school paper."

Pete chimed in, "Well, they say a picture is worth a thousand words." He turned to Lana as if all that was a done thing and his need for her attention was greater. "Anyway, Lana. You know I'm working part-time for the Hiram Welles campaign?"

Chloe frowned impatiently. "Listen, you guys. I have dish! Joel Beck saw a ghost in the cornfield."

Lana was startled. She knew Joel a little. "What?"

"Wait, wait," Pete insisted. "I have a mission. Then we can move back into bizarro territory. Lana, the governor wants to have a special evening for his local supporters. Kind of a reunion thing—he hasn't been back to Smallville in a long time." He said to Ginger, "Governor Welles grew up here. He's running for reelection." To Lana, he added, "He used to go to the Talon back when it was a movie theater."

"And Joel is freaking *out*," Chloe continued doggedly. "He's stayed home from school all week."

"Whoa, and this is Tuesday," Pete drawled.

"How'd you hear about Joel?" Clark asked. Somehow he felt bad for Joel, as if this were a matter that should stay private.

"Talon," Pete insisted, vying for Lana's attention. "Governor. Reelection. Many cups of coffee. Good publicity. Money. Name of establishment in the paper."

Lana considered. "Sounds like a great idea. I'll check with Nell, see what she thinks."

"Don't you think you'd better check with Lex first?" That was from Chloe, and she sounded a little sharp.

"What do you mean?" Lana asked, puzzled.

"Well, now that he owns the Talon, he might want a say in whose politics go on display there."

Thanks, Chloe. There's a reminder I didn't really want. It was hard not to think of the Talon as hers—her aunt had owned it since Lana was a baby, and she'd grown up with it as part of her background. The idea that she'd have to ask anyone about it except Nell was sort of disturbing.

But that's business, I guess.

"I guess I will," she said.

Then Chloe looked a little abashed. She said, "I'm sorry, Lana. That was a cheap shot."

Lana shifted her attention to Clark and the new girl, who was explaining to Ginger how Lex tended to rile people up.

"I'll say he does. His dad wiped out my family's corn factory," said Pete.

"Corn factory?" Ginger echoed. "Hybridized?"

Pete laughed and explained. "Sorry, I should have said *creamed* corn factory. Smallville used to be the creamed corn capital of the world—before the meteors, I mean."

"So, Pete," asked Ginger, catching up, "I've always wanted to know—does creamed corn *really* have cream in it?"

"Depends on the recipe," said Clark. "My mom's does."

"My dad tried to get Martha Kent's recipe for years to improve our canning process," Pete said. "But she insisted it was a family secret, and wanted to keep it that way." He shook his head. "Maybe if we'd gotten it, Lionel Luthor wouldn't have been able to buy us out . . ."

Clark whacked him on the shoulder, nearly knocking him off his chair. "Come on, Pete."

Lana watched Clark as he joked with Pete. She liked to be around him. She liked it when he was *here*, interacting. The problem was, he was hardly ever really *here* with them. He always seemed to be hurrying off somewhere, or distracted by some deep *Clark* thought.

He had helped her out so much this year, helped all of them out. If only he'd focus, stand up, and just *be* himself—

Then what, Lana?

She didn't know.

Then a tall, redheaded boy approached the table and said, "Chloe? The scanner's not working."

Chloe rolled her eyes. "Argh. I've been after Kwan to buy the *Torch* a new scanner. So far, he says it's a luxury. Of course, the football team has just gotten a second full set of weights for the training room."

"Hey, weights are important," Pete cut in. "They really needed them."

Chloe snorted. "Right. Because weights wear out."

Before Pete could say anything more, she got up. "Okay, later you're all hearing about the ghost. Bookmark it."

They ate, moving on to other subjects. Ginger was a little overwhelmed, but she tried to keep up. Then the bell signaled the end of lunch, and it was time to go back to classes.

"See you," Ginger murmured to Clark, who smiled back at her as he gathered up his books.

She and Lana moved off. Lana saw her glancing Clark's way, and she was surprised at the tingle of unease she felt.

Ginger asked Lana, "Is it true that Clark saved Lex Luthor's life?"

Lana nodded. "Lex drove off a bridge. Clark jumped in and pulled him out of his car before Lex drowned."

"Wow. No wonder Lex let him drive his Porsche."

Lana tried to picture Clark behind the wheel of one of Lex's cars speeding along. Calm, reserved Clark Kent.

No way.

"Now that's something I'd like to see."

Ginger laughed. "He was a little timid but still pretty good."

Lana still couldn't picture it. And the idea that Ginger had gone off in a Porsche with Clark was kind of annoying as well, for some reason.

They reached the location of Ginger's next class, and she started to go inside. Then she turned and looked at Lana.

"Thanks, Lana. For . . . everything. I'm glad to have met you."

Lana smiled. It was nice to be appreciated, and she was surprised to discover that she was glad to have met Ginger, too. Meeting someone who understood about her parents . . .

"Me, too. If you get lonely, give me a call at home. I live

with my aunt, Nell Potter. I'll give you my phone number."
She smiled as she quickly jotted it down on a piece of note-
book paper and handed it to Ginger. "Stick around for a little while after school, okay? The buses always leave a little
late. We'd better listen to Chloe's ghost story, or she'll be
hurt."

"We'll listen to the ghost story," Ginger said, but this time
her smile didn't reach her face.

I upset her somehow, Lana thought. *What'd I say?*

"See you later," she added, and this time, Ginger smiled
back.

"Looking forward to it," the new girl said sincerely.

CHAPTER THREE

I am here.

Joel Beck stood at the perimeter of the cornfield and opened up his Book of Spells.

Mine and Holly's, he corrected himself.

He couldn't believe that he'd done it. He'd finally made the connection. But Holly wasn't in town to hear about it. He'd gone to her house to tell her yesterday, but she was out of town again. Her mother had started getting her little acting gigs, and they were gone a lot.

She's gonna freak.

I'm still freaking.

He remembered being called to the field, as he often was called, after dark on Mother's Day. He had been so filled with rage; his dad had ruined the day, making his mother cry. Instead of it being a happy occasion, his father had gotten drunk before noon. Joel's mom had pretended not to notice. That was her way, and that made Joel even angrier.

Then when he had set down his present for his mother, his father had looked at him, and said, "It was the cord. The doctor was so stupid, he didn't realize it. You nearly choked to death. Huh. Couldn't even get born right." Then his father had staggered toward the kitchen, where he kept his Scotch.

And Joel had boiled over with fury that his own father could be so mean, and he had left the house so that he wouldn't do or say something that would make things worse.

So he climbed out of the window, as he often did, and gone over to Holly Pickering's house to cool down. He had an open invitation to stay whenever he wanted.

But they weren't home. He found a note from Holly in the kitchen that said, *"If you find this, hi! I've got a gig!"*

He'd knocked around for a while, watched some TV, trying to figure out how he was going to make it through senior year. His father's drinking was getting worse. His mom was fading away, disappearing into fear or denial or maybe both. It was pretty much just him and his old man anymore.

And I hate him.

He was pretty sure that if he asked, Karen, Holly's mom, would let him live with them until he turned eighteen. But he wasn't completely sure. If he asked, and she said no . . .

I would have no hope left. I wouldn't be able to stand it knowing I had to live with Dad.

And that was when the real rage hit; he had never been so angry in his life. He was tired of being told he was a loser; tired of being afraid to invite anyone over; tired of his mother hanging back, looking so scared and old and downtrodden . . .

Then it was as if a voice had called to him from the field; and without even realizing what he was doing; he had grabbed up the Book of Spells and trudged like a sleepwalker from Holly's house to the field.

Now his mind was clouded. He was so angry, so very angry.

He opened the book.

And he chanted . . . and a huge green sort of vortex had taken shape directly in front of him, swirling and whirling while he cried out and backed away. It whipped around him like a tornado as he turned to go; then it swallowed him up, yanking him somewhere else . . . somewhere terrifying.

There was nothing around him, just an all-encompassing gray. He was so frightened he started yelling.

Then something started racing toward him; all around him, a green-glowing mass that became a skeleton, and then the merest suggestion of a man. Echoing from every direction as if in a terrible nightmare, shouts of horror and white-hot anger rattled Joel's eardrums.

The figure had run at him, getting closer and closer . . . the shouts grew louder . . .

And Joel had run . . . and run and run . . . running in some strange otherland, a barren gray limbo where terror lived and moved and had its being . . .

. . . and it wanted to kill him.

It wanted that very much.

The late-afternoon light dusted the crop fields of the Kent family farm with sunflower kisses. Fresh, overturned earth mingled with the comforting odor of something baking in the oven. Home at last. The only place in the world where Clark Kent could just be *himself*. No need to pretend, to try to hold back. Clark smiled as he opened the decorative screen door at the back entrance to his house. He stepped inside, careful to wipe his feet first, and closed the door behind him.

He made his way to the dining room table and plopped his backpack on one of the Windsor chairs. *History paper*, he reminded himself, as the world of school began to melt away, with all its homework assignments and gossip and things that seemed very important when he was there, but not now, not at home.

All he had to do was pick an event from Smallville's history—"not counting the meteor shower," his teacher had warned the class—and use a few local sources to investigate it. It wasn't supposed to earn him a Pulitzer Prize, but if he didn't do it tonight, he would be slidin' home to a D. The problem was, now that he was late, he was even more intimidated by the assignment, and the more he put it off, the more difficult it seemed to be.

Chloe would toss this off in less than an hour, he reminded himself. *Pete, too*. Then he brightened. *Hey, she's probably got all the documentation I need on her Wall of Weird. And maybe for extra points, I could ask Ginger Brucker to illustrate my subject,*

Go, Kent. He shoots . . . he scores!

Footsteps interrupted his thoughts, and he turned to see his mom. She was carrying a potted plant of mint. She grew herbs in the kitchen window.

"Hi, honey," she said warmly. "I didn't hear you come in."

"Hey." Clark grinned and gave her a hug. As always, he was careful not to squeeze too hard.

Martha Kent patted her son on the back, set the pot among its brothers and sisters in the sunlight, and walked over to the refrigerator. Without missing a beat, she pulled out a large white-paper-wrapped package. She set it down on the counter, then leaned into the fridge again to get more ingredients.

"How was school?"

"Fine," he told her, glossing over his late assignment, Chloe's lunchtime report about Joel Beck, and the arrival of a new girl. "The governor is coming to town. Pete wants Lana to rent the Talon out to him for an evening."

"Pete Ross?" As she spoke, his mom opened the package she'd pulled from the fridge. Inside was a big hunk of meat, looked like a roast. *Yum*. He was starving.

Clark wandered over to see what he could do to help her. "He's campaigning for him."

She started slicing onions and peppers on the big cutting board near the stove. She'd already pulled down one of the big pots from over the island between the dining room and the kitchen.

In the Kent house, the kitchen was the center of things. A

huge stainless-steel vent hood hung over the stove, and the wooden-topped island between the dining room and kitchen held hundreds of spice bottles, as well as cloves of garlic, bottles of flavored oil, and Martha's pots of fresh herbs.

Rich brown-checked curtains framed the gauzy sheers over the window behind the sink. Kansas sunshine shone through the window, illuminating the stove and cutting board in a soft glow. All about the room were elements of the Kents' history. In the corner was an old-fashioned wood-stove that Clark's dad fired up on cold winter nights. It had been in his family for over three generations. A Tiffany-style lamp hung over the dining room table. Clark and Jonathan had found it in an antique shop downtown and given it to Martha for her fortieth birthday.

Clark had always thought that it was exactly how a kitchen should be, particularly one on a farm. It was here that the produce, eggs, and meat that they worked so hard for were "tested" for quality and general deliciousness.

"I'm not crazy about Hiram Welles," she said at last, scooting aside and nodding gratefully when he took the knife from her and began to chop the onions. "There's something about him . . ." She trailed off. "His politics are not always farmer-friendly. And his environmental policies stink."

"He'll get the Luthor vote, then," Jonathan Kent said as he walked into the room. "Clark," he added, by way of greeting.

Clark waited for his father to say something more. He was obviously upset about something.

He finally said, "Hi, Dad."

Clark felt that he had a good relationship with his parents, but as he got older, he noticed that it was tougher sometimes to talk to them about things, particularly his dad. They still talked about tough subjects, but sometimes it was like a coded message. Instead of saying, "Hey, Clark, let's talk," it had become, "Son, you want to help me with this motor?" Then, gradually, the talk.

Before Clark could ask, Martha did.

"What is it?"

Jonathan walked to the sink and washed his hands. Farmers washed their hands a lot. "You remember that boy we almost hit."

"We were talking about Joel at lunch," Clark told his parents. "It's all over school." He added, "Chloe wants to interview him."

"That's going to be difficult, for the time being," Jonathan replied as he dried his hands on a kitchen towel, then looped the towel back around the wooden towel rack. "He's missing. No one's seen him since Sunday night."

Martha looked puzzled. "But we dropped him off at his home. It was Mother's Day. Just two days ago."

"His father said he checked his room about midnight. He was already gone."

"I'd leave, too, if I had a father like that," Martha bit off, then took the knife back from Clark and resumed chopping the onions with more force than before.

Clark was taken aback. "I should go look for Joel," he ventured.

"You have homework," Martha said quickly, grabbing another onion and whacking it to pieces. She looked upset.

"Mom," Clark protested, "I could search faster than anyone."

His father shook his head. "You're not a detective, Clark. You have gifts, true, but you can't do everything," he insisted, backing Martha up. "You can ask around at school tomorrow."

"But . . ." Clark began, then he read the expression on both their faces.

They're afraid. For me. But why? I'm not going to run away from home.

Martha looked at her husband. "Have his parents checked with his friends?"

Jonathan shook his head. "His folks don't know his friends. They have no idea where to look for him. How he spends his time, where he hangs out. Nothing. And speaking of hanging out, you've got homework *and* chores," his father added sternly. "Enough to keep you busy around here this evening."

"But . . ."

Both his parents gazed at him with firm authority. He could almost hear the voice of the weatherman on the local Smallville TV news: "There's a united front moving in, so we all might as well stay home and avoid the storm."

"I do have a history paper," he conceded.

"And some hay to buck," his father added. He gestured with his head for his son to follow him out of the house. "And there's a fence . . ."

Clark sighed, passing his mom, who had moved on to some russet potatoes. She was whaling the daylights out of them. Suddenly she reached out a hand, and said, "Clark, be careful."

"Of the hay," he added, trying to tease her a little. "You never know when it's going to turn on you."

To his surprise, tears were welling in her eyes. She murmured hoarsely, "Go help Dad."

Clark blinked at her. "Okay," he said, and followed his father out of the house.

After school, Ginger had listened to Chloe's story, which sounded disappointingly like an urban legend. Somebody she knew had overheard someone else talking to this guy

Joel's mom at the drugstore about how her son had seen a
ghost in a cornfield and now he was missing.

*And there was a disappearing hitchhiker in the backseat
of his car,* she thought sarcastically.

Now she made her way to the bus she'd been told would
take her home, and hopped on, book bag in hand.

The day had gotten better and better, and she was feeling
pretty positive about the move to Smallville. Sure, it was
smaller, but the people were nice and the classes more inti-
mate, which meant she'd gotten more attention than she was
used to from her teachers. Mrs. Owen, the art teacher, had
been pleased with her work in class and had suggested she
put together a portfolio.

"Can't start too soon, ya know," she'd said, in her curt,
North Dakota accent.

The bus driver, an older woman, looked at Ginger sharply
as she got on the noisy bus.

"Don't believe I know you," she said. "What's your
stop?"

For a moment, panic swelled in her chest. But then she remembered.

"Ah . . . the real-estate lady called it the Welles place?"

"Oh." The driver was clearly taken aback. "Huh. How
about that." She stirred herself and smiled at Ginger. "I'm
Dorothy. Some of the kids call me Mom. Welcome to Smallville."

"Thanks," Ginger said, half-turning her head to look for a
place to sit.

Dorothy blared her horn at someone, muttering, "Those
Gutierrez twins are always late." Then to Ginger, she added,
"Good luck living out at that old place. There hasn't been a
family there in *years*."

"Oh."

The woman picked up a clipboard on the dashboard and

plucked a pencil from behind her ear. She checked off something and put the clipboard between her seat and the side of the bus.

"I'm leavin' 'em," she muttered. "Now, listen, no smoking, eating, or drinking, no throwing stuff, no cursing. You follow my list of 'To Don't's,' we'll get along fine." She flashed a smile at Ginger and laid onto the horn again. "I'm leaving them," she grumbled.

Ginger turned and faced the sea of unfamiliar faces. She was disappointed to see that neither Lana nor Clark was on the bus.

"Here," said a girl a couple rows back. She had short dark hair and severe goth makeup, moving over toward the window so Ginger could sit down. "Take a load off."

"Thanks." Ginger was grateful for the kind gesture.

Two dark-haired boys about sixteen years old flew onto the bus. Dorothy gave them a miniature blast about making her wait. Then the bus pulled away from the school, the beautiful scenery quickly focusing Ginger's attention on the potential for landscape painting. It was *beautiful* here, the great vast wheatfields moving restlessly in the wind contrasted sharply with the serenity of the blue sky, broken up by the occasional tree.

She'd been told there was a forest at the edge of town, and thought she'd go exploring when she got the chance.

But not today.

Then they passed a vast field of corn, the stalks waving in the breeze, and the girl beside Ginger flattened her hand against the window and chanted something in a foreign language under her breath. She looked at Ginger, and said, "That's a protection spell. I said it for Joel. And for me," she added under her breath.

"Oh?"

"The cornfield is cursed," the girl continued. "It sucked him in."

Ginger glanced past her earnest, heavily lined eyes to the stalks of corn waving in the breeze. *This person*, she thought, *has seen way too many bad horror movies*.

"I can get him back," the girl said. "The same way he went in. With magic."

"That's . . . interesting," Ginger replied, trying to sound earnest. But the girl narrowed her eyes and pursed her lips.

"I shouldn't be surprised that you don't believe me," she snapped.

"Um, why not?" Ginger ventured.

"No one ever does."

As if on cue, the bus rolled to a stop and the goth girl stood up. She glared at Ginger, and said, "This is my stop, do you mind?"

Ginger stood up, and the girl flounced away, stomping down the aisle toward the front of the bus. The doors opened, and she was gone, charging across the dusty road toward a distant farmhouse surrounded by yet more corn.

The bus started up again. With each stop, more students left, and Ginger began to wonder if she was going to be the last passenger.

The early start had made her tired, and the warm seat of the bus, the whistling of the wind from the open window across the aisle, and the rumble of the big motor lulled her nearly to sleep as she gazed out the window.

"Hey, sweetie, we're at the Welles place."

The bus driver's voice broke her trance, and she got up, stumbling slightly as she walked to the exit. There were still a few more kids on the bus, and it was nearly dark. *Long commutes. That's farm life for you.*

"Take care, now," Dorothy said. She looked very earnest.

"Thanks."

Ginger stepped off the bus, and with a roar it sped off, to outlying farms even farther away.

She was home.

As she approached the house, she thought she saw movement in one of the windows—a curtain flapping upstairs.

Is Mom home? Did something go wrong at work?

But the front door was locked.

"Mom?"

There was no answer.

Take it easy, Ginger. It's okay. You're just tired.

She walked up the stairs to the room she'd picked for her own, a huge space, big enough to hold the entire living room of the Metropolis apartment they'd lived in.

She had asked her mother if she could have Daddy's desk, and Janice had agreed. With a wave of melancholy, Ginger laid her books on the treasured object, which looked like something from a Charles Dickens novel, complete with pigeonholes.

As she opened the fold-down leaf, she heard a noise.

Downstairs, she thought. *That old clock. Maybe.*

"Mom?" she called, and the sound of her own voice startled her. "Are you back early?"

There was no answer. Ginger edged down the stairs. Shadows from the banister threw bars against the wall, and she was unnerved. It was such a big old house; maybe a rat or a raccoon had gotten inside.

Maybe something bigger, she thought, then, *Don't go there, Ginger. This is the country. You're fine.*

At the foot of the stairs, she hesitated, trying to re-create the sound in her mind. *Maybe it was the wind. Maybe we forgot to close a window . . .*

She went into the living room. An opened Bible lay on the floor.

I didn't even realize we owned a Bible.

With a frisson of anxiety, Ginger glanced down at the thick, leather-bound volume. It lay open, as if someone had been lying on the floor and reading it. In the center of the page, something like a drop of water had stained the lines of one of the verses.

"23: If any harm follows, then you shall give life for life, eye for eye, tooth for tooth, hand for hand, foot for foot, burn for burn, wound for wound, stripe for stripe."

Wow. Talk about zero tolerance.

She touched the water stain. It was wet.

Startled, Ginger glanced around the room. The window was closed, and there was no sign of any animals.

She put the old Bible back on the shelf, wedging it more firmly than it must have been before, between a copy of a novel titled *Indistinguishable from Magic* by her father's favorite author, Robert Forward, and a biography of the physicist, Richard Feynman.

Still creeped out, she looked around the room, and decided she would like to be just about anywhere else.

Outside, she thought. *But I can't just* sit *there.*

She trotted up to her room and grabbed a set of pastels, a few sticks of charcoal, and a pad of toothed paper. Back downstairs, she hurriedly snagged a Diet Coke from the fridge and nearly jumped out the back door.

A series of inlaid stones formed a patio; the yard had been well kept up to the edges of the stones, where a few wood lawn chairs sat in overgrown clumps of grass and weeds.

Those chairs are gorgeous.

Unfortunately, their beauty couldn't disguise the fact that they were heavy. She managed to drag one under a faded awning and gazed out at the fields beyond the house. A local farmer had leased part of the land the house sat on, and was growing wheat.

She put her sketch pad on her lap and stared out at the field.

Drawing, she had learned, was an analytical process more than anything else. There might be the rare fluke among thousands who could draw exactly what they saw, but most of the time it took practice to learn how to look at things, to break down the relationships between objects, and then to figure out how to re-create those relationships on paper.

The wheatfields, for instance, had a continuity to them. If she tried to draw exactly what she was seeing, she'd miss the overall flow, trying to get a line here or there. Instead, she looked at the rhythm of the wind, saw how it parted the fields just so, in a ripple effect that moved across the individual stalks.

Seeing the underlying currents made the drawing much easier.

She took the charcoal first, working up a black-and-white sketch to get the lines.

There wasn't anything in the picture to provide scale, so she decided to add one of the lawn chairs. That meant dragging another chair out so she could see the way it looked in front of the field.

She sketched it in, making it small to show the immense scale of the field. She added a few trees deep in the picture, giving it more of a sense of depth.

Then, hardly knowing why, she went back to the chair. It seemed wrong somehow to not put someone in, watching the field, looking at it the same way she was.

She focused on the chair in the sketch and tried to imagine a person sitting in it. Without conscious thought, she could suddenly sense the figure, as if he or she were actually modeling for her.

She worked fast, sketching lightly with short strokes,

feeling the person in the chair, but having no model to work from.

It went against most of her art instructor's teachings: Always work from life.

But it felt right.

She worked faster, breaking one of the charcoal sticks from pressing too hard. She paused for a moment and sharpened up a fresh one on a sandpaper pad, then went back to the work.

After a few minutes, she realized she was finished. She made a perceptual shift, going from creator to evaluator, and looked at what she'd done.

It was a young boy, sitting in the chair, looking at the fields.

Somehow she knew he was seriously ill. He was looking wistfully at the fields, as if he wished he could be out in them. One of his legs was pulled up on the lawn chair, and it looked smaller than it should have. Smaller, and twisted.

And he was pale, squinting slightly in the bright sun, something he wasn't accustomed to.

A chill ran down her spine.

There's something about him. Something about this house.

Before she realized what she was doing, she was sketching again. This second figure was larger than life. He was a big man, broad-shouldered and red-skinned. He wore overalls with no shirt, and had a large nose. Thick brows sheltered tiny eyes, and huge hands cradled a large scythe. The farmer glared at the viewer, his gaze frightening and angry, his stance aggressive.

Ginger couldn't stop herself from throwing the pad to the ground. She rose from her chair, taking several steps back.

The eyes of the farmer seemed to watch her.

Unnerved, she glanced back over her shoulder and hesitantly opened the back door. She tried not to think about the Bible that had fallen out of the bookshelf. She tried not to notice the eyes of the farmer as she left the drawing pad outside and went into the kitchen.

There was another noise, and she cried out in alarm. It was louder this time. She could *feel* it.

In her toes.

It's in the basement, the thought rushed to her. Goose bumps broke out along her arms and over her features.

What's in the basement?

From her vantage point in the kitchen, Ginger saw the cellar door. The key dangled from a hook. She reached for it.

If this were a monster movie, this would be a bad idea.

But it wasn't. This was Smallville.

Grimacing, she opened the door. Below was blackness, way too much of it for the kind of afternoon she had already had. In the waning sunlight from the window, Ginger saw the switch on the cellar's interior wall and quickly threw it.

A series of yellowed lightbulbs came on, illuminating the cellar's stairway.

Nothing moved. There were no sounds, no vibrations, no nothing. She could see nearly everything from the top of the stairs, except for what was directly behind them.

With a deep breath, she went down just one step. A loud haunted-house creak greeted her effort, and she reflexively pulled back her foot. Her heart was thundering.

Okay, I did it, nothing there. Right. Checked it out. I'm done.

One of the lightbulbs went out, its filament popping in a sharp actinic white.

Ginger jumped back across the threshold and slammed the door hard. Her hand shook as she stabbed the key in the lock, twisted it, and took another step away from the door.

Ka . . . thump!

It was another sound, louder, and right underneath her . . . from the empty cellar.

Ginger jumped straight off the ground, her heart about to leap from her chest.

Time to call Mom.

Ginger punched her mother's cell phone number into the portable beside the stove.

And her mother answered. "Hello?"

Science Indistinguishable from Magic, she murmured to herself, like a mantra. *Lots of reasons for things to happen . . .*

The grandfather's clock chimed, making her shriek, "Mom?" into the phone.

"Ginger? What's wrong?"

"Um . . ." What to say? How to explain it, when even now, it was all beginning to seem kind of lame? "Are you coming home soon?"

"Why? Are you *okay*?"

"I'm fine . . . it's just that there are some weird noises here . . ."

Her mother paused, and Ginger had a sinking feeling that she wouldn't be coming home.

"What kind of noises?"

"Thumping, bumping, the usual haunted-house ones . . ."

And, listening to herself, Ginger realized just how ridiculous it must sound. Having her mother on the phone was like adding light and reason to the house; there were no thumps or bumps, and everything seemed normal again.

"Ginger, I've just started a tour of my new lab. But if you want me to come home now, I will." She sounded exasperated.

Sure, mess up Mom's first day on the job. No way.

Besides, everything was quiet now.

"No, I think I'll be okay." She laughed a little. "Just new

house jitters. Because, well, it's an old house." She thought of trying to make a joke about their "new" old house, then thought better of it.

"Good." Her mother sounded distracted. Disinterested. "Hold on."

There was a pause.

"I won't be able to get calls for a while. If you can't reach me, just call the main number and they'll page me."

"Sure. It's cool. I'll be fine, Mom."

She said good-bye, and hung up.

There was a thump from the study.

Ginger jerked. She took a deep breath and stood rooted to the spot, spied the rolling pin in a half-open drawer, and grabbed it, feeling both stupid and terribly afraid, and wishing with all her heart that she had insisted her mother come home *now*.

She walked toward the doorway of the study, trying to stay as calm as possible, alert and ready to defend herself against . . . whatever.

The Bible was on the floor again.

And even from where she stood, Ginger could see something red on the page.

Something that looked like blood.

The clock chimed again.

Ginger grabbed her purse and pulled out a small piece of paper. Lana Lang's phone number was on it.

As fast as she could, she dialed the number.

"Be home, Lana," she whispered. *"Please."*

CHAPTER FOUR

Feeling mildly exasperated, Janice Brucker disconnected from her daughter's phone call.

I think Ginger's having more trouble with this relocation than either of us expected.

I think I am, too.

Janice put her cell phone in her purse and looked at the security guard, the one who had informed her that she was going underground. Lex had postponed their initial meeting, and she had spent the day hanging out at their new house, putting things away and answering e-mails from colleagues, still doing some damage control about the lab accident even after all this time. She was trying very hard to protect the secrecy of her and George's work, but if all the regulatory bodies investigating what had happened compared notes, she wasn't sure they would buy her version of what had happened. She was still afraid that the reason she was here was that Lionel had figured it all out and wanted her to try it again in another setting. Certainly, the fact that she had returned to work at LuthorCorp, albeit a different branch in another city, had not been lost on the scientific community at large, nor on the politicians and administrators who oversaw their work.

Now here I am, knee deep in . . . product, she thought with grim humor. *At Fertilizer Plant Number Three.*

If she hadn't seen the LuthorCorp trucks pulling in and out of the huge property, just past the domed storage tanks, she might have missed it. A small granite obelisk with the purple-and-black LuthorCorp logo announced the location in tight, terse letters.

Lex likes to keep things low key.

That was smart. Modern fertilizer production used a wide variety of toxic materials: the acids, gases, and other catalysts used in the process were bad enough—the by-products were somewhat worse. Janice had sensed a general unease about the plant from people she'd talked to, so downplaying its presence was a smart move.

Fertilizer production was one of the sleeper issues of modern science. The Haber-Bosch process invented in the first part of the twentieth century had given mankind a way to develop nitrogen-rich fertilizer for the first time in its history. The result had been a population explosion, as land that previously couldn't support agriculture on any significant scale suddenly fed nations. Now a third of the world's protein came from fertilized crops. Humanity had started a conveyor belt it couldn't stop; without fertilizer, large numbers of the population would starve.

The more troubling, long-term prospect was the environmental cost. Global warming, caused by the greenhouse effect, was exacerbated by excess fertilizer unutilized by crops. Some of the unused nutrients broke down and wound up in the atmosphere as nitrous oxide—a gas that was notoriously bad for the environment.

While not an immediate concern compared to other greenhouse gases, like carbon dioxide and CFCs, the future was another story. There was no way that humanity was going to stop using fertilizer, but there was no way to tell what kind of harm nitrous oxide would wreak in years to come. No one was going to tell their children they would have to starve to death to protect the environment.

Janice had driven toward the main parking area beyond the four domed silos near the entrance to the plant and parked. She got out, taking her briefcase and computer and headed for the entrance. As she entered the building she saw the LuthorCorp logo everywhere, the geometric black 'L' with purple, sharp-edged 'C' a perfect expression of what she knew of the company. Behind the reception desk was the LuthorCorp motto: "We Make Things Grow."

She thought that the many companies purchased and then dismantled by Lionel Luthor or the many billions of insects killed by his pesticides might have come up with a different motto:

We take no prisoners.

She chided herself for the thought.

Now Janice, it doesn't pay to bite the hand that feeds you.

As a high-level researcher for most of her life, she'd taken the bread of some questionable employers. She'd never done anything illegal; but the motives of some of the corporations she'd worked for had probably been less than ethical, the profit motive overshadowing all.

As a scientist she ignored all of that. All that mattered was the search for new discoveries, the ability to conquer ignorance and understand how to affect the world.

Or to put it more crudely, as George and I did: fame, fortune, and a place in the history books . . .

As a mother, she'd occasionally been troubled by some of the research she was asked to do. Most of the very questionable projects had been without results, so she'd never been forced to make a choice about whether an employer should have something she discovered, and she hoped she'd never have to. Far simpler to concentrate on getting results than to try to foresee the impact of her discoveries and the ethical consequences.

The guard at the reception desk—there could be no doubt he was a guard, with his ear receiver and his body-by-Nautilus build—had been polite.

"Hello, Dr. Brucker," he'd said, before she had a chance to identify herself.

Then he punched a button on a keyboard behind the desk, the monitor a dressy black flatscreen, and a laminated card ejected itself from a small printer nearby. He snapped a spring clip to the card and handed it to her.

The card had a head shot of her on it, taken only moments ago as she'd walked in the door, the blue Kansas sky the background.

She'd glanced up behind the reception desk and saw the minicam that had taken her picture. She wondered how people's badges looked on days with bad weather.

Janice clipped the card to the left lapel of her suit and waited. That's when Ginger had called, and the anonymous guard had warned her that her phone might not work once she was taken on her "tour."

"Would you care to make any other calls?" he asked politely. Janice shook her head.

The guard picked up a handset behind the desk and pushed a button. Within a few seconds a man in a nice suit and a headset showed up. He was tall and muscular, like the first one, and Janice figured they could moonlight as bouncers in an elegant establishment if they had a yen to.

Guard #2 smiled, and said, "This way, please, Dr. Brucker. Mr. Luthor's waiting."

Janice followed him as they began to walk down a long corridor.

"Very nice security, Mr. . . . ."

"Wilcoxen." He nodded pleasantly at her. "I'm Jim Wilcoxen, Dr. Brucker." Then he tapped his own badge, clipped to his suit lapel.

"A smart chip keeps track of your access level. Helps us find you if you get . . . lost."

Janice nodded. "Understood."

They continued down the long corridor, heels clicking on tile. As they walked, Janice thought about the number of times she'd started at new facilities. She and George had always enjoyed that first day, getting set up in the system and getting their new spaces.

And defining the mission, as George liked to call it.

The pain in her chest was real, but no cause for alarm. Her heart was broken. It was so hard to be starting without him. She had lost a part of herself; she would be working handicapped, a piece missing. It was harder than she had ever imagined, living without him, yet so incredibly easy to blame herself for his death.

Yes, George had been a little too anxious to get near the new isotope; it'd been a risk, and he'd known it. But if he hadn't been so trusting that her calculations had worked, hadn't been so confident in *her*, then maybe he wouldn't have. And she had been too eager to tell him that they could get started. Lionel Luthor had been getting anxious about their apparent lack of progress, hinting that perhaps their work wasn't going to be cost-effective after all.

"I have to watch that bottom line," he'd told George. "LuthorCorp spends huge sums on research and development, and I need to give my shareholders a return on their investment."

That had concerned them both; they had a good setup at LuthorCorp, with the ability to work on their secret project without being scrutinized by their employer. They had agreed that they had to pump up the volume.

I had a bad feeling. I wanted to wait, but I didn't want to disappoint George.

He believed in me, and died for it.

She hoped that she could do whatever it was that Lex Luthor was asking. She needed to vindicate herself, both professionally and emotionally. Survivor's guilt. Mother's guilt.

When I look at Ginger, all I see is how much she misses him. How haunted she is.

Truth was, she was worried. Beyond worried—scared. If her theory was flawed, it could take years to try and replicate the radiation from the meteor rocks. Worse, what if she did develop something—and it was unstable, like last time? And it imploded?

She sighed again and gripped her briefcase a little harder. Lex was smart, and he was rich. She'd make him provide safeguards, and safeguards on those safeguards. The redundancies she would demand would make the space program look downright foolhardy.

Okay, no contest there.

She took a deep breath and recited a personal catechism she'd made up years ago to calm herself down.

Determine objectively, empirically, and confirm.

There were the fundamental principles of science all wound up in one phrase. Everything had a cause, and on the average, such behavior could be predicted. That was determinism.

All results that could be found could be presented for replication. That was objectivity.

And as for empiricism, gathering data through systematic observation revealed the orderly relationships in the world. Theories could be tested and confirmed or disconfirmed.

The words soothed her, made her feel confident that she would seek out yet again the answers to the questions she sought.

I'll do it for you, George.

And maybe in so doing, she could finally put her guilt to rest.

Jim, the big guard slowed suddenly and opened a large metal door with the words MEDIA ROOM chiseled into it.

They stepped inside.

The room was large, maybe twenty by forty, with a large, heavily polished cherrywood conference table in the center. Flat panel monitors ringed the table, and everything was a subdued gray. On the wall nearest the table, there was a huge white movie screen. A projector aimed down at the screen from the ceiling.

Lex Luthor and another man were sitting at the table. Lex sipped a coffee from a mug that read "The Talon," and the other man drank from a nicely shaped glass. There were bottles of Pellegrino and Perrier on a small Japanese lacquer tray, as well as beautifully presented vegetables, crackers, and cheeses.

Both men stood as Janice and her escort walked in.

Lex stepped forward.

"Sorry for the delay," he said. "Something came up."

"My time is your time," she replied steadily. The young man was pleased.

The other man looked familiar, and Janice tried to remember where she'd seen him before. He was black, and older, maybe in his fifties. He looked as though he'd seen more prosperous years, and there was an air of leery secrecy about him.

Maybe I can feel it because I have one, too.

Lex gestured to the stranger. "Dr. Brucker, this is Dr. Steven Hamilton."

Hamilton! Of course!

She'd read his papers all the way back in middle school. He'd worked at the Astromaterials Curation Center at the Johnson Space Center for years, identifying and analyzing samples of moon rocks, meteorites, and other space-exposed artifacts. The Astromaterials Center was a specially constructed fireproof, hurricane-proof, tornado-proof, and theft-proof building where various collections of extraterrestrial materials were kept for study. His comments about the effects of the solar wind on moon rocks, and the potential energy for future space flight had thrilled her.

She couldn't recall any citations about his work in any scientific journals for a few years. *Wait a second.* There had been some scandal a few years back, she remembered now, something at Metropolis University . . .

We have a plot thickening here, she thought anxiously.

"Dr. Brucker."

She took Dr. Hamilton's hand and shook it.

"Dr. Hamilton. I'm a fan of your moon rock work from way back." She smiled, and he returned it, somewhat distantly.

"Ah yes, back in the good old days." His smile was still very cool as he added, "And now we're colleagues."

"Oh?"

"Dr. Hamilton and I share a mutual interest," Lex said easily. "He's been researching the Smallville meteors for some time now."

Before Janice could ask any questions, he added, "We've put together a background presentation that you might find interesting." He gestured in the direction of the conference table.

"Please. Have a seat."

She lowered herself into a chair that looked like it had escaped from an Italian design studio and was surprised to find it comfortable.

Dr. Hamilton reached for a silver remote in the table and punched a button. The lights in the room dimmed immediately and a state-of-the art viewing screen lit up. A computer-generated picture of a sign, similar to the one she'd seen on the drive into Smallville, leapt onto the screen.

WELCOME TO SMALLVILLE, CREAMED CORN CAPITAL OF THE WORLD, it read.

Hamilton keyed another button, and a voice-over came out over wafer-thin speakers. It was his own voice. He sounded calm, yet passionate.

"Twelve years ago, Smallville changed."

Another visual replaced the sign. This one showed the same field with the sign destroyed, burnt stumps where it had rested before.

"The Smallville meteor shower was the most significant meteor event in the history of the United States."

A montage of other images, impact craters in cornfields, burning cars, shattered sidewalks. There was that famous picture from *Time* of the terrified little girl. Home video footage came next, probably digitally cleaned up, of meteors screaming through the atmosphere, sonic booms, and loud hissing sounds as they arced through the air. The impact crashes made her jump.

I never really comprehended how bad it was, she thought. *My God. The sky really did fall.*

As if mirroring her thoughts, Dr. Hamilton's narration resumed. "There were over three hundred falls, which we define as meteorites found after they were seen to arrive. There have been even more finds, defined as meteorites discovered after the fact. After they landed, in other words."

A computer graphic showed the definitions pictorially. First there was a starfield, with hundreds of glowing greed dots and coordinates. In the upper right quadrant were the words FALLS: PLOTTED TRAJECTORIES, 300, CORRECTED TO ± 5%.

Then a map of Smallville appeared, dotted with hundreds more glowing pixels. It read, FINDS, TO DATE, VERSION 27.3, LUTHORCORP/HAMILTON.

"Thanks to the nearly rock-free soil of the Great Plains, the finds have been easy to identify," Dr. Hamilton said seated beside Janice.

On the screen, there was a pan of hundreds of meteorites labeled on pristine lab shelves.

The screen went dark for a few moments, and then bright again, several photos of newspaper headlines appearing on it. *Man Gains Finger on Left Hand*, read one, with a shot of a man's hand, a supernumerary digit emerging from beside his thumb.

Farmer Grows Square Watermelons, read another, this one also from the local paper, the *Smallville Ledger*. A third headline proclaimed *Boy Carries Sister Through Wall of Fire!*

Dr. Hamilton's voice-over continued. "After the meteor shower, the people here began noticing some strange things."

A low-quality video of a young girl opened in a window on the screen. The interviewer was calmly asking her some questions.

"And then what did you see?"

The girl's eyes were huge. Her ponytail bobbed as she spoke.

"He just *jumped,* like he was some kind of giant *grasshopper*! Thirty plus feet over the tree, the fence, everything! And he made these noises . . ."

"What kind of noises?"

"Like he was a *bug*! A ratchety, scraping sound! It was horrible!" She began to cry.

Another video window opened up. This one was a little higher quality than the first. Again, an interview was being conducted.

"Tell me about the cars."

The interviewee looked uncomfortable. He was a middle-aged sheriff's deputy, and clearly not used to being on camera.

"When we arrived at the call-out, we found the house

quiet. We'd had a report of possible domestic violence, so we didn't want to go in without backup."

"And then what happened?"

The man's eyes widened. "Then it was like there was the *rushing* sound. Things started happening . . . Cars started getting knocked over like they were toys, and I saw . . ."

"Please go on, Officer."

"I still can't believe it." He shook his head. "This *kid*, couldn't have been more than sixteen—he picks up one of the patrol cars and throws it on top of the house."

There was a moment of silence on the tape.

"And then what did you do?"

"What do you think?" The man laughed, but his face was transfixed with fear. "I got the hell out of there."

A time line graph morphed onto the screen. The last thirteen years were shown. Numbers appeared on the line, the first in 1990, a number '1.' The numbers got higher and higher with each successive year.

"While analyzing the data from the shower, I developed a theory that they are affecting the environment they landed in."

The flat line graphic suddenly became a bar graph, showing an exponential curve of incidents heading up into the current time.

"I came to believe that the meteorites had somehow affected people in ways that we only used to find in comic books."

Dr. Hamilton paused the presentation for a moment.

"Dr. Brucker, I formed a hypothesis. You know what I had to do next."

Almost whispering, Janice replied, "You had to test it."

Hamilton nodded, a light in his eyes she hadn't seen before.

He triggered the remote again and the presentation resumed. This time there was a picture of a seed in a small glass bowl. A small digital clock sat next to the bowl. A hand reached into the shot and set a meteorite next to it.

"The seed you are seeing is a seed of the formerly extinct Nicodemus flower. It was suspected by many to have caused a general uprising on the site of the Smallville township over a hundred years ago, because of some hallucinogenic properties of the pollen of the flower."

The hours flashed by on the time-lapse photography, and suddenly there was a break in the seed. A tiny tendril of green moved from the seed, and a leaf unfurled.

The extinct seed had just come back to life.

Wow.

Another video window popped open, this one revealing a huge cavernous room, illuminated by grow lights. Rows of soil stretched along the floor of the room. It looked like a farm that had been taken indoors.

"Other experiments have been performed with the meteor rocks as well. This soil was fertilized with a high proportion of meteor rock used as a base for a standard nitrogen, potassium, and phosphorus mix of nutrients."

As Janice watched, a man wearing a white suit started working his way down the tilled soil, pushing something into the ground every few feet.

He's planting something.

By the time he'd reached the end of the first row, the first seed had sprouted.

Janice stared at the video, shocked. *Nothing* grew that fast.

She looked at the video, but there was no jump, no glitch to show it had been doctored. The same man started on the second row, and he was now joined by a second man, probably to get things finished sooner. A fine mist of water obscured the men slightly; an overhead sprinkler system watered the plants, giving them the water that they would drink in weeks—months—in just minutes. The men continued with the planting process. By the time they had finished the second row she could tell what had been planted.

Corn.

Another video window appeared on the screen. Seven mice sat in a wire cage, with two ears of corn nearby. The corn was an odd shade of yellow, with almost a greenish cast to it.

"The remarkable speed of the corn production had some unusual side effects."

One of the mice bit into one of the corn cobs. He looked pleased with himself, munching and crunching.

A few moments after he'd started eating, he stopped, and stood stock-still for a moment, but only a moment. Then he began to *jitter*, moving like he was going through some incredible withdrawal symptoms. The mouse reached for the corn, and his speed, his jittering was so fast that when it touched the corn, the cob snapped away from him, accelerated by the even more rapid tremor of the creature's paw.

My God.

It looked like the fast-growing corn was also a physiology accelerator.

Dr. Hamilton pushed a button, and the lights came up again. The presentation was over.

She looked at Lex.

The billionaire's son smiled. "We're planning to add a conclusion, once we figure out how to make everything work right."

Dr. Hamilton spoke.

"The trick will be controlling the emissions of the radiation so that we can maintain the benefits with few or any of the negative side effects."

Janice nodded, but her heart was pounding. *I brought my*

kid here, she thought anxiously. *What have I done? And now that we're here . . . have we been exposed? How can I know?*

More to the point, what can I do about it?

Oh, my God, George, have I done it again? Put us in harm's way?

"I see this project as not an end in itself, but as a means," Lex said. "We need to see if we can harness this energy, figure out how to get this stuff to do things we want it to do. The meteorites are too valuable to use up—if we can figure out a way to emulate them, to get the same radiation, we can work out our theories with little or no wasted material."

She looked at Lex and wished that George was with her now. She was terrified, horrified . . . and fascinated.

Dr. Hamilton picked up the thread. "We seem to be having either a hybrid type of ionized radiation—not really gamma, or beta, or alpha but rather a mix—or something completely new." He looked hard at Janice. "I know you're scared," he said gently.

She swallowed. There was no denying it.

"We are all. But this . . ." He gestured to the remote. "It's already happened. It's here. We need you."

Lex gave her the moment she needed, then she nodded, decision made.

"Yes," she said. "You do."

CHAPTER FIVE

In the waning light, the goth girl trudged with her weighty black velvet bag in both her arms. In it she carried several Smallville meteorites and some ritual arcana—candles, incense. What was missing was the Book of Spells she and Joel had created together.

The cornfield loomed ahead, and she inhaled sharply. She was very, very scared to go there.

But I have to.

For Joel.

Her name was Holly Pickering, and Joel Beck was her best friend.

It had all started so long ago. In the first grade, Alexis Catalano had started calling her Holly Picks-Her-Nose, and everyone had taken up the terrible nickname. And Holly, with her brand-new first-day-of-school outfit and her brand-new Ghostbusters running shoes and her big girl Alf lunch box, had dragged herself off the school bus sobbing with misery.

Joel had gotten off the bus with her. She still didn't know if that had been his original intention, because there was one stop closer to his home. She hadn't noticed him at first; she'd turned around in a little circle, weeping, expecting her mom to be there, only she wasn't, and the big boy looked at her, and said, "Rough day, huh."

That was when their friendship had been born. She had told him about that so very rough day, from the fact that she didn't get to sit in one of the new desks down to the dreaded new nickname. With consummate kindness, he had listened to her outpouring of disappointment and frustration. All her life, she had been waiting to be old enough to go to big kids' school, and frankly, it sucked. When she had finished, trailing off from sheer exhaustion, he had shaken his head sadly.

"Don't pay any attention to them, Holly. Take away their power, and they'll fade away."

He had waited with her until her mother had shown up, and then for that first year, he'd kind of checked in on her from time to time, on the bus mostly. Her mom liked him and had him baby-sit her. They went on walks and to all the kids' places in town. He showed her the library and they went there often; it was he who introduced her to Susan Cooper and J.R.R. Tolkien. The books were steeped in alternate worlds filled with legends and magic, and she escaped into them like Alice stepping through the Looking Glass.

When Holly found out that Joel's dad was an alcoholic, she realized that he had seen how hurt she had been, and that had drawn her to him. They had shared so much . . . but their ages made sure they would never be more than very good friends. In a way, Holly was grateful. It kept their relationship focused on themselves and kept away bogus distractions like dating.

About the time she went into the third grade, they started going to the cornfield, and that had sealed the bond between them.

First they went because they had heard the stories about the cornfield's curse. They would take sandwiches and S'mores, and Joel started reading Edgar Allan Poe to her. Then they realized there was something there—a presence, a spectral force, call it what one would. They were sure of it. She could feel it, and so could Joel. They spent long afternoons after school trying to contact it, and she was thrilled. They developed all kinds of little rituals, little "secret club" stuff, created mostly by her.

Looking back with the perspective of a little maturity, she realized that at first Joel had just followed along, maybe just to please her. He'd helped her gather up a few of the Smallville meteorites they found in the field and made ritual Circles with them. Wearing his black sweatshirt, he'd chant medieval summoning spells with her, and researched incantations on the net for her until he taught her how to log on by herself.

He never invited anyone else to go with them, and it never occurred to her that *she* could have invited anyone else. Not that she had any prospects. . . .

Because while Joel was wonderful and cute and smart, he was wrong about school. It wasn't true that if you ignored the bullies, they would lose their power. Even though she ignored the mean girls, they got meaner through the years. It was as if they had branded her forehead with a big "L" on the very first day of first grade. For a while she fought the outcast label, then she finally went with it and became a goth. And it was weird, because once they had the proof that she was a loser, they left her alone.

But the truth was, she didn't really like being an outcast and suspected many of the other goth kids felt the same way. She knew gravers and tribals, Edwardian goths, and cybergoths, and although nobody ever came out and said it, there was a tinge of wistfulness in everybody's voices when they talked about the popular kids. Even though they mocked the conformity and swore to each other that they would rather die than be like *that*, she had a feeling they were making do with the kind of popularity they could snag.

But Holly's life was changing . . . big-time. Holly had been in a play in middle school last year, and her teacher, Mrs. Jeret, had taken Holly's mom aside and told her that Holly had real acting talent. At Mrs. Jeret's suggestion, Holly's mom had signed her with Metropolis Talent Management, and Holly had begun to get work doing voice-overs for local commercials.

Since they were gone so much, they had made sure Joel had the keys to their house. He watered the plants and got the mail—and in return, had a place to cool off when his father drove him too hard.

Now she wasn't sure who her friends could be. She had kept her voice-over work a secret from the other goths and made Joel keep it a secret, too. He kept insisting that her friends would be thrilled for her, but she wasn't so sure. What if they resented her success?

"Self-esteem issues much?" Joel had teased her.

Oh, yeah. No secret there. Joel so understands.

She knew he had been there until last night. When they had returned home this morning, she had assumed he had gone home, but everyone at school was talking about how he'd been missing since Sunday. And that was when she'd noticed that their spell book was missing.

Now, in the dying day, shadows impaled themselves on the tall stalks, which waved back and forth at her like long, thin spikes. She shuddered and licked her lips, repeating the protection spell she had said on the bus.

That stupid girl was looking at me like I was insane or something. I was an idiot to try to be nice to her.

Figuring she had done everything she could possibly do to protect herself, she deliberately set foot on the earth in the field.

No matter what I have to do, she thought, *I will get him back.*

On the Kent family farm, Clark and his father worked in silence for at least an hour, but Clark told himself that was because of the chipper. With his superstrength, he ripped some old, dead trees out of the ground, chopped them, then his dad put them through the chipper. The machine growled and hiccuped, and they both watched it as if they were silently begging it not to break down. Clark couldn't count the number of times his mom had fixed it.

After that, there were some fence posts to mend and the cows to milk. Like any other farm boy, he sat on a stool and milked all three of them by hand—milking not a good job for superspeed or superstrength—while watching his father move through his own chores.

Though Clark worked in a blur, the sun was outpacing him, and he wondered if they'd get everything done before dark.

Farm life is hard, he thought. But then he took a breath and looked out at all the things his parents grew, and he thought, *Hard, but worth it*.

After the milking, there was still some sunlight left, and he and his dad drove to the hay field. It was almost dark, and in the distant, deep blue sky, the moon was rising.

They had baled all the hay except for a few errant stacks on other days. Now all that left was to truck the bales into the barn. Clark did the hefting, and his dad kept the big squares organized on the flatbed.

With his tongs, Clark would pick up each bale and toss it onto the bed—a job no ordinary man could have done, much less with such ease. His father shook his head and pushed the bales up against their many brothers and sisters. Working together in silence, they had succeeded in clearing the field of all but a few bales near the barn.

"What, Dad?" Clark asked, concerned. "Did I throw it too hard?"

The mood had been somber, each of the Clark men lost in thought. Clark kept thinking about Joel Beck and wishing he was out looking for him. As for his own father . . . *I don't know what my dad's thinking about*.

"No, you didn't throw it too hard." Jonathan smiled faintly. "I'm just thinking how lucky we are that you've got powers." Wiping his brow with a leather-gloved hand, he gestured to the hay and added, "This would have taken a regular guy like me hours to do."

Clark smiled back, but inwardly he winced. *I am a regular guy*, he wanted to remind his father. But of course it wasn't true. *Sometimes, all I want is to be your son. Really and truly your son.*

His dad clambered out of the flatbed and got into the cab. Clark joined him; they were on their way back to get the bales closer to the barn. Jonathan had left them for the last on purpose, so they wouldn't have to haul them around while they gathered up the others.

"Sure would be nice to have a round baler," Jonathan added, by way of trying to make conversation. Now it was Clark's turn to smile faintly. Some men dreamed of fancy cars; his dad wanted a slick new hay baler. He thought about the truck Lex had tried to give him shortly after Clark had saved his life and wondered if it had been a hay baler, if his dad would have had as easy a time of it giving it back to Lex.

"I'll get you one for Father's Day," Clark teased. The two shared a faint smile. Hay balers were so expensive that some of the other farmers in the county could only lease them. These days, the local family farms were struggling on all fronts . . . making offers of buyouts from the Luthors that much harder to resist.

"Now, about Mom," Jonathan began, and Clark knew they had finally reached the subject on both their minds. "You know we're right about looking for Joel, Clark. There are other people who are better at that than you. Professionals. You don't have to do everything, son." He looked at him very seriously. "You can't save everyone."

"But Mom was so upset," Clark ventured.

"She's afraid for you."

Clark blinked. "Me?"

His father nodded. "It's such a dangerous world, son. So much can happen to you. If your mother and I really sat down and thought about it, we'd probably both go crazy."

"But I've got my powers, Dad. I can take care of myself."

His father put the truck in gear; as he looked in the rearview mirror, his voice got a little softer, a little sadder. "I still remember when we kept trying to have a baby. You know, when we got married, it never occurred to either one of us to wonder if we could have children. We just assumed it would happen. It's one of those normal, everyday parts of life.

"But it didn't happen for us. It nearly killed her, I think. The one thing she had her heart set on. She felt so betrayed . . . by her own body. One day she said, 'My innocence is gone, Jonathan. Bad things really *do* happen to nice people, and for no good reason. One of us could die tomorrow. Anything can happen to us.' "

He paused, and gazed at Clark. "Then the meteors struck."

Clark paled. *The meteors were my fault. They came to Earth with me . . .*

"And out of all that death and destruction came the thing she wanted most in this world," Jonathan went on. "A son."

Touched, Clark swallowed. "It's . . ." he began. *It's hard being wanted that much. Mom must have had a lot of daydreams about what her son or daughter was going to be like. I don't know if I'm measuring up. And she sure didn't dream about adopting a baby from another planet . . .*

"So we get scared," Jonathan finished. "Scared you'll get hurt. Scared someone will find out about you and try to take you away from us."

"But . . ." Clark trailed off, unsure of what to say.

"But you have to grow up," his dad said. He sighed. "It's hard to let you do that. But we're trying."

"I know." Clark nodded. "For what it's worth, except for the no football thing, I think you're doing a great job."

"So do I, son," Jonathan replied. "So do I." The expression on his face was one of great pride, and a surge of love warmed Clark from the crown of his head to his toes.

"Look. There's your mother." Jonathan pointed toward the house, where Martha Kent stood on the porch, waving at them. "I'm starving. How about you?"

"Starving," Clark agreed.

They drove on in, and his dad said they could unload the bales tomorrow. Clark started to follow Jonathan, then stopped beside the house and picked a couple of sunflowers. Then he carried them in and found her putting a basket of freshly baked biscuits on the table.

Giving her a peck on the cheek, he handed her the large brown-and-yellow blooms.

"Oh, Clark," she said warmly, "how thoughtful. They're so beautiful."

His dad came into the room, took note, and gave his son a small, pleased wink. Clark said, "I'll put everything else on the table, Mom. You sit down." Then he pulled out her chair and waited for her to sit.

"Mother's Day was Sunday," she joked.

"I'm practicing for next year."

He went to get dinner.

Lana had just returned home from a very busy shift at the Talon when she got Ginger Brucker's call.

"I'm so sorry to bother you," Ginger said in a tiny voice. "But I . . . I'm alone here in the house, and well, weird things are happening."

Lana's brows rose in alarm. "What kind of weird things? Is there an intruder?"

Ginger hesitated. "Maybe."

"Ginger, your teeth are chattering."

"I'm in the front yard," Ginger told her. "I'm scared to go inside." She hesitated. "I don't have a car or anything ... um ..."

Lana got it. She said gently, "I'll be right over. Stay put, okay?"

"No worries there." Ginger laughed uneasily. "No way I'm going in there alone."

Lana hung up and looked regretfully at her aunt, who had spent the last hour making homemade caraway-carrot soup—a wonderful dish Lana was considering for the Talon's menu. Her aunt gave her a questioning look as Lana crossed the kitchen to go to the hall toward her room, to get herself a coat.

I'll take my green jacket, too, for Ginger, she thought. To her aunt, she explained, "That new girl, Ginger? She's home alone, and she's pretty nervous."

Her aunt frowned. "Poor thing. Bring her back here. We'll have soup together."

"You go ahead," Lana urged her. "Her mom's probably on her way home from work. I'll just stay with her until she gets there."

"You're a sweet girl." Nell took the napkin ring off her lavender napkin and laid it in her lap. "I'll heat some up for you when you get back."

"Thanks."

Lana got the coats, then gave her aunt a quick wave and left the house. She climbed into their truck, got it in gear, and drove away.

On her left, she passed the Kent farm. There were lights on in the farmhouse dining room. The Kents were probably sitting down to an excellent meal. As a rule, farmers ate very well.

I'll ask Clark's mom about her corn chowder recipe, Lana thought. *She may not part with the creamed corn secret, but maybe the chowder's another story . . . or recipe . . .*

Country roads are dark roads, with no streetlights as there are in the city. Only the truck's headlights illuminated Lana's way as she trundled along, recalling what Chloe had told them about Joel Beck. So many strange things happened in Smallville; she hoped there was a simple explanation for Joel's disappearance. Maybe he had had a falling-out with his parents; and he was staying with friends to cool off . . .

The headlights played over the road; she turned the radio on for company. Her aunt had left the radio tuned to a classic rock station, and Lana smiled faintly, imagining her parents listening to this music—the Clash, the Stones—and turned it up.

Then she realized she was hunched over the wheel and her fingers were clamping hard. A gaze to the right told her what her mind already knew: She was nearing the cornfield Joel had darted out of.

The one where he saw a ghost. Or said he saw a ghost.

Lana tried not to look at the moonlight on the stalks, but she did. There was a variation in the way the light fell, sort of a like a shadow in reverse, something that seemed to suck in the light.

After a few more seconds, she was past the field, and she relaxed and concentrated on her driving. She wasn't exactly sure where the Welles house was, and Ginger's directions were a little hazy.

At last she saw the weather-beaten sign for Waitley Lane. The road was old, and her tires bumped through a number of potholes. There it was: a large farmhouse with a sloping roof, a few lights on in a couple of the rooms, and a girl standing well away from it. She was silhouetted against the moon, and, even from a distance, she looked frightened and very, very alone.

As soon as Ginger saw Lana, she waved and hurried toward the truck. Lana slowed and rolled to a stop. She gathered up her coat and jacket, opened up her door, and hopped down to the ground.

"Hi. Thanks so much for coming," Ginger blurted, by way of greeting. "Oh, God, Lana, I'm so scared." She bit her thumbnail, then raked both hands through her hair and nearly burst into tears. "You probably think I'm crazy . . ."

"No," Lana replied kindly. "It's okay, really."

"I don't know anybody else. Well, Clark, but . . ."

Lana handed Ginger the jacket. "It's chilly tonight." She looked at the house. "It's a big place. Someone could probably break in without you hearing it."

Ginger hesitated. She said, "I . . . I don't think anyone broke in. I think . . . someone was already inside before Mom and I moved in." She took a deep breath and half closed her eyes, as if she was about to say something she really didn't want to say. "Lana, I think the house is haunted."

Lana's stomach clenched. She cocked her head, and Ginger rushed on. "We have a Bible . . . I didn't know we had one, my parents aren't religious or anything. It fell out of the bookshelf. Just fell, and to this passage about smiting your enemies and stuff." She took another deep breath. "Twice."

"Oh." Lana didn't want to panic Ginger; she was upset enough as it was. "Old houses settle . . ."

"Not like this." The other girl's eyes were huge. "Lana, there was water on the page, then I swear it looked like blood. The second time, I mean. First water, and then blood. And, you know, everyone at school was talking about that guy who saw a ghost . . ." Her shoulders sagged. "I'm wondering if the same ghost hangs out here . . ."

The two looked at each other. Lana couldn't help shivering in the cold . . . at least, that was what she told herself she was doing. But her scalp tingled as if someone was kneading her head with a bunch of toothpicks. Her cheeks were hot.

Ginger's gaze ticked past Lana to her truck.

"Do you want to go to my house?" Lana offered.

The other girl shook her head. "My mom should be home any second. I keep trying to reach her cell, but I can't get through, not even to leave a message."

Lana tried to put her at ease as she said, "Well, we can wait for her. We can sit in the car, turn on the heat, and listen to the radio."

Ginger looked tempted. She glanced over her shoulder at the house. "I don't want my mom to go in there without me at least trying to figure out what's going on," she said with an air of protectiveness. "She's been through a lot. She was . . . she was there when my dad died." Her gaze grew solemn and downcast. "It'll scare her if she comes home and I'm not here."

Lana was touched. *She really loves her mom.*

"Because what . . ." Ginger took a deep breath. ". . . what if it's my dad, and he's . . ." Her eyes welled and she looked down at her hands.

After a beat, Lana prompted, "You think your dad is in the house? That he's trying to contact you?"

Should I tell her about me? Lana wondered. *Should I confide in her?*

Ginger didn't look up as she nodded. Lana waited for Ginger to go on, and when she didn't, Lana offered, "But that would be a good thing, wouldn't it? If your dad was here."

"I don't know," Ginger whispered.

When she finally did look up at Lana, her face was contorted with pain. "Lana, I think . . . he might be very angry. You know, Earthbound. That Bible was open to a verse about vengeance." A single tear rolled down her cheek. "I think my mom had something to do with . . ."

Ginger buried her face in her hands. "Oh, Lana, I haven't slept in months! Mom has these terrible nightmares. She talks in her sleep, and she tells him she's so sorry for . . . for killing him."

Lana was shocked. "Are you saying that you think that she . . . ?"

"Killed him?" Ginger cried out.

"Oh, my God!" Lana covered her mouth, then gathered Ginger into her arms. "Oh, no, Ginger, that can't be right!"

Ginger began crying in earnest, sobbing against Lana's shoulder. "It's like he's haunting her dreams. She's been so different since it happened. So distant."

"Your father wouldn't try to hurt you," Lana asserted. "I'm sure he loved you very much. And I'm sure your mom didn't do anything. She's just feeling guilty because she's alive, and he isn't."

That sounded brutal, and Lana was sorry. "What I mean is—"

"I know what you mean." The other girl wiped her eyes. "But you can see that I don't want my mom going in there alone."

"Okay, then. Let's try to figure out what's going on." She raised her eyebrows and her shoulders at the same time, a sort of nonverbal question mark, and stuffed her hands into her pockets.

Ginger sighed, and said, "Okay."

The house loomed large as Lana approached. The slanted roof looked like a giant forehead, angrily titled forward. The porch was a jutting chin, and the door . . . a mouth. The windows, fierce eyes . . . *and I have been watching way too many scary movies. They're just windows.*

And all the green-glowing rocks in town are just rocks.

They walked side by side, Ginger unconsciously slowing her gait as they climbed the porch. Lana was nervous; she wondered if Ginger had any idea how many strange things went on in this country-bumpkin town. If this was any other town in America, she would probably be more excited than afraid about doing some ghostbusting. But given that this was Smallville, there was no telling what was going on inside the Welles farmhouse.

The wind picked up, rustling bushes and rushing through a crop field somewhere nearby. It was cold for May, and Lana wondered if that was due to whatever was going on.

Someone had to go through the front door first. Lana took the lead and pushed open the door. She could feel Ginger falling back. She glanced over her shoulder to reassure the other girl and went inside.

Lana alone stood in the dim foyer. There was a grandfather clock; she could hear it clacking away. The moon glanced off the walls and cast elongated squares of light on the floor.

Like teeth, Lana thought uneasily.

Nothing happened.

At the door, Ginger watched her, looking very uncertain. After about thirty seconds, she came into the house and shut the door.

"This is a beautiful old place," Lana said enthusiastically. "Turn-of-the-century."

"They don't build 'em like they used to," Ginger replied, obviously trying to make a joke. But her voice cracked. The tears in her eyes were threatening to spill down her cheeks.

She is really, really scared.

"I want to show you the picture I drew," Ginger said. "It's on my bed."

"Where's your room?" Lana asked, still trying to sound upbeat.

Ginger gestured toward the stairs. Now it was Lana's turn to feel uncertain. She wasn't sure she wanted to go up there, isolate herself from making a rapid exit, if that was required. . . .

"How about some tea?" she asked. She rubbed her arms. "We can wait for your mom in the kitchen. You know, it's cold in here."

Ginger bit her lower lip and half turned her head to the left, where Lana assumed the kitchen was located. "There's . . . there was a noise. In the cellar. The door to it is in the kitchen."

"Okay. Then we can . . ."

There was a thump. It sounded as if something had fallen, and it came from deeper in the house. Ginger looked stricken.

"That was in the study," she whispered. Frowning as she gazed in the direction of the sound, she added anxiously, "The Bible kept falling out of the shelf."

"Maybe the shelf is tilted," Lana suggested. "Where is the study?"

"I really don't want to go in there," Ginger demurred. "Please, Lana." She drew Lana's green jacket around her shoulders. "Let's go back outside."

"Fine," Lana said. "And we can leave. Your mom will understand."

Ginger looked torn. "I can't reach her cell phone. I can't even leave her a message." She sighed heavily. "I don't know what to do. She thinks I'm making all this up . . ."

"We can leave her a note."

Just then, a loud thump rattled the floor beneath Lana's

feet. She cried out and jumped to one side . . . a useless gesture, as the thump was followed closely by a second.

"Out," she ordered Ginger as she wrapped her hand around the doorknob of the front door and—

—it wouldn't turn.

"Oh!" Lana cried.

Ginger eased her aside and turned the knob. She stared at Lana.

"I didn't lock it. *It locked itself*," she cried.

Lana put both hands around the knob and gave it a hard twist. She yanked on it.

Nothing happened.

"Oh, my God," Ginger cried, beginning to panic. "Lana, we're locked inside here with a ghost!"

"Okay, okay," Lana soothed, struggling to gather her wits about herself. "It's an old house. We tripped the lock somehow. The thumps . . . do you have a boiler?"

"I don't know!" Ginger wailed. "You're just making all the stuff up so we won't be scared!"

"Do you have a hammer? Maybe we can . . ."

"Lana. Let's get out of here."

Lana capitulated. "Okay. Okay. Do you have a back door?"

Ginger closed her eyes. "We have to go through the kitchen to get to the back."

"We can do that," Lana said firmly. "We can." She reached out her hand. Ginger took it firmly. They gave each other a steadying gaze, and walked together to the kitchen. Ginger turned on the light switch and headed across the light green linoleum.

Lana looked around as they headed for the back door. It was an ordinary kitchen, pleasant enough, with green-and-yellow-checked wallpaper and a green tile floor. Dated, but still homey. Just a regular farmhouse kitchen . . .

The thump sounded again.

It came from the cellar.

"Boiler," Lana muttered to herself, trying to steel herself, fighting not to panic. Ginger was really starting to lose it, and they had to get out of there. "Boiler."

Then, without a moment's warning, the temperature in the kitchen plummeted. One moment it was chilly, and then it was icy. Lana could suddenly see her breath.

Ginger reached the back door and rattled the knob. She burst into tears, and said, "It's locked, too!"

Lana felt as if someone had just poured a bucket of ice water over her head. She said, "We'll call for help." But as she reached in her coat pocket for her cell phone, she realized she had left it in her purse . . . in the truck.

Barely coherent, Ginger ran to the cordless and picked it up. She stared at Lana, and said, "Call Clark."

"We should call the sheriff," Lana suggested.

"Call Clark!" she insisted.

Lana nodded, took the phone, and punched in his number.

Clark was in the loft, gazing through his telescope and feeling nostalgic for a time and place he didn't know . . . his infant years. So many stars glittered in the starfield; which ones had his birth parents seen when they had looked up at the sky?

Did they have eyes the same color as mine? Did they even have eyes? Did they make me look human so I could live here?

The phone next to his telescope rang, startling him. He had taken the cordless phone up with him; his mom had to watch a movie for one of her night school classes, and his dad offered to watch it with her. Clark volunteered to take any calls so they could watch it in peace.

He picked up it, connected, and said, "Hello?"

"Clark, oh, thank goodness!" It was Lana. His heart skipped a beat; then she was rushing on, and he could barely understand her.

"We're locked in Ginger's house. The Welles house. There's . . . there's something in here, Clark."

"I'm on my way," he said, and almost hung up. Then he said, "That's why you called, right?"

"Yes, yes!" she cried. "As fast as you can. Do you know where it is?"

"I was there with Lex," he told her. "I can find it."

"Hurry, please!" She sounded frantic.

"On my way," he said again.

As he hung up, he thought, *If I run, I'll get there faster. But if I run, there'll be way too many questions.*

He dashed into the house. The smell of microwave popcorn filled the air, and he found his parents on the couch . . . not watching the movie. They were kissing.

He cleared his throat. They broke apart like guilty teenagers, his mom smoothing her hair.

"Clark," she said, a bit too brightly.

"Mom, Lana called. She and Ginger are in some kind of trouble at the Welles house."

"Did they call the sheriff?" Jonathan cut in, looking worried.

Clark took a deep breath. He had to tread carefully, or he might get ordered to stay out of it . . . again. And this time, it was Lana who was in trouble.

"I don't know, Dad. I do know that she called *me.*"

His parents looked concerned. They glanced at each other. Over their hesitant, what-shall-we-say? expressions, he said, "I need to go this time, okay? I really need to."

"Okay." His mom bobbed her head and glanced sideways at his father, who sighed and nodded, too. "Truck keys are on the hook in the kitchen."

"Thanks, Mom. Dad."

He blurred at superspeed to the key hook, then out to the truck. It was then that he realized it was still loaded with hay bales.

The mileage is gonna suck, he thought, and put his foot on the gas pedal.

As fast as an overloaded old farm truck could speed, he was out of there.

Clark had a curious sense of déjà vue as he tore down the highway, acutely aware that he was on the same stretch of road where he and his parents had almost run down Joel Beck. There was the cornfield where it had all happened . . .

Hey, he thought, as he trundled past, *there's someone in the field.* Something was flickering—firelight, flashlight, he couldn't tell . . . but he couldn't stop.

Is Joel camping out there? I'll have to check it out after I make sure Lana's okay.

He made a right turn onto a road whose sign he couldn't read, but he recognized the beat-up old mailbox from his first trip out, with Lex.

What I wouldn't give to be behind the car I drove then . . .

As he approached the Luthor house, he saw a large black Hummer heading out toward the road. Clark took the time for a glance and saw that Lex was going out.

Wonder what the occasion is?

He tried to make the truck go faster, but it was old and tired, like a lumbering trail horse, and he tried his best to stay patient.

Then the front tire blew.

No, he thought stunned. *No!*

He got out, glanced at the tire, thought briefly about

changing it, and decided to just go for it. Lana was in trouble, and he could fix the truck later.

He began running at superspeed along the country road. At night he could be a little less careful with his powers, particularly when moving this fast . . . and there had been no traffic so far. A little blur in the rearview mirror? Most people would think they just imagined it.

He figured he was going to damage his shoes; the first few times he'd gone out for superspeed runs he'd laid down rubber when executing tight turns. Suspending friction and momentum unfortunately weren't among his powers.

He didn't want to have to explain to Lana or Ginger why his shoes were trailing smoke . . .

He slowed further, managing to avoid many sharp scuffs on the road, and turned at his best maneuvering speed. Only a little farther now.

A vehicle lumbered in the distance; it looked like some kind of appliance delivery truck. It was moving at a pretty good clip toward the Welles place, but he'd beat it there—no risk of being seen.

A wind blew across the wheatfields, cooling his skin. It always amazed him that he could still feel the wind when he ran this fast, but it was not a problem unless he was running directly into or away from it.

He could see the Welles place now—the large framed house, the sloping roof. Hardly any lights on.

And then he heard a scream.

Lana!

Clark increased his speed.

As he neared the house, everything came into crystal-sharp focus. He could see the delivery truck approaching, the shutters on the house painted with light from inside, nearby trees swaying in the breeze.

And *there*, spilling out from the house—out a large broken window—were Lana and Ginger. They were screaming, and it galvanized Clark in a way that he couldn't explain, a primal, protective urge.

The two girls looked horrified; then Ginger ran past Lana's truck directly toward the road, where she'd be in a few seconds. Lana chased after her, waving her arms.

Right in front of the delivery truck.

Lana!

His heart suddenly beat faster, and a bolt of terror ran up Clark's spine. One of his greatest fears was that somehow, someday he'd fail to protect someone he loved with his powers. There were many things he couldn't do, and he didn't expect he'd be able to stop acts of God—a heart attack, or cancer.

But a speeding truck *was* within his capabilities.

If he could get there in time.

Ginger stumbled out into the road, still completely freaked out. She didn't even see the truck yet.

It was going to be close.

Clark pushed himself hard, getting every ounce of speed he could out of his powers. The scene seemed to still, as if time had stopped.

Ginger had noticed the truck at last, and she was screaming again, this time at the new danger. Lana stood at the side of the road, frantically shouting at her.

Clark's problem now was that he was traveling extremely fast *toward* the truck. He had to stop his momentum, but he wasn't certain how.

Sometimes thing around him seemed to slow. It was as if he had all the time in the world to take note of each detail in his environment, carefully considering his course of action. Now was one of those times. He looked up at the truck, a huge, flat fronted vehicle with a big window and M-A-C-K spelled out above the radiator grille. The truck driver looked panicked; he was standing on the horn. The sound pervaded the still scene, adding an extra-low-frequency thrum to it.

Clark slapped the front of the truck, pushing as he did so, using his years of practice to slow his body to a neutral speed before grabbing Ginger. If he'd grabbed her at high speed without care, she might get hurt.

Once he had her, he leapt to the side of the road, and they fell to the ground. There might be a dent where he'd hit the front of the truck, but it was worth it.

The scene sped up, sound became normal again, and Clark found himself looking at a very surprised Lana Lang and Ginger Brucker.

Lana ran toward him. "Clark? How'd you get here? The *truck*—"

Clark helped Ginger to her feet. "My tire blew."

Lana's eyes widened. "Are you all right?"

"Sure. You guys sure do like to live dangerously though. Shouldn't play chicken with delivery vans."

Ginger threw herself into his arms, and cried, "It's haunted! It tried to kill us!"

"Whoa."

He tried to ease her away, make sense of what she was saying, when Lana interjected, "There's something going on in there." She was panting from her run; her cheeks were rosy in her pale face. Her gaze was troubled, and she was trembling.

"It locked us in," she added. "It wouldn't let us out."

"I'm sorry I freaked," Ginger told her. "I ran right past your truck!"

"I should take a look," Clark ventured, and Ginger cried, "No!"

But she didn't know what kind of look he meant. His

work boots crunching over pebbles and weeds, he used his X-ray vision to scan the house.

Whoa, he thought again.

Something was in the cellar, and it was glowing the familiar green glow of the Smallville meteors, the ones that sapped his strength and could kill him if he got too close for too long.

Is that what's "haunting" this house?

"Could it have been a trespasser?" Clark asked Lana, who had the cooler head of the two girls. "Someone in the house?"

Lana shook her head. "It was . . . not something like that," she said carefully.

Ginger spoke again. "It was a ghost. It kept making books fall out of the shelves . . . our Bible, and it locked the doors. And it made this horrible sound."

Lana nodded in agreement. "She's right." She looked over her shoulder at the house and shuddered. "There's something in there, Clark." She looked at him. "What could it be?"

I'm not sure I can go in there. If that was a meteorite I saw, I need to steer clear.

He took a step toward the house.

Lana blurted, "Clark, please, let's just get away from here. We can talk about it on the way, okay?"

I don't want to just walk away, he thought, but both the girls were staring at him with terrified expressions.

He thought for a moment. Then he said to Lana, "We'll talk to Chloe about it. This is definitely her territory. Meanwhile, I need to fix my truck. Then you can go to Lana's house Ginger, and wait for your mom there."

"Okay," Lana said. "Good plan."

"You have to believe us. It's haunted," Ginger said.

He scanned the house again. There was the glow of green,

still there, and *something* went from one room to another, before fading out completely.

The hairs stood up on Clark's neck.

"I believe you," he said.

CHAPTER SIX

Lex Luthor sat in his home office, resting his elbow on the adjustable armrest of his Aeron chair. He stared at the active matrix screen of his Titanium PowerBook, reading the figures for the plant's monthly variance report.

Things were looking good.

When he'd come to Smallville—or rather when he'd been *exiled* here—it hadn't been that way. Fertilizer Plant Number Three had been on the skids, with high turnover, low earnings, and a public who hated it.

Lex had hated it, too. Transferring him to Smallville had been a particularly nasty move in the game his dad played with Lex to help the young overcome his fears, to be strong, take charge, and "be a Luthor, Lex!"

It had been here, after all, where *it* happened—where he'd lost his hair during the meteor shower, where he'd run away from a flaming ball of rock in a cornfield. He'd only been nine at the time, his hair had come out in great clumps almost immediately, much to the discomfort of Lionel Luthor, his very virile father. The older Luthor had been disgusted with Lex's hairless head and had covered that disgust with gifts . . . and trips to medical centers all over the country.

But nothing had worked, not implants, not even that very special Hair Club for Men—at ten, Lex had been its youngest member, and one of the few unsuccessful ones. Nothing.

The ridicule from his classmates, and the combination of pressure and disgust from his father, whom he could never please, were constant companions.

"Hey, Baldie! Hey, Chemo-Boy! Hey, Cueball!"

"Why don't you be a *Luthor*, son?"

But a curious thing had happened. With no one else to turn to, he'd turned to himself.

Never particularly physically strong, and with no allies to go against the classmates who bullied him, he'd backed down in public—and gone after his tormentors when they were alone. His father had insisted that he learn self-defense at an early age, and those skills had been put to use as he sought his revenge.

After a while, even the few he hadn't been able to defeat respected him.

He kept all of this from his father, however.

In that arena, he'd spent a great deal of time crafting the image of the spoiled rich kid. It was the one weapon he had, the one trump card he could play.

To *not* be ready to take over LuthorCorp.

His father, a man who'd worked his way up to become the head of a multibillion-dollar chemical-manufacturing empire, had fought his recalcitrance at every turn. He'd pushed Lex, lectured him, threatened him, trying to get him to shape up. He'd even hired other kids Lex's age to befriend and manipulate him.

But Lex had resisted.

The irony was that he really had become more capable as a result of all the years of teasing and neglect—just not in the manner of his father.

Lionel attacked openly and cleanly, taking over other companies, firing people, dueling with a foil for stock options. He was a bear or bull, depending on the goal, and charged forward swinging, both fists ready to go. Sometimes the elder Luthor would play the fox, waiting, but he would always resort to a frontal assault for the endgame, relishing the hot-blooded sense of accomplishment.

Lex, on the other hand, was cooler, more calculated. He

slid sideways to avert confrontation, outsmarted his enemies, and never met them head-on if he could avoid it. His route, forced on him by necessity, was more circuitous, but worked equally well.

It just wasn't how his father wanted him.

Ostensibly, it had been his problems in Metropolis that had been the final straw that sent him here, but Lex knew better. His dad was putting the pressure on again, to see if he would try harder, be a model son and prepare himself for the mantle of the Luthor legacy.

And Lex had almost given up, let his image become the reality. He'd had enough from his father, enough of the games.

But Smallville had inspired him, although not exactly as his father had intended. Rather than trying to escape the terrifying place where he had been stigmatized as a child, he'd found himself adopting a new strategy.

It had been the people. He'd never been anywhere where people were so openly opposed to his father. It was refreshing, even though he was included in the grudge, cast into the same role as far as the town was concerned.

Lionel Luthor could have written a book on domination in the workplace: Treat your employees like dirt and make them take it. He'd used the same practices in child-rearing.

So the younger Luthor could empathize with the people in Smallville, could understand their anger.

And was in a position to do something about it.

He'd made changes at the Smallville plant—added education programs, increased the pay, and even reduced hours. That it had actually improved the bottom line was a bonus he hadn't anticipated. His latest attempt to thwart his father had also made him into a success.

And he liked it.

But more than that, he liked it that his father's way wasn't how he'd achieved it.

How about that, Dad?

The second part of his Smallville turnaround had been the meteor rocks.

They'd proven his nemesis in childhood, providing terrifying nightmares and casting him as the Caliban in every real-life school play.

And then he'd started seeing their potential. The rocks' strange radiation could give incredible power to whoever learned to harness them. And there was no one in a better position to do it than he. With the rocks . . . who knew how far he could go?

He had a personal interest, too—he wanted to understand how they had changed him, and why. What other effects from their exposure might be lying dormant?

Now that he had two top scientists working on the problem, he hoped he'd see progress soon. The creation of an artificial isotope, or better yet, a machine that could replicate the radiation, would give him the means to perform more experiments to see how he could best use the radiation to his advantage.

Which might or might not be to his father's advantage . . .

He smiled, a tight-lipped grin, imagining how his dad would react if Lex returned to Metropolis, not as an errant son come crawling, but as a victorious entrepreneur, ready to buy out controlling interest in LuthorCorp.

It was a nice dream.

Abruptly, the cell phone on his desk rang.

It was not the usual phone that he carried, but a cheaper one, purchased for this one use.

Lex picked it up and pressed TALK while simultaneously activating an antibugging suite of devices with a switch on his desk. The interface was simple; a red LED, a green LED, and the switch.

When the LED was red, he was bugged.

It was green.

"Hello?"

"Hello, Mr.—"

"No names!" he said sharply, cutting off the caller.

Even though the line didn't appear to be monitored, it didn't pay to take chances. If there was anything Lex had learned in the corporate world, it was that.

"Do you have them?" Lex asked.

"Yes, we do. There is the matter of price . . ."

They talked for a few minutes, haggling, and came to an agreement. The caller gave Lex a location, and a time, and the younger Luthor agreed to be there.

He hung up the phone and hurled it across the room into the huge stone fireplace. The plastic shattered on the hard stone, destroying it.

Lex rose from his chair after shutting his computer down.

He had preparations to make, and people to see.

Lex threaded his way through his many-car garage, walking past a veritable who's who of sports cars. There were Ferraris, Lamborghinis, and Porsches—Lex's favorite for general around-town driving. He had several of them, including a street-illegal gray-market 959 that he'd slipped past customs, and a Ruf CTR2, one of the fastest production cars in the world. There was also the regular assortment of Targas, turbos, and Cabriolets.

Over in the corner sat a McLaren F1 GT, probably the rarest of his collection, since only three had ever been made. The 6.1-liter quad-cam V12 engine in the sleek, silver car produced no less than 629 horsepower, and held the top acceleration record for a production car, taking only 3.4 seconds to reach 60 mph. Its top speed was 240 miles an hour, just second to the Vector Avtech at 249. It had been custom-fitted, with seats built based on his body measurements.

Each car sat in its own pool of metal halide light, like artwork in a museum. Some were covered with protective cloths, while the more frequently driven were not.

Lex appreciated a fine car. The efficiency and the control were what he valued most. Everyday cars were for everyday people. These were thoroughbreds, made for use by experts.

Yeah—experts who drive off bridges.

He grimaced at the memory. It wasn't *his* fault that a passing truck had spilled a spool of barbed wire on the road, now was it? No one could have anticipated *that*.

It wouldn't do to use one of these for the meeting he was going to. No, he needed a packhorse, not a racer. Something that he could carry cargo in, and something that wouldn't attract as much attention as one of these.

Beyond the exotics were more utilitarian vehicles—limos, trucks, and others. Lex walked past a few covered shapes, his shoes scuffing the concrete, and came to a large blocky silhouette covered with a white tarp.

He reached down and tugged it off, revealing a black Hummer H1. The vehicle was the 4-door wagon type, with an enclosed cargo area and black-tinted windows. Silver hubcaps gleamed on the huge 32x12.5 R-17 tires.

It was beautiful in a Bauhaus form-follows-function way. The H1 had been designed for the military to carry people and cargo over demanding terrain, and that was just what he was going to put it to use for tonight. Although he doubted he'd encounter twenty-one-inch vertical walls to go over, if he did have to go through streams of water up to thirty inches deep, he could do so with ease.

He got into the car and put the silver Zero-Haliburton briefcase full of money on the floor of the passenger's seat before grabbing the plain black steering wheel. There was so much space inside he felt for a moment that he was nine again and had just climbed into his dad's car.

Lex started the huge 6.5-liter V8 turbocharged diesel and turned on the lights. Analog dials lit up, telling him everything he'd ever need to know about the engine's performance.

He put the car in drive and pulled out, feeling like he was driving a tank. At over three-and-a-half tons curb weight, he might as well have been. It handled like a beast, but it was what he needed.

He'd had it modified by a professional security company called Ibis Tek with several interesting features, including bulletproof glass and Kevlar panels in the doors. There was no point in going to meet a black marketeer in anything less, particularly when you were Lex Luthor, and even more so when you were going alone.

And, of course, the fact that the items he was going to get were radioactive isotopes, *strongly* regulated by the government, well, it made things just that much more interesting.

He smiled wryly at the irony. Here he was, Lex Luthor, a millionaire in his own right, sneaking out in the night to buy black market isotopes for a pet project, when he could buy them legally—as part of the normal business of the plant.

But of course, if he did that, if he purchased the isotopes through normal channels, two things would result. First, he'd waste time locating them, getting the approvals, and having them shipped. There would be a sea of paperwork, which would lead to the second problem: lack of secrecy.

If any hint of what he was doing got back to his dad, any surprises he planned with the meteors would be blown. His father would come storming out at the first hint that something was going on, would want to dictate the terms of the research.

And, of course, there was damage control to consider. If anything went wrong with the project, if there was a lab accident, for instance, he needed total deniability. Pull the plug, pay off his Ph.D.s, and deny everything.

"Why no, I have no idea about any secret project. You're welcome to check the records, of course."

Now that Smallville was going well, his new image shining up, he wanted to keep it clean.

Ethically he didn't feel that this was a problem—if no harm was done to anyone, why worry? The potential benefits both for himself and mankind far outweighed the risks as far as he was concerned. Of course, other regulatory bodies might not feel that way.

He was far from worried about the safety aspects anyway. After Dr. Brucker's accident in Metropolis, he was reasonably certain her safety protocols would be superb. People were always more careful after a problem—that's why it was safer to fly after a crash. Safety overcompensation.

After hours of brainstorming and theorizing, "alpha decay" this, and "beta accretion" that, Dr. Brucker had given him a preliminary list of materials she'd need to start experimenting.

"I know it'll probably take a few weeks to get them"—she'd sighed, obviously anxious to get started—"but it'll give us some time to tune the equipment."

Lex had stared at the list for a few seconds, recognizing several of the metals she was asking for—the benefit of a science degree—and had shook his head.

"I think we can do a little better than you might think," he'd said. "I'm excited by the project, Janice, and I'll do what I can to get these fast."

He left her looking hopeful, and had forwarded the list to his contacts in Metropolis.

And because there was no one else to trust, he had to pick

up the goods himself. There was simply no one else to delegate to.

The H1 thundered along the dark country road, pushing seventy, the Kansas speed limit. Getting stopped on the way to Metropolis wouldn't be a big deal, but coming back would be a different story.

Secrets didn't bother Lex. That gift was something he'd had ingrained from his earliest years in the Luthor household. Amid servants who reported his moves to his father, friends of the family looking for an edge, and a father who was always judging him, they were something to be treasured.

Maybe that was another reason Smallville spoke so strongly to him. It was *full* of secrets, good and bad.

Even his straight-arrow friend Clark Kent was shrouded in mystery. Adopted at age three with no knowledge of his parents, and with a strange knack for being in the right place at the right time, Lex just knew there was more to the Clark story than met the eye.

No problem there; he respected his friend, and found his day-to-day honesty and open mind refreshing. Clark was one of the few people who didn't judge him because of who and what Lex's dad was and could do; and that, plus his utter lack of greed even after befriending a billionaire's son, was probably the most astonishing thing of all.

It was ironic that Jonathan Kent didn't like his son hanging around Lex. Lionel Luther would probably feel the same way, not wanting his son to have a penniless farmer as a friend.

Not that his dad even believed in friends.

"Luthors don't have friends, Lex," he'd said once, "only allies or enemies."

Ahead was a sign—"*Metropolis 15*."

He'd made good time.

Lex pulled out a portable GPS unit he'd brought and checked his location. He triggered the "list directions" option on the built-in map. The exit he needed to take was just ahead.

Lex drove the last few streets toward the meeting. It was an old brewery that had been abandoned when the bottling company consolidated its operations back East. There had been some talk about turning it into a museum a while back, he remembered, but no one had been able to raise the money.

Now that he was close it was time to make final preparations.

Lex had done a few deals like this before, and the key was always to be sure that you were ready for whatever might happen. Walking in blind, trusting that everyone would stick to the terms agreed on, was stupid. These people were criminals for skirting the law like this; so was he.

And criminals, by definition, aren't trustworthy. There is never, ever, any honor among thieves.

Lex pulled the car over and opened the briefcase with the money. Sitting on top of the stacks of banded bills was his laptop.

He got it out and tabbed it out of sleep mode, the screen's light casting his shadow upward, lighting his face from below like something from a monster movie.

The billionaire's son used the cellular modem to access a high speed Internet service and went to a military website. Once there, he used codes he'd purchased to log into a control server that had access to a geosynchronous satellite hanging high in the sky over Metropolis. The codes had cost nearly as much as the isotopes he was coming to buy, but they'd be worth it if they worked.

They did.

After he logged on, a menu of options came up, giving
him effective control of the satellite. He checked to be sure
that there were no other jobs running, then accessed a navi-
gation menu to target the brewery.

It took only a few keystrokes to zero in on it. Once locked
on, Lex had several options available for imaging. He se-
lected a general view first, which gave him a nighttime
bird's-eye view of the loading bay near the back of the
building, where he was to meet the sellers.

A few streetlights illuminated the scene, and it looked de-
serted.

Let's see.

One of the key selling features of the codes he'd purchased was the thermal imaging the satellite was supposed
to be capable of. Lex triggered that function, and the scene
changed dramatically. Infrared radiation showing different
levels of heat overlaid the nighttime scene, and Lex could
suddenly see much more.

It looked as if the sellers were already there, waiting. Lex
zoomed the camera in, and tracked at least three separate hot
spots in and around the parking lot. One was on the loading
dock, one far to the right, in what looked like (and which he
confirmed) was a Dumpster, and one on the opposite side of
the parking lot.

Interesting, since the meet wasn't scheduled for nearly an
hour.

Was it trouble? Or simply sellers wanting to be sure that
they weren't ripped off?

Lex used several of the camera functions to identify the
number of people he was dealing with. Two were on the
dock, one in the Dumpster, and one across the parking lot.
The resolution of the camera during the daylight would be
so good that he could read the labels in their suits, but at
nighttime it was somewhat less crisp. He was able to discern

that they seemed to be carrying what *could* be weapons, but couldn't identify them.

Well, well, well.

He logged off the website, but not before picking a parking space that would put the H1 in a corner of the parking lot, well out of the triangle made by the three groups. If they wanted to cheat him, it would be harder. He shut down the laptop, putting it under the seat, and pulled out again, moving toward the meeting.

Lex drove the H1 into the parking lot, heading over toward the far corner that he'd picked. His position there put two of the three hot spots he'd identified in a line, and the other one off to his right, instead of behind him.

A much better vantage point.

He killed the engine and turned off the lights. He was still early for the rendezvous and didn't want to let his hidden watchers know that he knew about them.

So he waited.

Even though he was far better prepared than the people he was meeting, he still felt a little thrill run through him. It didn't get much more exciting than this.

The minutes ticked away, and as the appointed time arrived, a white Ford van pulled into the parking lot, stopping in the middle of the fields of fire Lex had identified with the satellite.

His stomach churned slightly. He couldn't be sure—yet—but it was looking more and more like a sting. He was pretty sure it was of a criminal nature, since he'd seen no sign of police anywhere, but there was only one way to find out.

Lex grabbed the briefcase and hopped down from the H1. He hit the concrete with a jarring thud, and waited to see what would happen.

A man, probably forty or fifty, stepped out of the van.

From this distance it was hard to see him clearly, but Lex made out a beard and tiny round glasses.

"Come on over," the man called to Lex. "It'll make the transfer easier."

"No thanks," Lex called out, "I like my spot here just fine. It's got lots of money."

He opened the briefcase and pulled out a stack of bills. He waved it in the air and tossed it toward the van. The bundle landed at the driver's feet. He reached down fast, grabbing the money.

"Okay, you got it. Coming your way."

But instead of moving the van, the man went around to the back of it and opened it up, grabbing a heavy-looking toolbox.

He lugged the box toward Lex's H1 and stopped when he was just in front of the car.

He said, "I'll have the rest now, if you don't mind."

Lex shrugged. "But I do. Let's see it."

The man sighed and opened the box. Within were partitions made out of a thick material that Lex bet were lead. The driver took a small LED flashlight from his pocket and pointed at the isotopes, calling them out by name.

"Looks good," said Lex.

The man smiled.

"Mr. Luthor, there's been a slight change in plans."

Lex's stomach tightened. What he'd expected, but still frightening.

"We think maybe we ought not sell these to you."

Lex started to move backward to the Hummer.

There was the sound of a gun being cocked—it was the man in the Dumpster— and the driver held up a hand.

"The money, please, Mr. Luthor."

Without hesitating, Lex set the silver briefcase on the ground and slid it over toward the bearded driver. The man smiled again and popped the case open, whistling at the stacks of bills.

"Guys, wait till you see *this*."

Lex took advantage of their distraction to move his right arm down, somewhat sharply. A black remote control slid down his sleeve from the pocket he'd had it in, and he caught it in his hand.

He tapped a large round button on the unit and waited to see what would happen. If the men were smart . . .

Lex watched the face of the driver. Although it wasn't as interesting as what Lex was hoping was happening behind him, it was more critical to how this was going to play out.

Behind him, a specially constructed roof panel of the H1 rolled back and a scissors jack activated, raising the fifty-caliber machine gun he'd had hidden in the back of the Hummer above the roof. Ibis Tek specialized in vehicles like these, used for corporate protection. Lex pointed the remote control toward the driver and tabbed another button. Behind him he heard the gimbals and gears whir as the machine gun oriented itself on the bright ruby laser spot he was painting the driver with.

The man stood there, his mouth a huge 'O' of surprise.

Lex heard curses from the men hidden on the loading dock and Dumpster.

"Plans seem to be changing a lot tonight," he said. "I think I'll take that box now."

The driver just stood there.

Lex tapped another button, and a loud click was heard in the now silent night.

"It *will* fire," Lex said. "Want to see?"

The man shook his head no and slid the heavy case toward Lex.

"Now get out of here, all of you," said Lex. "Keep the

money. It's what we agreed, and *go*. You two, you, and you,"
he said, pointing to the hidden men.

The driver of the van's eyes grew hooded, even admiring.
Everyone slunk into the vehicle like the bad little rats they
were and, aware that Lex's machine gun followed their
every move, drove away.

Lex waited until everyone was gone before loading the
heavy lead-lined box of isotopes into the cargo area. Once
he had done that, he hopped into the truck and triggered the
machine gun release to lower it back into the cargo area.

He was glad the men had decided to act reasonably. If
they hadn't, he'd probably have let them keep the money.

He was no killer.

Happy and relieved with how well things had gone, Lex
started up the Hummer and headed back toward Smallville.
Dr. Brucker would be pleased.

CHAPTER SEVEN

Clark, Lana, and Ginger stood beside Clark's truck as he rummaged around looking for the jack. He couldn't find it, which meant he couldn't change the tire without lifting up the truck himself. So he would have to catch a ride from Lana.

Lana drove. Ginger got in next, then Clark, who wondered aloud *why* a ghost would be haunting the place.

"Don't they always want something?" he asked rhetorically. "I don't think there are any old Indian burial grounds around here . . ." He trailed off.

"Lots of meteors, though," Lana said softly. "Lots of ghosts." She murmured, "Or maybe only two."

She and Clark both fell silent.

She's thinking of her parents, Clark realized. *I wonder if this is upsetting her.*

Squeezed between the two of them, Ginger fidgeted anxiously as if she were still too afraid to believe she was safe. *She may be right in thinking that*, Clark thought. *First there was no green-glowing meteor, then it was there, and Joel saw something . . . and now the house . . . for all we know, whatever this thing is could be hitching a ride with us right now.*

He didn't care for how spooked *he* was feeling.

"Maybe . . . maybe if we can figure out why it's here, we can help lay it to rest," Ginger ventured.

The other two remained silent. Then Lana cleared her throat.

"Like . . . have a séance," she said.

Clark leaned past Ginger to gaze at Lana. She blushed and

stared straight through the windshield. He didn't need X-ray vision to read her body language. She was about to tell them something she would just as soon not share.

"Promise you won't think I'm too weird," she began. Her voice dropped almost to a whisper.

Clark nodded. He'd promise Lana almost anything.

"A while back I . . . I had this idea that maybe I could contact my dad and mom."

Oh, Lana, Clark thought, feeling another protective surge. *I wish I could fix that wound in your heart . . . I wish the . . . whatever I feel for you could fill it.*

We're so alike, you and I. We're both orphans, and we both don't remember our parents. But I have so many more questions than you'll ever know . . . about what it's like to know that they loved you, and wanted you, and never, ever thought of sending you away . . .

"So I bought a book on séances," she continued. "And I . . . tried. To see them. Hear them." Her voice cracked, and Clark could almost see her in the graveyard, with candles and maybe some incense, trying desperately to make contact. "It didn't work." Her voice was hushed. "But I still have the book. Maybe if we put our heads together, we could try again to contact the . . . someone who isn't alive any longer." She looked at Ginger. "If there's someone like that in the farmhouse."

Clark saw something in Lana's expression beyond her embarrassment. It was hope.

He understood. *If there is a ghost in the Welles farmhouse, and we can figure out how to make contact with it, she might be able to contact her parents as well.*

"A séance in the farmhouse," Ginger murmured. She swallowed hard. "That's . . . that's so amazingly terrifying," she said, and she and Lana shared a look that took Clark out of the picture for a few beats.

"Yeah, it is," Lana agreed. "Amazingly terrifying."

Ginger said to Lana, "But if . . . if we could answer some questions by doing it . . ."

Lana's lovely eyes were shining, as if she was on the verge of tears, but none came. Then she said, "There's no guarantee, okay? I mean . . . it didn't work before. It might not work this time, either."

"Maybe this isn't a good idea," Clark ventured, seeing how shook-up both the girls were. "You two just had a big scare. I'd think that house is the last place you'd want to be."

Ginger opened her mouth to speak. Then she sighed, and said, "You're right. We might as well try."

Gently, Lana touched Ginger's arm. "Let's go to my house. We can wait for your mom there."

They rumbled down the road toward Clark's and Lana's houses. The moon seemed to chase them; it was low in the Kansas night sky and tinged with a luminous pink.

Then headlights flashed up behind them. Lana frowned slightly, muttering, "Please, no brights," while Clark glanced in the side mirror.

He smiled faintly, and said, "It's Chloe."

Lana pulled up to her house, and Chloe followed her, killing the engine and popping open the door. The chop-haired blonde emerged from her car with a handful of folders and notebooks, and said, "Clark, I guess you forgot I was coming over. I brought you some stuff for your paper."

"Oh, man, my *paper*." Clark shook his head. "I'm headed for a D at this point."

"Not to worry." Chloe looked triumphant. "I have over a century's worth of history for you here. Meaning that it's going to take you a century to read it."

She loaded the material into Clark's arms. Then she looked at Ginger, and said, "Hi. Hey, are you okay? You look like you've just seen a . . ." She narrowed her eyes and peered at Lana. "Okay, what's happened?"

"My house is haunted," Ginger announced.

Chloe's eyes widened, and a delighted smile stretched across her face. Lana nodded, as if to corroborate the story, while Clark shrugged noncommittally.

"No kidding?" she squealed. "For real?"

Ginger moved her shoulders. "I don't know. I—I—"

Chloe didn't seem to notice how upset Ginger was. "First Joel Beck and now this. I'd say we're swiftly moving into Wall of Weird territory." At Ginger's puzzled look she explained, "All these strange things happen here. Guys who suck the warmth out of people, guys turning into insects . . . wait, this sounds like your average high school boy."

Clark grimaced. "Thanks, Chloe."

She smirked, then grew serious. "I have a theory that it's all in the rocks. The meteorites. You know about the big shower, right?"

"Oh, yes," Ginger said softly, glancing at Lana. "I know about that."

"Well, I've collected all kinds of articles about mutations and strange occurrences—come by and see my clippings at the *Torch* office. A haunted house fits right in with the rest of the weirdness, in my opinion."

"Oh." Ginger blinked as Clark and Lana nodded in agreement. "I had no idea."

"Well, lots of people don't want to believe it," Chloe said. "To us, it's pretty obvious. But we're just"—she made air quotes—"kids." She rubbed her hands in anticipation. "Are you guys going to try to contact it? This spirit or ghost or whatever?"

Ginger grimaced. "I don't know."

Chloe shifted her weight, her eyes glittering with excitement. "We should do it now while the ectoplasm's hot." She laughed. "Or whatever."

Lana said, "Maybe we should take this a little slowly."

Ginger nodded. Then she said to Lana, "We may as well look at the book, anyway."

"A book?" Chloe echoed. "For contacting dead people?"

"For the right way to hold a séance," Clark cut in.

Chloe took that in. "A séance tech manual." She made a "scoot" gesture to Lana, saying, "*Please*, let me sit in." She chuckled and added, "That's a little séance humor. The word 'séance' comes from a French root meaning 'to sit.' You sit to call spirits."

"No calling necessary," Ginger murmured. "They've already made a connection."

Lana said, "I'll get the book. Please, come in."

"Don't mind if I do. It's cold for May," Chloe commented, quickly following Lana inside. "Weird." She clicked her teeth. "Just like my favorite farming community."

Lana's aunt Nell had left her some soup and a dinner roll on the dining room table, as well as a note that read, "*Gone to the grocery store. Back in a bit. Hope your friend is all right.*"

Lana went into her room while the others stood around. Clark realized he was hungry—the soup smelled good—and he wondered if his parents had left any popcorn.

If they even ate any. Maybe all they did was kiss.

Lana came back with an oversize hardback book bound in black open in her arms. She was thumbing through it and tapped a particular page. "Now I remember. We need six candles. And some cheese. And some bread."

"White or wheat?" Chloe asked, picking up Lana's roll.

◆◆◆

While the three girls gathered supplies, Clark went over to his house to get a piece of plywood for the broken window, located a jack, and told his parents about the truck. His mom's movie was over, and she was hunched over what looked to be a textbook. His father was cleaning some farm equipment. They both looked very upset when he told them about the tire blowout. Jonathan put down the crankshaft and Martha laid down her book.

"I'm going back to Ginger's with Lana," Clark added. "I'll ask her to give me a ride to the truck, then I'll fix it and drive it home."

"I knew that tire needed to be replaced," Jonathan said, grimacing an apology at both him and Martha. "I'm sorry it blew out on you." He added, "I hope you weren't driving very fast."

"No," Clark fibbed. *Okay, lied.*

"I'll come with you to take care of it," Jonathan said, half-rising from his chair.

"No, it's okay, Dad." He smiled and made a mock-muscle with his biceps. "I can handle it." His mother frowned. "Really, Mom. I'll be okay."

He smiled at them both.

Neither smiled back.

They caravaned back to the Welles house, Chloe alone in her car while Lana, Ginger, and Clark rode in Lana's. As they trundled down Waitley Lane, both girls visibly stiffened.

Lana murmured to Ginger, "It'll be all right."

Clark cleared his throat. "Look, we don't have to do this."

Ginger turned her gaze at the house. "I think . . . I think we do."

"And she's not going to do it alone," Lana added.

Then they were there, the house looming over them; the

three fell silent. Ginger tried her mother again from the safety of the front yard. Still no luck.

"Then let's do it," Chloe enthused, rubbing her hands together. "I want to commune with the spirits."

First, Clark insisted on boarding up the broken window with the plywood he had tied to the hood of Chloe's car. Ginger was impressed at his resourcefulness—he had brought a hammer and nails—and he actually got a little embarrassed by all her compliments. Chloe just grinned at her.

Then they went in, Lana and Ginger hanging back, while Chloe swept across the threshold and started flicking on lights.

"So, this is the scene of the crime, huh?" she asked brightly. She traipsed from room to room. "Yo, ghost!"

"Don't joke," Ginger said uncomfortably.

"Sorry." Chloe had led the other three into what looked to be a parlor. The room was small, set off the main living room. It looked as if it might have been used as an office at one time. Dark walnut bookshelves, mostly bare, lined the walls. A few held decorative baubles that could have come straight from the Victorian era. The tall windows facing the group were topped with a large valence supporting thick green velour drapes. These were held open by pale gold ropes with tassels that could have graced the Talon back when it was a movie theater. White sheer curtains completed the picture.

In the center stood a round table covered with an old embroidered tablecloth, the pattern on it something that looked vaguely Middle Eastern.

Chloe raised her eyebrows at Lana, who nodded. The contrast in their demeanor was striking—Chloe was eager to begin a new adventure, while Lana and Ginger were completely nerve-racked.

"It's perfect," Lana conceded. "Circles are supposed to be very important for calling spirits."

She opened the duffel bag Clark recognized from her cheerleading days. Inside there were six candles and some bread and cheese. As she unpacked, she explained that spirits were supposed to be attracted to the light and warmth of candles, and natural, aromatic food was also believed to draw them. According to Lana's book, *Spirit Mediumship and How to Develop It*, the only other things they needed were a good, harmonious sense of spirit and open minds.

At the Welles house, the séance was about to begin.

Clark looked around the room, his acute senses probing for any sign of the supernatural.

Nothing.

There was no debilitating green glow, either.

As Chloe would say, weird.

"I think it's really valuable that we're doing this now, while paranormal activity is still recent," Chloe continued. At Clark's less-than-enthusiastic expression, she said, "Look. We've handled a lot of very strange occurrences in Smallville. We've never gotten anywhere by pretending they weren't happening."

Ginger spoke up. "If . . . if this is my dad, I want to know." She took one of the candles from Lana and put it on the table. "I think we both want to know."

Lana nodded.

If someone had told Clark this morning that he'd be sitting around a candlelit table holding hands with three girls, it would have sounded like a fantasy. Sitting there, with Ginger on his left, Lana on his right, and Chloe in front of him, trying to summon the dead, was awkward and exciting.

Clark wasn't sure how open his mind was—sure, he'd seen a lot of strange things in his life, and he'd even seen *something* in the house earlier. But a real ghost? Were they *really* going to contact spirits? He could almost see his mom and dad rolling their eyes.

"Okay, let's start with a basic attempt at contact," Lana suggested, as she glanced down at the book, which was open to her right. "The book says there are several ways for that to happen. Let's see . . . if someone feels the impulse to start drawing something, or even writing, they should do it."

"Writing?" Ginger echoed.

"It's called automatic writing," Chloe cut in. "It'd be your hand doing the writing, but not *you*, if you get my drift."

"Too bad I can't do that for my history paper," said Clark, aiming for an attempt at humor to defuse some of the tension.

Chloe chuckled.

But Ginger and Lana didn't.

"Hold on," Ginger said. "I want to get my sketches."

"I'll go with you," Clark said, pushing back his chair.

"Okay, wait, let's all go," Chloe said, suddenly looking nervous.

They left the room in a group, Clark going through the doorway first. Ginger pointed at the stairs, and said, "My room's up there."

"Making a fast getaway impossible," Chloe drawled, her tone of amusement giving way to a squeak of anxiety.

Clark took the stairs, the others behind him. He was on alert for telltale signs that a meteor was nearby, but so far, so good.

Ginger's room was furnished with a four-poster bed, an antique desk and matching bookcase, and a few moving boxes. On the walls hung several framed cross-stitcheries of the alphabet, and an oil painting of a green vase of fat pink roses.

"The house came furnished," Ginger observed as she crossed to the bed. "That still life is hideous."

She picked up a thick piece of paper and showed it to the other three.

"Scary," Chloe said, gazing at the drawing of the farmer.

Clark was impressed. Ginger could really *draw*. He'd spent his entire life working in wheat and cornfields, and in a few lines she'd captured the flow, the essence of them.

"Nice work," he told her.

"It's okay," she said. "But this is what I wanted to show you."

She jabbed her finger at the figures in the drawings.

"When I drew those, it was almost like what Chloe said. I didn't know *why* I was doing it, it just . . . came out."

The two figures she'd sketched struck them all with their intensity. The sad look on the little boy, and the menacing farmer only heightened the sense of unease they were all feeling.

"Still *skeptical*, Chloe?" Lana asked gently.

Chloe tilted her jaw forward, like she was heading into a storm. "It's part of the job."

Clark checked around the room, kneeling to look under the bed, opening the closet door and flicking on the light.

"Nothing here," he told them.

"Okay." Chloe regarded the others as she picked up the sketches and cradled them against her chest. "Shall we go do this thing?"

Lana and Ginger nodded.

Clark took the lead again, and the group trooped back downstairs.

"I'm still not loving the stairway," Chloe muttered.

They went back into the downstairs parlor and took their seats.

"Okay." Lana scanned some more pages. "The basic séance uses yes or no questions directed at the spirit being contacted. The . . ." She looked up at the others and licked her lips. "The table might tip slightly, or we might hear tapping."

"Or the sound of the entire cellar trying to walk up the stairs," Ginger cut in.

"Wow, was it really like that?" Chloe asked.

"Yes," Ginger and Lana replied in unison.

"Wow," she said again, and glanced over her shoulder.

Lana read directly from the book. "More advanced events can allow the departed spirit to talk through one of the attendees."

"No way," Ginger blurted. "Drawing, maybe. Talking, uh-uh."

Lana turned back a page. "Besides the writing, or the drawing . . . here's the table tap part. Three tips of the table usually means yes, and one means no."

Chloe looked puzzled. "How do the spirits know that?"

"I guess we have to tell them," Lana suggested. She looked nervous.

"One and three so it's a little clearer," Clark ventured. "If it's one and two, they might sound too similar and . . . the . . . the séancers might not know what the answer is supposed to be."

"That sounds reasonable," Chloe said. "So let's ask yes and no questions and see what happens."

"We might hear a tapping sound," Lana continued, eyes glued to the page. Her hands were shaking, and her voice wavered. "If we ask a question that requires a longer answer, we can ask the . . . the spirit if it can respond to the alphabet, then read off each letter, waiting for either a tap or a tip."

"Sounds like we could be in for a long night," said Clark.

Chloe smiled. "You have anything else to do, Clark?"

He shrugged. "Just a history paper. It can wait."

So they lit the candles, placed the food in the center of the table, and dimmed the lights. After sitting down, they all held hands.

"We're all supposed to think calm thoughts, something that relaxes us. Be open to listening."

"We're supposed to *relax*?" Ginger echoed, her voice shrill.

Clark did his best to relax, thinking about Ginger's drawings, the peace and serenity of the Kansas fields. Ginger's hand gripped his tightly, and Lana's was damp from nervousness. It was remarkable how very *good* it felt. Not too large, or too small, but just right in his own hand.

"You have strong hands, Clark," said Ginger.

He could feel the blush moving up his face and was glad for the dim light.

"Ah, it's all the chores. Toughens your skin."

Yeah, particularly if you're from another planet.

"Quiet you two. *Focus*," Chloe remonstrated.

They sat still for a few more seconds. Clark became aware of the ticking of a grandfather clock, which he hadn't noticed before. It hung over the scene like a metronome.

"Say something," Chloe said to Ginger.

Ginger sat helpless, and looked to Lana.

"'Spirit of the house,'" Lana intoned, reading, "'we bring you gifts from life into death. Commune with us, oh spirit, and move among us.'"

A whisper of sound seemed to go through the room, and the temperature seemed to drop at least ten degrees.

"Yikes," Chloe murmured happily.

Clark's eyes widened as he felt the table lift from the floor. His hearing and vision sharpened of their own accord, and a chill ran up his spine. He heard Lana gulp and saw a look of shock on Chloe's normally calm face.

Clark focused on remaining calm. It wouldn't do to get

scared and accidentally squeeze too hard on Ginger's or Lana's hand.

He scanned the room with his X-ray vision and had a sense of pale, ghostly streamers holding the table up, like some kind of ectoplasmic rope.

If they're from meteors, I'm not feeling the effects yet, Clark thought.

"Are you the spirit of this house?" Lana asked breathlessly.

The table bobbed. Once.

At the same time, there was a loud tap against one of the bookcases. Ginger cried out, then clamped her jaw shut. Chloe whispered, "Stay calm."

Clark looked over at Lana. She stared back at him, eyes wide, and gripped his hand a little harder.

Lana Lang was holding his hand. Even in the atmosphere of the room, that was a pretty cool thing.

"I guess that's a yes," muttered Chloe from across the circle.

"Is there something you want us to know?" Lana asked.

Again the table tipped, and a tap came. This time it was from the bookcase on the opposite side of the room.

And then there was a second tap, and a slightly smaller tip of the table.

"What's that?" Chloe asked. "One tap or two?"

"Should we go on?" Clark whispered to the group. Lana and Ginger both did nothing, as if frozen in place. But Chloe's nod was echoed by the table.

One tip.

"Okay then," Lana breathed. She inhaled before she went on. "Did someone do something . . . wrong . . . in this house?"

The table jumped at least another couple of inches, the candles bouncing slightly, making Clark worry for a moment about whether or not they'd fall over and set the tablecloth on fire.

But they didn't. Whatever was holding the table up had a hold on the candles as well. For some reason the very thoughtfulness of that act gave a greater sense of presence to the spirit.

Wow.

Then the table jumped again, and Clark heard two taps— not as if they'd been struck in succession by a single hand, but almost simultaneously, like *two* hands had struck them at nearly the same time.

"Will you tell us what happened?" asked Chloe.

And suddenly things went crazy.

The table crashed down, and the parlor window flew open. The white sheers suddenly blew inward—no, wait; it wasn't a wind—it was as if there were a figure within the folds, a tall human shape, pushing through them.

The sheers took on the look of a bag being pushed at from within, the faintest impression of a hand or a face, or both, or maybe more than one appearing on it.

There was a loud popping sound, and the books on the top shelf of the bookcase behind Lana began falling off one by one.

The door to the room burst open, then shut, opened, shut, slamming over and over again.

The sound of footsteps marched around the table.

Ginger cried, "Stop it! Stop!"

She let go of Clark's and Chloe's hands.

Everything stopped. The door hung open. There were no footsteps. The drapes fell straight and unmoving.

"I'm done," Ginger murmured. "Now let's get out of here and—"

On the shelf, the books that had fallen over righted themselves just as the table jumped back into the air. It bobbled wildly.

One. Two. Three.

Three taps knocked from across the room.

Three means no, Clark reminded himself.

Clark used his X-ray vision again. Ghostly green trails floated through the air, stretching and pulling. They were eerie, like elongated shadows of fingers sliding against the wall . . . creeping toward the four of them, eager to grab someone . . .

Can the girls see them?

Suddenly the trails clumped together into a giant ball . . . no, there were *two* balls, a large one and a smaller one. They bunched together, and the table hit the ground again, jarring his shin.

Had he been a normal guy, he would have yelled. As it was, he was glad it hadn't hit any of the others.

Then all the books flew from the shelves, cascading to the ground. The sheers blew until they flapped and rippled like pennants. Ginger sobbed in terror. Lana gripped her hands against her chest, and Chloe—God bless her—appeared to be mentally writing the story of her entire career thus far.

Without discussion, the four ran out of the house, off the porch, and into the front yard.

Ginger was crying in earnest now; flinging herself into Clark's arms and burying herself against his chest. He held her, looking over her head at Lana and Chloe. Lana was somber, but Chloe looked more excited than terrified.

She said, "We need to debrief and I need to get home sooner rather than later. So let's go to the Talon on the way home and talk, okay?"

As they left the house, Ginger started to lock the front door. Chloe stopped her.

"If anyone is stupid enough to break in, I kind of think he or she will be sorry."

"The door'd probably lock on them anyway," said Lana.

Ginger laughed, at last, and the four of them started down the porch steps.

Lana stumbled slightly, and Clark quickly caught her.

"You okay?" he asked.

She smiled gratefully at him, then gently took a step away. Was it his imagination, or was she the slightest bit regretful about having to do so?

"Uh, yeah, kind of. It's just—it was *real*."

Clark understood. It was one thing to believe in an afterlife, but something else entirely to have proof that there was *something*.

"Do you mind driving?" she asked. "I'm shaking too hard."

"Sure," he said.

She handed him the keys, and he climbed into the driver's seat. Lana climbed into the passenger side, then seemed to realize that Ginger was waiting to get in, too, obviously wanting to go with her and him.

Chloe signaled that she was ready to go. Clark started up the truck. It was turning into quite the week for driving. First Lex's Porsche, and now Lana and Nell's truck. He'd fantasized a number of times about driving Lana around. It wasn't *precisely* how he'd like it to be, but sometimes, as his dad said, you had to take what you could get.

He put the old truck into gear and they pulled out onto Waitley Lane. The gears were stiffer than in his family's truck, and he had to take care not to grind them. *That* would make an impression on Lana, but not in a good way.

Clark accelerated away from the Welles house, looking back over his shoulder to be sure that Chloe was following.

Which was lucky.

Because as he turned his head back to the road, he saw a flicker of movement in the field at the edge of the road. A second later and he would have missed it. It was someone running.

And that person would be in front of the truck in seconds. *Oh no!*

Time seemed to slow to a halt, as it usually did for him under extreme stress. In the time he had to think at all, he frantically tried to figure out a course of action. If he jumped out of the car at superspeed, he'd give away his secret *and* risk injuring or even killing Lana and Ginger.

If he slammed on the brakes too hard, he'd risk having Chloe ram into him; if he veered off the road, *she* would collide with the runner.

The thoughts flashed through his mind, faster and faster, different options suggesting themselves based on speed, momentum, and his limited driving experience.

As he pondered the alternatives, he recognized the runner. *Joel!*

The boy who had gone missing was back again—just as before.

Except this time it looked like he'd really be run over.

The thoughts flying through Clark's mind didn't click perfectly, but he had no more time—he had to act now.

As the girls screamed, Clark shouted, "Who's that?"

He swerved slightly to the left, then back to the right, tapping his brakes so quickly that the old truck skidded slightly as he turned to the right again.

The old Chevy shot to the right side of the road just as Clark braked and swerved *again*, this time skidding back to the right, tracing an arc around Joel—who was now out of the danger zone.

As soon as the car had stopped, Lana turned to him. "Oh, my God, Clark! Who is that? We almost hit him?"

Clark got out of the truck and dashed toward Joel, who was racing toward him. By now, Chloe had also seen the boy in the road.

"Isn't that Joel?" she cried as she rushed forward with her hand extended.

"Hi, Chloe Sullivan, from the *Torch*."

He just looked at her.

Then he turned back to Clark. "Get me out of here," he begged him. His voice was low, practically a whisper. "Now."

CHAPTER EIGHT

I miss you, he said. I want to touch you again. I want to be back . . .

And then his fingertips grazed her forehead . . . .

The tears rolled down her cheeks, then Janice opened her eyes and realized she had fallen asleep in her new lab at LuthorCorp. She stirred, looked around, and saw that she was alone. There were a few workstations on soft gray consoles, a lot of cardboard boxes, and her empty coffee cup.

No one had come to check up on her. *So, do I not have a smart chip in my badge yet or are they respecting my privacy?* she wondered. She checked her watch, saw that hours had passed since Ginger had called, and felt a rush of mother-guilt. Her own mother—Ginger's grandmother—used to say to Janice, "Why did you have a baby? You never see her. She's always with those sitters."

Ginger had been a happy baby, and George, especially, had spent a lot of time working from home so one of them could be with her. True, there had been nannies and sitters, but Ginger hadn't seemed to suffer. It was just that Janice's part of the work often entailed long hours in labs, on security-secure computers and equipment . . . and so she had to be away.

But still, that maternal guilt never let up.

And add that to the guilt I feel over George's death . . . if I had any free time, I'd be spending it in therapy.

She rose unsteadily, drowsily rubbing her face . . . and that was when she remembered the dream. His touch, his voice. Her throat tightened, and it was difficult to swallow.

It had seemed so real, as if George was really trying to contact her, to speak to her . . .

. . . *wishful thinking,* she thought mournfully, *My heart, grieving while I'm asleep.*

She realized she was still underground, and looked around for a phone so she could check in with her daughter. She didn't see one. There wasn't much equipment in yet . . . *but one would have expected at least a phone . . .*

She tried her cell phone, but as she had anticipated, it didn't work. Nor had Ginger left her a message . . . or been able to. Janice was certain that she'd at least tried.

Something around here is affecting my phone. My messaging system should have been able to pick up something . . .

Finally, she located an intercom on the wall and pressed it.

There was no answer.

She blinked and tried it again.

Still no answer.

"Well, hell," she blurted. She started jabbing at it with her index finger.

Am I going to spend the night in here?

Joel was practically catatonic; he seemed unable to speak to anyone.

"You have to tell us what happened," Chloe insisted, as the group gathered around him.

He nodded. "I can't believe I did it twice. It's like I had no control over myself. Like someone was making me do it . . ." He doubled his fists. "I was so *angry* . . ."

As the others looked on expectantly, he said, "There's always been something here." He gestured behind himself, then said, "Get me out of here."

"We have to know what's going on!" Chloe said.

"Not here. It's not safe here," he said. "Take me to Holly's."

Clark frowned apologetically. "Holly?"

"Friend of mine," Joel bit off. "She lives close by. I don't know if she's even home. She goes out of town a lot. We can't stay here."

"Okay, okay," Chloe said, placating him. "Clark, we'll follow you." She gestured for Lana and Chloe to go with her. They did so, leaving Joel and Clark in Lana's truck.

"We could practically walk there," Joel said.

Following Joel's directions, Clark soon pulled up beside a small one-story yellow house. All the windows were dark.

"No car," Joel muttered, disappointed. "They must still be in Metropolis."

Now what? Clark thought, but he said nothing.

As the two sat in silence, Chloe got out of her car, and said, "No luck?"

"I'm not going home," Joel said harshly.

Chloe looked at Clark. "Lana forgot some things at the Talon. How about we go there as planned?"

Clark looked at Joel, who said, "I don't care. Fine."

Chloe went back to her car, and Clark started up Lana's truck again. As they pulled away, Joel gazed out the window, muttering, "You have no idea. Oh, my God, I thought I was *dead*. I thought that . . . *thing* . . . was going to kill me."

Clark nodded as if he understood, but he didn't. First the séance, then this.

It's gotta be the meteors.

As Clark glanced from the road to Joel, they hit a dip in the road that had been there since Clark could remember. But Joel gasped and grabbed the armrest as if he had never encountered such a thing in his life.

He's on the edge, Clark thought. *What on Earth happened to him?*

Clark kept driving, gazing at the rearview mirror. The moon was still low, still pink.

Joel murmured, "There's blood on the moon tonight. Someone's died. Something's happening."

There was a beat. Now that he was talking about other people dying, Clark decided he'd better push Joel to open up a little. He said, "Joel, how do you know that? Did you see—"

"I feel it." He made a fist and pounded his chest. "I feel it right here, okay?" His voice shook; he was shouting.

"All right, it's okay," Clark soothed. "We'll figure this out. We'll all help."

"I'm not sure anybody can help," Joel said desperately.

They were barely seated in the most private booth at the Talon before Joel started talking. Ginger, Lana, and Chloe all leaned forward, hanging on every word.

"There's always been something there, in the cornfield. Holly and I both sensed it." Joel put his hand to his forehead. His hands were shaking badly. "We wanted to find out what it was. So we started doing magics."

"Magics?" Chloe echoed incredulously.

"What's the difference between that and a séance?" Ginger said, jumping to Joel's defense. "What's the difference between that and any of this Wall of Weird stuff you keep talking about?"

"Sorry, sorry," Chloe said quickly.

A waitress bustled over, beaming at Lana as if she was eager to prove her job skills. Coffee was mindlessly ordered all around, and the waitress bustled off, clearly pleased with herself.

Joel took advantage of the break, composing himself, starting over.

"We called it the ghost in the cornfield." He looked steadily at the group. "And that's what it is."

"Go on," Clark said.

"Things changed a while ago. We'd tried for a long time before that to make contact. But then . . . we got through. We both felt it. All there is is so much anger . . ."

Ginger gasped. Lana put her hand on Ginger's forearm; neither girl spoke.

"Then on Mother's Day, I was so pissed off. My father . . ." He gritted his teeth and clenched his hands together on the table. "It was supposed to be a happy evening. For my mom, you know? But he . . ." He closed his eyes.

"I'd had it. I went to the field. I said the spell. And this big green . . . column . . ." He paused, searching for words. "It was like a whirlpool, spinning on its side. Stuff crashing around inside, like waves of energy . . ." He shuddered. "I tried to run, but it . . . it swallowed me up."

Chloe picked up her cup. Clark could see her taking mental notes.

"Then I was in. Everywhere around me it was gray, just gray. I figured I was in limbo. Or hell.

"Then I saw two green-glowing things inside. They were like figures; running in the distance. One was tall, and one was small, like a kid. The kid was chasing the tall one.

"I just stared at them, like I was hypnotized. I began to wonder if I was asleep, having a dream. I could feel all this rage, and fear . . ."

Ginger said softly, "No."

Joel didn't register that she had spoken. "Then the small one stopped. It turned and looked at me. And I don't know why, but I was more terrified than I have ever been in my entire life. I turned and ran. I ran faster and harder than I ever had in my whole life . . ."

He exhaled sharply and looked at Clark.

"And that's when I ran in front of your truck."

"What?" Chloe cried. "You never told us that, Clark. Here I was going on about all this at lunch and you never said a word!"

Clark flushed but said nothing.

"Why'd you go back?" Lana asked Joel. "If it was so terrifying—"

"I don't know." He covered his face with his hands. "I couldn't stop myself. It wasn't really even a conscious decision."

Chloe pondered that. "Was it the same experience? The figures chasing each other, then the one coming after you?"

"Chloe, give him a chance," Ginger said.

"No, it's okay," Joel assured her, then looked at Ginger as if for the first time. He looked bemused and said, "You're new."

"I'm from Metropolis," Ginger answered. "But Mom got a job to come here . . . of all places . . . and I pushed her to take it." She gestured as she talked, realizing that he was listening very carefully to her; she was grateful for his attention.

"My mom's a prominent scientist. There was this accident in their lab . . . her and my dad's . . . and my dad . . ." She shook her head. "She dreams about his death all the time. I think she . . ."

Chloe half raised a hand. "Of course she feels guilty about surviving."

Now Lana looked down, and a wave of guilt washed over Clark. He imagined the horror Lana must have endured, watching a meteor crash into her parents' truck and kill them both.

"Go on," Ginger said to Joel. "Please."

His gaze on her was soft, kind.

"This time I was in a dark room, or something. There was a floor, not ground. Brick, maybe. I could hear laughing. Very cruel, very out of control. I knew I had to get out. I knew I was in danger."

"Nothing chased you?" Chloe persisted.

"I didn't see anything. It was dark. But then I was running, and I could hear that laughter . . . and then it all became a jumble I heard tapping, and voices, and then I was back in the field, running. And then you guys came along."

He buried his face in his hands. "Oh, my God. I can't believe any of it really happened."

There was a long silence as the others took that in. Lana murmured, "I think you were somewhere near our séance."

Then Ginger spoke up. "There was a girl on the bus. A goth. She said a protection spell for you."

Clark said, "I'm guessing that was Holly."

Joel nodded, wiping his face. "I guess we just missed each other. She and her mom go to Metropolis all the time. They're talking about moving there."

"It wasn't like that at all in the house," Ginger said. She said to Joel, "We held a séance."

At his surprised look, Chloe chimed in, "Books falling off shelves. Doors locking. And these terrible noises."

"I was thinking it was just a run-of-the-mill poltergeist," Chloe said. "But now I'm not so sure it's that harmless."

"It sure didn't feel harmless," Joel said.

"Not to me, either," Ginger murmured.

"Maybe it's someone a meteorite got," Lana broke in.

" 'Got?' " Ginger said.

"Affected," Chloe amended.

"It's science plus 'magic,' and I use air quotes around magic," Chloe announced. "All magic is, is something happening for which there appears to be no scientific explanation. You did magic spells here in Smallville . . ." She waggled her brow. "And if there's a meteorite nearby took that energy, all that anger you have, and transformed it into some images, impressions . . ."

"Or amplified them," Lana added. "Maybe we did the séance near a meteorite . . ."

"Bet there's two," Chloe said. "One in that cornfield and one in the house."

"You said . . . you said that things changed a while ago." Ginger looked hard at Joel. "How long ago?"

He thought a moment. "About six months. Why?"

Ginger leaned forward on her elbows and covered her face. Her shoulders shook, and she began to cry again. "Six months ago, Lana!" she wailed. "He made contact with someone who was very angry six months ago! Oh, God!" She began to panic. "Where's my mother? Why isn't she answering her phone?"

"Come on," Lana said gently, urging Ginger to her feet. To Clark, she said, "I'm going to take her to the employees' lounge, give her a minute."

"Lana, let me borrow your cell phone," Clark asked.

"Sure." She fished it out of her purse and handed it to him as she shepherded Ginger out of the booth.

As the two moved away, Joel said, "Why is it important to her that all this started happening six months ago?"

"Her dad died six months ago," Chloe supplied, looking grim. "Maybe there's some kind of connection."

Clark punched a very familiar number into the cell phone and waited for it to ring.

"Clark," Lex's voice crackled as the connection was made. "What's up? It's late. Well, not for me," he added. "And you know you can call anytime."

"Lex, you won't believe . . ." he began, then saw that

Chloe was urging him to get on with it with urgent hand gestures.

"Ginger Brucker's trying to find her mom," he said. "She hasn't come home yet, and her cell phone isn't working."

"Janice'll be in her lab then," Lex said reasonably. "Has Ginger called the main desk? Security's there, of course."

"We tried a bunch of numbers," Clark said. "We get these menus and—"

"Okay," Lex cut in. "I'll handle it."

"Thanks, Lex," Clark said. "I thought about driving out there, but Ginger didn't want to embarrass her mom . . ."

"Got it," Lex said. "Please tell Ginger not to worry."

"If you reach her, please give her Lana's number," Clark said.

"*When* I reach her, I will," Lex assured him. Then he paused and said, "You okay, Clark?"

"Yeah." Clark flushed. He felt as though he were lying to his friend. *I guess I am lying. I'm not a hundred percent okay at all.*

"I'll track her down."

Lex disconnected.

Inside the employee lounge, Ginger cried for a long time, then began to calm down a little.

She must be exhausted, Lana thought. *Carrying all this fear and worry around for so long, plus no sleep.*

Finally, Ginger said, "I thought it would be so quiet here, kind of, you know, boring . . ."

"Oh, it can be," Lana assured her, and they both chuckled grimly at that. "There's a lot that's normal small town, Ginger. Honest. It's . . . well, the meteors make a lot of weird stuff happen. Or that's what Chloe believes, anyway."

"What do you believe?" Ginger went into the bathroom

stall and grabbed some toilet paper. As she crossed back to the sink, she turned on the water.

"I believe she's right." Lana cocked her head.

Ginger tested the water, then rinsed off her face. She glanced in the mirror and grimaced. "I look terrible," she grumbled. "Trust me to have like no makeup when Clark's around." She smiled very weakly. "Does he have a girlfriend? My luck he does."

Lana opened her mouth to speak, but she realized she wasn't sure what she was going to say. *Clark doesn't have a girlfriend . . . but he wishes I were his girlfriend and if I didn't have Whitney . . .*

She felt horribly guilty for her thoughts, and disloyal both to Whitney and Clark, although she couldn't explain why, in Clark's case. *Because I'm trying to keep him all to myself, even though he's not mine to start with?*

"Ah," Lana said, hesitating.

The door opened. Chloe stuck her head in. "Are you okay?" she asked Ginger. "I don't mean like, 'the hills are alive.' Just, are you going be able to keep on ticking?" Ginger nodded, and Chloe visibly relaxed. She smiled kindly. "That's good. Lana, Whitney just showed."

"Oh." Lana flushed, feeling even more guilty over her thoughts. *And my confusion.* "Thanks."

Chloe gave her a nod and shut the door again, leaving the other two alone.

"No," Lana said firmly to the girl who was crushing on Clark. "He doesn't have a girlfriend."

Ginger visibly cheered up. "Cool."

They went back out, catching up with Chloe. Whitney was walking toward them. His hair was wet and he smelled good, of soap and the fresh T-shirt beneath his letter jacket.

"I was working out," he said. "What's up? You guys working on some kind of group project?"

Lana sighed. *Where to begin?* "You might say that."

As usual, Chloe jumped in with both feet. "Ginger's new house is haunted. Well, not her 'new' new house." She gestured as if she had just realized that she used an awful lot of air quotes. "An old house. The Welles place."

"Get out." Whitney looked amazed. "The spook house?"

Ginger wrinkled her brow. "That's what they call it?"

He nodded. "Some people. Even my parents are afraid of that place. Lots of bad history."

"Well, Clark," Chloe said ironically. "You could use that for your topic."

"My paper," he echoed thoughtfully. "Huh."

Lana said to Whitney, "Clark hasn't turned in his Smallville history project."

Whitney grimaced. "Dude, Mr. Cox lowers grades one letter a day for late homework."

"I know," Clark said sighing. "And I've got to get my parents' truck tonight, too." He said to Whitney, "Tire blew. I've got the jack and stuff in the back."

"It broke down near the *cornfield*," Chloe emphasized. "The haunted one. Coincidence? I think not."

"I can drive you over," Whitney offered. "I have a meeting at coach's house."

"Thanks, but . . ." Clark glanced at the others. Lana was touched that he didn't want to leave them, and embarrassed that Whitney so clearly did.

Ginger laid a hand on Clark's forearm. Pink bloomed in his cheeks. She said, "I'd feel better if you stayed. It was so nice of you to show in the first place."

Hey, I went, too, Lana thought. *And I had to go inside all alone. And I broke the window. He just showed up.*

Oh, my God. I'm jealous of her!

Oblivious—or did he really not care?—Whitney brushed her lips with his. "You're okay, right? This sounds really cool, but we're doing this midnight thing . . ." He looked embarrassed. "It's an end-of-the-year team thing—an old Smallville tradition."

"Rah, rah," Chloe said dryly. "What kind of thing? Want to tell me for the *Torch*?"

"It's a secret ritual," Whitney said, sounding embarrassed.

"Oh, like your coach setting things on fire?" Chloe shot back.

"Easy, Chloe," Clark said.

"I'm okay," Lana said, very much wanting to put a stop to the sniping. But she was hurt that Whitney was leaving. She needed him right now.

Then tell him.

What if he still wouldn't stay?

"Good." He kissed her again. "I want to hear about all this stuff later," he added. Then he kissed her again. *Right in front of Clark.* "I'll see you."

She kept smiling, but she didn't really feel like smiling. *I'm busy, too. That's the way our lives are. I understand that, even if it . . . it makes us look to others like we're not that much of a couple.*

"Got it."

He peeled off from the group and headed for the door . . . just as Pete came barreling in. The two guys registered each other's comings and goings; then, as Whitney continued out, Pete rushed over, all excited.

"Lana, your aunt said you were here . . . Listen, I talked to Governor Welles's aide and . . ."

"Welles," Ginger blurted. "I knew that name was familiar. You guys, that's his house!"

"Welles. Of course," Clark said, nodding at her. "Didn't you know that?"

"Whose house?" Pete asked, surveying their faces. "What are you guys talking about?"

"Governor Welles's boyhood home is haunted," Chloe informed him. "Ginger just moved into it, and it went completely Amityville on her."

"And us," Lana added.

Pete looked mystified. "Slow down. *What?*"

"Governor Welles's farmhouse. It's possessed," Chloe said carefully, as if she were speaking to someone with a hearing impairment. "Or maybe it's a poltergeist, but y'know, I really doubt that, now that I think about it. Too . . . hauntingish."

Pete guffawed. "Get out."

"That's what the house said to us." She glanced around the table and Clark, Lana, and Ginger. "More or less, that's what it said. And look." She gestured to Joel. "He was trapped in the cornfield."

"Trapped . . ." Pete echoed. "In a cornfield." There was no mistaking Pete's skeptical tone.

"C'mon, Pete. You've seen a million weird things here in Smallville," Chloe chided him. "This is no weirder than any of the other weirdness. It's just a lot scarier." Her frown deepened. "Well, maybe scarier. A football coach setting my office on fire with his mind, that was pretty scary." She turned to Lana. "And if the jocks are off doing voodoo at midnight . . . also not liking that."

Pete gestured to the guy making coffee drinks for his usual. "So my candidate reputedly owns a haunted house."

"*Does* own a haunted house," Ginger cut in.

Pete smiled slowly at Chloe. "You must be in pig heaven, girl reporter."

She flashed him a lopsided grin. "Despite the terror-of-Witchboard thing we've got going here, it has not escaped my attention that this could be the story of my fledgling career thus far."

Pete didn't look pleased. "A story that the governor would probably dislike."

"Hey, it's public record that his family owns a haunted house," Chloe said indignantly.

Pete shook his head. "No one has verified that."

"Oh, yes, we have," Ginger shot back. "We more than have."

There was a moment as everyone retrenched. Lana found her mind wandering back to the house and how terrified she had been . . . and how moments ago, Whitney had given her a peck on the lips, asked her if she was okay, and split.

Okay, two kisses. But both very short. What would have happened if we had called him instead of Clark? she wondered. *Would he have told me he was too busy to come?*

Pete looked as if he were about to say something, then closed his mouth and exhaled. Chloe gave him a hard look, and said, "What?"

Pete sighed. "I don't know why I'm even telling you this. I'll probably get fired from the campaign . . ."

"You're a volunteer," Ginger said, then moved her shoulders. "But I guess you could be asked to quit . . ."

"Go on," Chloe practically commanded him.

"Well, LuthorCorp did some research into ghostbusting a while ago. After that deal with that girl who stole Lex's watch and stuff? He got all inspired. You know, all that vidcam heat tracer stuff like in the movies. They were looking for . . . what's the word? Ectoplasm?"

Chloe rolled her eyes. "Why am I *not* surprised?" Then she frowned, "And why do you know about it and not me?"

"It was no big deal at the time," Pete said. "We were both sitting in here one day. He had a guy with him, and they were talking about building some of the equipment."

"You eavesdropped!" Chloe cried.

"Hey, free air space," Pete rejoined. "I . . . listened carefully."

"I'm so proud of you," she added, grinning. Then she turned to Clark. "Maybe you could ask Lex if we can use his equipment to investigate the house. It could be pretty exciting. Lex likes exciting stuff." She smirked. "Like dying in accidents."

And we are back to death, Lana thought uncomfortably.

"Wait, wait." Pete held up his hands. "I don't think my candidate would like us to go on a ghost hunt in his boyhood home."

"We've already had a séance in his boyhood home," Chloe challenged. She raised her chin. "Maybe we should just call oh, the *National Enquirer* and let *them* come take a look."

"Hey, wait a minute." Pete frowned at her. "That's not fair."

And Lana's cell phone rang. *It's Whitney*, she thought happily. *Checking in on us.*

"Hello?" she said as she pressed the talk button.

"Um . . . I'm trying to reach my daughter, Ginger. Lex Luthor gave me this number?"

Even though she was disappointed, Lana glanced at Ginger and smiled. "She's right here. I'll pass you over to her."

She held out the phone, and Ginger took it.

Ginger took the phone. She could hardly keep from crying as she heard her mom's voice, saying, "Ginger?"

"Mom?" Her own voice was shrill. "Where are you?"

"Well, it's the dumbest thing," she said. "I've just gotten unlocked from my new lab. I fell asleep and I guess everyone went home. Lex just came in and got me out." She laughed uneasily. "It was creepy."

"I'll bet," Ginger drawled. She knew her mother wouldn't

catch the irony in her voice. It was almost funny that her mom was creeped out from being locked in a nice, safe, sterile lab. She had no idea what was waiting for them at home.

"Where are you? Whose phone am I calling?"

"Mom," Ginger said, choosing her words carefully, "there's something wrong with our house. Big-time wrong."

"Oh, great. Is it the plumbing? I had a feeling—"

"Mom, it's . . . there's something wrong," she repeated awkwardly.

There was a pause. Ginger could almost see her mother's scientist brain working overtime, analyzing her daughter's mental health.

"Ginger . . ." she began.

"You can talk to Lana. Or Clark. They were there," Ginger retorted.

"Who are you talking about? I don't know any of those people. Now what's going on? Why didn't you stay home?"

"Mom, Mom . . ."

"I know this transition is difficult," her mother continued.

"*Transition?*" Ginger asked shrilly.

Chloe gently took the phone from her, and said, "Dr. Brucker? I'm Chloe. I met Ginger at school. We think . . ." She glanced at the others and mentally crossed her fingers. "We think there may have been an intruder in the house."

"Oh, my God. Did you call the sheriff?" The woman was shouting so loudly that Lana could hear her voice.

"Well, no . . ." Chloe shifted. She looked at the five as if to say, *Wrong tack. So sorry.*

"Put Ginger on the line."

Ginger took the phone.

"I'm calling the sheriff. Where are you now?"

"The Talon. A coffeehouse," Ginger amended.

"You're safe there? The people you're with . . . are there any adults nearby?"

"Yes, Mom," Ginger said dutifully.

"Stay there. I'll call you back after I get to the house."

"No . . ." Ginger murmured, but her mother had hung up.

She looked at the others. "She's going to the house. She wants me to stay here."

Clark got it. "We'll head her off, meet her in the front yard," he suggested.

She nodded.

They all went outside to the parking lot, Clark hanging back with Chloe while Joel caught up with Ginger and Lana. Pete trailed behind, clearly uncomfortable with the whole thing.

"Joel likes Ginger," Clark said.

"She's likable." Chloe cocked her head. "But he's got a hard act to follow." When he didn't get her meaning, she shook her head faintly, and said, "You, Clark. She's crushing on you."

"Me . . . ?"

He watched as Ginger climbed into the cab and glanced back at him, then smiled politely at Joel as he stood behind her. He was surprised, a little flattered, and kind of sorry for them both.

I know what's it like to be in his position, he thought, *only Lana . . .*

. . . Lana what? Knows *that I want to be her boyfriend?*

Is that somehow better, that she knows and I'm still not her boyfriend? Because it sure doesn't feel better.

Chloe said, "Hey, are you jealous of him?"

"Who?" he asked, startled.

"C'mon," she said, "we'll take my car."

They climbed in, gesturing to Pete to join them, and followed Lana's truck. As they passed the cornfield, Clark said, "I think I've been on this road more times tonight than in my entire life."

"Clark," she said, "we can't leave her in the house. So her mom comes home, so what? Whatever is in there is going to respect her parental authority?"

He sighed. "I know."

"Come on, you guys," Pete groaned. "You're going all bad movie on me."

"You weren't there," Chloe snapped at him, "okay?" To Clark, she added, "We have to figure out exactly what's going on. Maybe it's just the meteors. Some anomaly." She looked thoughtful.

Clark watched Lana's truck as she slowed and swerved around his own family's truck. "Wasn't there a movie about that?"

"Lots of them," Chloe said.

Clark looked out the window. "I saw something when I drove out there to Ginger's house earlier. Something in the corn."

Pete cleared his throat. "It *must* have been Joel, in a fugue state or something. Maybe he takes drugs."

Chloe grumped, and Pete fell silent, leaning back against the passenger seat and yawning.

Then the house loomed before them. Clark felt icy fingers climbing up his spine.

There was the broken window, which Ginger was going to have to explain to her mother. And there was the front door . . . standing wide open, like an angry, hungry mouth.

"Not liking this," Chloe murmured.

"Me, neither," Clark said.

Pete walked around them and headed for the front door. Lana was climbing out of the truck on her side, and Joel had just dropped down from the other side and was holding the door open like a gentleman for Ginger.

She got out, and visibly jerked when she looked at the house.

Then lights came up behind them . . . car lights. Two pairs—one belonging to a Smallville sheriff's patrol car.

From behind the other pair, Janice Brucker appeared as she got out of her Jeep Cherokee.

She rushed to Ginger, and said, "Are you all right?"

Clark watched with concern as Ginger pulled back out of range. He saw the hurt on her face, heard the hesitation in her voice as she said, "Not really, Mom."

Then the deputy called, "Dr. Brucker, ma'am? Would you please come over here?"

She left Ginger and joined the deputy beside the window Clark had boarded up.

"It's a bad dream," Ginger murmured. "I'll wake up soon."

Lana crossed to her and flashed her an encouraging smile, but it didn't reach her eyes. Everyone was upset . . . Clark included.

The deputy opened the front door. Janice Brucker followed him inside.

"No," Ginger groaned. "Mom, don't go in there."

He must have waved her back onto the porch; she came back outside while the deputy searched the house. Clark watched his progress as he turned lights on in each room.

Finally, he reemerged, talked to Ginger's mother for a few moments; and then the two of them walked together toward Clark and the others.

The deputy was a young man with sandy brown hair and freckles. He said patiently, "I know it can be scary in the country at night. But there doesn't seem to be any sign of an intruder in your house."

Ginger parted her lips, then clamped her mouth shut and gave Clark a look that said, *What's the use in trying to explain?*

"I've suggested to your mother that you two spend the

night in a hotel, just in case," the deputy went on. "Would
that make you feel a little better?"

"Oh, sure," Ginger managed. "Thanks."

He half closed his eyes and smiled, pleased. "All right.
Now I want you young people to disperse. I'll stick around
for a while, have a look-see around the premises. Okay, Ginger?"

"That's great," she said wearily.

CHAPTER NINE

Much to Chloe's pique—there was so much more to discuss!—Lana drove Clark home and Joel went with Chloe and Pete since their houses were closer to each other. Joel said that he knew it was time to go home.

"Although I'd rather be stuck in the cornfield," he said, and Clark knew he hadn't meant it as a joke.

Now, Lana dropped Clark off, not saying much and looking tired and scared. They promised each other they would take care and try to sleep, and Clark went into his house.

His parents were in the kitchen, waiting up. His mom was in a nightgown and robe, and his father had his robe loosely belted over a pair of sweatpants and a T-shirt.

"What's been going on?" his mother asked.

Clark hesitated. At his mother's raised brow, he said, "I . . . we found Joel." His parents both visibly relaxed. "And some stuff happened at the Welles house. We held . . ." He flushed. "We had a séance. And . . . well, some books flew off the shelves. And other things," he trailed off.

His parents stared at him. "And you didn't think to call us?"

His cheeks reddened. *Now that I hear it aloud, well . . .*

"I'm sorry. Everything kept happening."

Jonathan Kent looked less than pleased. He said, "We'll talk about this on the way to truck." Then he grimaced. "Except Mom's car is in the shop."

"Dad, I'll go get it. I'll be fine." Clark yawned, realizing he was not promoting his case by doing so.

"We'll leave the truck until morning," Jonathan said reluctantly, "and I'll hitch a ride out there with Nell or Lana."

He held up a finger to quell Clark's ongoing protest. "It's too late, and there's apparently been way too much bizarre activity out there. "

"I agree," said his mom.

"Look, give me the cell phone, and I'll call if there's a problem."

Martha shook her head. "What if this 'ghost' is some kind of energy field or . . . or transporter device or who knows what? What if it's keyed to your DNA and it's searching for you?"

"Mom, what kind of movie did you and Dad watch?" he asked gently. "Science fiction?"

She sighed, and he knew he was halfway to convincing her.

"Besides, I want to check on Ginger and her mom, make sure they're okay."

Jonathan opened his mouth to protest. Clark said, "Cell phone."

"I'm on record as opposing this," Martha said. She walked to the stove and flicked it on under her kettle. "And I'm not going to bed until you're home safe and sound."

His father walked to the cabinet and got out a canister of tea bags at exactly the same time Martha grabbed two teacups.

Sometimes they act like one person, he thought. *I wonder if I'll ever have a relationship like that. That is, if I can find someone who will want to be with me, after she finds out I'm not . . . not from around here . . .*

"Call as soon as you get to the truck," Martha said, crossing back to the table. Her purse sat on the floor beside her chair. She dug around in it and fished out her cell phone. With a kiss on his cheek, she handed it to her son.

"I'll be careful," he promised again.

◆◆◆

Again, he ran like the wind down the dark roads and stopped by the broken-down vehicle. In quick order, he jacked it up and changed the tire.

Then he turned and gazed at the cornfield. The stalks rustled in the night wind; the moon made strange shapes out of the slender leaves and the budding ears of corn, a giant making finger games against the Earth.

An owl hooted plaintively, and there was an answering skittering in the corn.

Then he heard a crack, as if someone had stepped on a twig.

"Is someone there?" he called softly.

The phone rang, startling him.

"Hello?"

"It's Mom."

"I was just about to call in," he assured her, although, in truth, he had forgotten. "I just got the spare on. There's still lots of tread on it," he added, hoping to distract her.

"Clark, we just heard from Joel," Martha told him. "His friend Holly is missing."

"She's in Metropolis," he told her, confused.

"No. They got back yesterday. Mrs. Pickering is at the Becks' now. She went over to see if Joel knew where she was."

"I'll look for her." He gazed at the cornfield.

"No. I want you to come home. Now. Carry that truck on your back if you have to."

"Mom," he protested. "What if she's out here?"

"They're sending the sheriff over there."

Sure enough, he heard a siren. It must be the deputy who had been at the Welles farmhouse, he realized.

"I hear that," Martha said into the phone. "Finish up the tire the old-fashioned way and drive home, Clark."

"All right, Mom."

He disconnected.

Then he walked to the edge of the field.

"Holly?" he called. "Are you here?"

There was no answer but the rustle of the corn.

He took a few more steps, an eye out for Joel's spell book. And then he saw something on the ground and bent down.

Candles. Matches. And . . .

He broke into a sweat and lurched away.

Meteor rocks.

Chloe's theory that meteorites are involved might be right after all.

The deputy arrived, verified his identification, and began to search the cornfield for the missing girl.

Janice and Ginger spent the night at the Smallville Hotel, in the center of town. Neither slept much, and they both admitted defeat with the dawn.

As they knocked around the hotel room, the tension took its toll on them both. Her mother seemed more concerned that Ginger's new friend had "bothered" Lex Luthor by calling him at home than that her daughter had been frightened out of her wits by something in their house.

She doesn't believe me, Ginger thought. *She thinks I got together with a bunch of immature kids, and we freaked each other out with ghost stories.*

She was terribly hurt.

Her mother kept her distance, and Ginger found herself replaying the night in vivid detail.

What if it is Daddy? What if Joel channeled his energy to this place with his magic, and it was magnified because of the meteors?

What if he wants to tell me how he died?

Questions without answers, as the sun rose . . .

After a while, Janice announced that she was going to go into the lab. Ginger tried not to show it, but she was both hurt and relieved. Her mom told Ginger she could stay "home" from school if she wanted to. Ginger suggested a compromise: She'd sleep for a few hours, then catch lunch and her afternoon classes. Her mother looked relieved, and Ginger decided not to mention that at this point, she could care less about school. She was only going so her mom wouldn't worry about her watching TV all day. Besides, she wanted to talk to the others about what had happened before, during, and after they had left.

It was 8 A.M. and Lex, like all good Luthors everywhere, had been up for hours. He had put in what other men might call a full day's work, and had just concluded a session with his personal trainer, Ira, who, as usual, was wearing the most amazing shoes. The man was obsessed with two things: physical fitness and all kinds of shoes—athletic shoes, street shoes, exotic sandals—and that fascinated Lex.

Lots of things fascinated him, including the fact that he had to put Clark on hold on one line of his cell phone to take a call from Janice Brucker.

Both of them were talking to him about the same thing.

"My daughter was badly frightened last night," she informed him. "I think there was an intruder in the farmhouse. We spent the night in a hotel."

"I know," Lex responded. "The sheriff's office called me. I'm so sorry."

She sounded somewhat mollified by his soothing tone. "The kids she was with were certain that . . . something had gone on." There her voice changed. "It sounded like some sort of particle emission," she said, half to herself. "And it got me thinking that . . . we. . . ."

Then she became all business again. "We're at the Small-ville Hotel."

"Please stay there as long as you like," Lex said. "We'll find you another place to live."

"Good. Because there's the matter of the lease . . ."

"Don't worry a thing about it. I'll call Robin at the real-estate office and take care of the whole matter." He smiled into the phone, and added smoothly, "I'm so sorry, Janice, but I've got someone on hold on the other line. If you wouldn't mind, why don't we have lunch and talk about all this?"

"That would be fine." She took a breath. "You'll under-stand if I tell you that I have very mixed feelings about hav-ing taken this position."

"Naturally. I would be surprised if you didn't." He wasn't worried about her quitting however. He'd read her like a book—she was a scientist first, and everything else second.

Just like my father and business. He's a cutthroat corpo-rate entity first, and a human being . . . oh, about twenty-fifth thing down his list.

"Let's meet in my office, say around noon," he continued. "And we can discuss this . . . particle emission idea, and anything else you'd like to talk about." He knew he was baiting the hook—though he had no idea what with—by mentioning the particle emission.

"All right."

That taken care of—*for the time being*—Lex got back to Clark.

"Okay, so then the table rose up in the air," he said, to re-mind Clark where they'd bookmarked the conversation while he talked to Janice.

"And the books flew out of the shelves. There was this tapping. Did I mention the footsteps?"

"You did. And Joel flew back out of the cornfield." He touched his bald head. *Lots of strange things appear and disappear in the cornfields of Smallville. And why would Janice think that would have anything to do with particle emissions?*

"Yes. And Pete said that you had all this, um, equipment to track spectral things . . ."

"He did, did he." Lex made a mental note to be more discreet when discussing his business in public. "He's working on the governor's campaign, isn't he?"

"Yes."

"And you're talking about the governor's boyhood home? Being haunted?"

"Or something." Clark hesitated. "Lex, there's something going on. In a very big way."

Lex pondered the angles. *Governor Welles is running for reelection, and he's a friend of the family. He might actually enjoy the publicity of a ghost hunt . . . unless the Welleses have a skeleton in one of their closets . . .*

If he wants to keep this quiet, it's too late. Gossip flies through high schools faster than the Internet. And if I know my Chloe Sullivan, there'll be an article about it in the Torch, oh, yesterday.

"Lex?" Clark prodded. "You still there?"

Janice Brucker has a personal interest in investigating it. I should get her and Dr. Hamilton involved before the site is contaminated any worse with kids and séances.

"Okay, Clark. I'll play," Lex said brightly. "You can use my stereo." When there was a pause, Lex added gently, "That was a little joke." *But since you and I both never had brothers to share our stuff with, I guess it fell a little flat.*

"Thanks, Lex," Clark said gratefully. "For that, I'll let you read all my comics."

Now Lex grinned. Clark had gotten the joke after all.

I should never underestimate Clark Kent, he thought.

"Listen, Ginger's mother is very upset. I want you to keep her daughter out of this."

"Okay. Of course. It's your equipment," Clark assured him.

"Why don't you come down to the plant after school?" Lex suggested. "I'll call Metropolis after I hang up, get the ghost-hunting stuff out of the warehouse and driven down."

"That'd be great. But I'll have to check with my parents first. I have chores, as usual," Clark said, with such sincerity and innocence that Lex was envious. He couldn't imagine a time when he would have willingly told his father what he was doing with his time, much less ask Lionel Luthor to excuse him from any kind of obligations.

"Okay, farm boy," Lex quipped, to hide his wistfulness. "We'll be at the plant. I'll leave a visitor badge at the security desk." He let a beat go by. "By the way, I fired my entire security department. No one will be locking Dr. Brucker in her own lab at night again."

"I knew those guys would get in trouble."

"Big trouble," Lex affirmed. *And trust me on this, Clark—they won't be working in security anywhere, ever again.*

"So, we're on, then," Lex said, needing to move the conversation to a close. He'd love to spend an hour chatting with Clark—chatting with just about anyone—but he had a "To Do" list, and making general conversation wasn't anywhere on it.

"Yeah. Thanks, Lex."

Clark disconnected and smiled at Pete, Chloe, and Lana, who were grouped around him off the school grounds so he could make the cell phone call at zero tolerance Smallville

High, as far as drugs, weapons, pagers, and cell phones went.

Chloe gave him a thumbs-up and Lana smiled at him uncertainly. Pete seemed the least happy of the three, but Clark could tell that he was just as eager as the others to be part of an official ghost investigation team.

"Ginger's not allowed to participate," Clark said.

"She probably wouldn't want to anyway," Chloe said. "So Lex is taking it seriously."

"Yes," Clark said.

"Cool." Chloe smiled at him. "And speaking of Ginger, we've got first bell in about, oh, two minutes and she's not here. And neither is Joel."

"I'm sure Joel actually is about ready for a lunatic asylum," Pete said just as Joel showed up. "And . . . hey."

Joel said abruptly, "Where's Ginger?"

"I'm sorry, but she hasn't showed yet," Lana told him.

"But she's okay," Clark added. "Lex was just talking to her mom. About the house, and—"

Joel turned and walked away. Lana gazed at Clark with concern as Chloe raised her hand and said, "Yo? Interview at lunch?"

He didn't react.

"Not much with the social graces, is he," Chloe muttered.

"Chloe, chill," Lana said, watching the receding figure.

Clark caught her scanning the rest of the milling students and thought, *No Whitney. That's who she's looking for.*

And he's not here.

But I am.

As usual, he had mixed feelings about scoring off Whitney. The guy had his share of problems—sick dad, lost his athletic scholarship—but on the other hand, he seemed to take Lana for granted a lot.

I would never do that. I would consider myself the luckiest guy, treat her so well . . .

She focused her large, dark eyes on him and said, "We should all go to class." She sounded so sad that the small bit of triumph he felt at Whitney's lackluster boyfriend record was dashed.

She separated from the group and walked away, leaving Clark with Chloe and Pete. Chloe cocked her head and said, "Whitney is stupid, huh, Clark."

"Not stupid enough," he replied.

She chuckled faintly and said to Pete, "Thanks again for the tip on the equipment."

He shrugged, obviously still of two minds about the situation.

Then it was first period, and then history, where Mr. Cox told Clark he might as well cash it in and take the F, and finally lunch.

Ginger didn't show.

"So, ghost hunting," Chloe said as she sat down at their usual table. "Let's talk about it."

Pete looked conflicted. "This could turn my candidate into a laughingstock."

"If anyone wants a good laugh at his expense, all they have to do is look at his record on environmental issues," Chloe riposted.

"Hey. The governor has worked hard to protect the environment," Pete said.

Chloe rolled her eyes. "Now you're going to spout the party line."

"No party line needed," Pete shot back. "His record stands on its own . . ."

"Own *pile* . . ."

And they were off and running. But Clark lost the thread. Across the cafeteria, Lana had slipped both her arms through Whitney's, and she was gazing up at him with pure joy written across her beautiful face.

I'm never gonna win that vote, he thought.

Clark raced through his chores, got time off for good behavior, and took the truck to LuthorCorp. He got his badge, and Lex asked him if he'd like to see Dr. Brucker's lab while his couriers unloaded the ghost-detecting equipment off the LuthorCorp courier van.

Clark said yes, and Lex led him down a maze of sterile hallways and into an elaborate equipped laboratory.

"Wow, talk about complicated machinery," Clark said, impressed by the lab's layout.

"You're looking at a unique combination of particle accelerators, ion implanters, cyclotrons, and betatrons, controlled by software that turns them into one big isotope simulator," Dr. Brucker told him.

"Or, simplifying for the lay audience, several million dollars' worth of cool stuff," Lex said, giving Clark a smile.

"All this stuff . . . it's supposed to re-create the same kind of radiation the meteors give off?" Clark grimaced at the thought. "Don't we have enough meteors in Smallville? Maybe even a few too many?"

Lex chuckled. "I want to find out why they do all the strange things they do, Clark. Make 'em stop, if I can. Maybe make them only do good things."

"Your definition of good," Clark pointed out.

"My definition."

"Okay, everyone, we need to get back behind the shields," Dr. Hamilton said. "We're going to check out the radiation condensers."

Janice Brucker suddenly looked very pale. She said, "Not with . . . not with people unattached to the project in the room."

She's scared, Clark realized. *Maybe this is similar to what happened when her husband was killed . . .*

"I'd like to stay," Lex said.

"I insist." She gazed at him levelly, and added, almost beneath her breath as Dr. Hamilton walked away again to check on the readouts on the main monitor, "Remember what we talked about."

"Safeguards." He nodded, and tapped Clark on the shoulder. "That's our cue. I promised Dr. Brucker I'd be careful around this stuff." He smiled at Ginger's mother. "That we'd all be careful."

She remained steadfast and unsmiling. Clark found himself thinking, *No wonder Ginger was afraid to make her angry. She's tough.*

He followed Lex's lead out of the lab and into the corridor. Lex said to him in an aside, "We had lunch today. She's very frightened about what's going on in Smallville. And in that house. Though she won't say as much, I think she believes there may be something paranormal going on, too." He regarded Clark with a faint grin, and added, "She also mentioned that her daughter is 'smitten' with you."

Clark flushed. "It's that exotic air of farm life."

Lex shook his head. "You've got a lot going for you, Kent. If you'd just move on . . . Lana's not the only girl in high school. Ginger's pretty cute. And she must be at least half as smart as her mom . . . she cut you out of the herd pretty fast."

"Too bad Dr. Brucker's too old for you," Clark riposted, trying to rib Lex.

Lex moved his shoulders in a lazy shrug. "She's not too old."

Clark opened his lips to say something.

Then their conversation was interrupted by a thunderous

explosion back in the lab. It shook the walls of the corridor. The floor actually rippled.

Red lights flared on and alarms began to blare. Neither friend hesitated as they wheeled around and dashed back to the lab. Clark had to restrain himself from putting on the superspeed; it was too public a place and Lex was an eyewitness. So he satisfied himself by keeping up with Lex, footfall for footfall.

A phalanx of security guards arrived on the double as Lex keyed the door code into a monitor. As the door fwoomed open, one of the men barred Lex's way, and said, "You can't go in, sir, until we clear the area."

"No way!" Lex shouted.

In the ensuing confusion, Clark darted around the security guards and raced into the lab.

It was chaos. Dr. Brucker and Dr. Hamilton were on the floor; something was smoking and the room . . .

Clark staggered and dropped to his feet.

The room was filled with a fine, green glow . . . and he was feeling the effects. Immediately, he gasped in intense pain. He could barely move, barely breathe.

"Radiation leak," Dr. Brucker managed.

Clark crawled to her and picked her up in his arms. Then, with supreme effort, he draped her over his shoulder fireman style and struggled to his feet. As quickly as he could . . . which was not quickly at all . . . he lurched toward the door, where Lex was still arguing with a security guard. However, others fanned around Clark and headed for Dr. Hamilton, who was trying to get to his knees.

"Clark," Lex said. "My God."

Sweat poured down Clark's face. Lex helped him undrape Dr. Brucker, shouting, "Medic on the double!"

Relieved of his burden, Clark stumbled back against the wall.

"I'll be okay," he told Lex. "I'll be fine."

But as Dr. Brucker and Dr. Hamilton were taken away on gurneys, accompanied by at least six or seven medical personnel, the pain and weakness stayed with him.

Even after Lex made him sit in a wheelchair and got him back outside, it stayed.

Clark was alarmed.

What if I've been permanently injured? he wondered. *What if this time, I've been exposed enough times that I'm not going to come back a hundred percent?*

CHAPTER TEN

The next morning, Clark was still feeling the effects. His powers were severely diminished. His strength was only slightly greater than that of a strong man, and as for speed . . . he wasn't going to set any records.

"Now's the time for me to sign up for football," he told his father at breakfast, trying to joke about it.

His father tried gamely to smile. But it was clear he was worried about Clark.

There were more chores after breakfast. Clark moved through them slowly, painfully, until finally his dad came out to the field where he was trying to mend a fence and told him to get ready for school.

On his way to take a shower, he overheard his parents—overheard in the normal, everyday sense of the word—discussing his situation. They were in their bedroom, and their door was slightly ajar, as if they hadn't closed it carefully enough. Though their voices were low, he could hear every word, and to his shock, he realized that his mother was crying.

"What's happened to him, Jonathan? He looks *awful*. What if his powers don't come back? What if it means something even worse?"

Worse? Clark wondered. *What could be worse?*

"He'll be fine," Jonathan replied. But he sounded less than sure. "It's just those damn meteors. God knows what Lex Luthor is up to at that fertilizer plant."

"I'm scared." His mom's words were muffled; Clark could picture her pressed tightly against Jonathan's chest, her husband's arms tightly around her.

"We both are." Jonathan was quiet, too.

They said nothing more.

Flushed and frightened, Clark went into the bathroom and stared at himself in the mirror. He did look awful. His skin was burned, and his cheeks were gaunt. His eyes were bloodshot.

Before, whenever he moved away from a meteor, its effects on him disappeared immediately. It wasn't happening this time.

He studied his features in the mirror. *What's happening to me? Does it have something to do with the cornfield and the house?*

Am I dying?

Maybe if Dr. Brucker learns enough about the meteor radiation, she can help me. Would I dare tell her the truth about myself?

If it meant saving my life?

Joel left school. He wandered the streets of downtown Smallville, astonished that life could just go on, business as usual, after what had happened to him and considering that Holly was missing.

There should be a notice in every store window with her picture on it, he thought. *The sheriff's office should be looking for her everywhere.*

He stopped in at the Talon and used the pay phone, checking in again with Holly's mother.

She was frantic. "The sheriff won't do anything until she's been missing for another day," she told him.

"I'll find her," Joel promised her. "I will."

Then Ginger Brucker came through the door, looking as upset as he was. He waved to her, and she joined him at his table.

"Hey," she said. She looked tired. "Long day, huh. I had

a bad night with my mom." She cocked her head. "How'd it go with your dad?"

Joel swallowed. "He said something about getting mixed up with 'some little weirdo' and told me to get a girlfriend my own age. He also told Karen—that's Holly's mom—that if she ever let me stay there again without informing him, he would sue her." He made a face. "For what, I'm not sure. He was drunk when he said it. Of course."

"Oh, I'm so sorry."

"She's not my girlfriend," he said. "She was this little kid, and we became friends. She looked up to me, and no one else did. Then she went all goth, and for a while I was embarrassed to be seen with her." He looked sad. "Then I realized I was already socially dead." He laughed. "I'm whining."

"No." She shook her head. "I totally get it. And . . . I'm glad you're telling me these things."

He smiled at her gratefully. "She was always there for me." His voice caught. "She understood what it was like between me and my dad."

He sagged, feeling utterly defeated. "I want to go back, see if I can find anything to help find her. But . . ." His face fell. "I'm scared, Ginger."

They stared at each other.

She nodded. "I get that, too. I'm scared, too. But . . ." She straightened her shoulders. "I'll go with you, if you want."

He gazed at her. "To the cornfield? You would do that?"

"Yes."

As one person, they rose from the table. Joel got out his wallet and put down some money for the cup of coffee he had not touched.

Since neither of them had a car, they took the bus.

As the wheels coughed up dust, they stood across the country lane from the field.

It's like it's waiting for us.

Joel took Ginger's hand. She let him.

It was late afternoon; the shadows were lengthening across the corn. Joel was very tense; he said, "I want you to wait here."

"No way." She raised her chin. "I'm going with you, Joel."

He sighed, and she shook her head.

She was going.

They crossed the road, skirting the dried fissures caused by rainstorms and snowy days. As if in greeting, the rows of stalks dipped and eddied, like the wheatfield behind Ginger's house the day she had drawn the little boy and the farmer.

Joel crept to the perimeter of the field, releasing Ginger's hand and urging her behind himself. She was touched.

He licked his lips, and called softly, "Holly?"

There was no answer except the rhythmic waving of the stalks, but as they stood in silence, Ginger was chilled.

They sound alive.

They sound like they're breathing.

Eager to get away, yet not wanting to seem callous about his worries for his friend, she offered, "I don't think anyone is here."

Joel squinted at the waving stalks.

Then he pointed down at his feet. Nestled in the grass were some stubs of black candles and a couple of Smallville meteorites.

"She was here," he said. Then he turned to her, and said, "I'm going to get her back, Ginger. If it's the last thing I ever do."

"I'll help you," she promised.

He gazed down at her—he was much taller than she—and

she felt a tingle from head to toe. He murmured, "You're so brave . . . and sweet."

"I'm just me," she said, her voice barely above a whisper.

"I . . . I like just you."

Her face burned. She didn't know what to say . . . except that she liked this guy back.

Huh. I thought I was going to be all crushy on Clark Kent. But Joel's here . . . for me.

"We should get away from this place," he said. "Let's stop in and see Holly's mom. I'm sure she could use some company."

"Okay."

They held hands as they walked away from the cornfield.

Then a familiar car rolled past them. Joel couldn't quite place it; but it stopped and pulled to the side, the driver giving a quick honk.

Joel and Ginger hurried over.

It was Chloe. Through the open passenger-side window, she said, "Um, I thought you weren't coming."

The two looked back at her. Joel said, "To what?"

"Oops." Chloe bit her lip. "Never mind. Gotta go."

Like that was gonna happen.

The last rays of sun set on the green fields surrounding the Welles farmhouse. In the shadows, the ghost hunters made their final preparations.

Clark, Lana, and Pete sat on the empty cases that had housed the equipment Lex had sent over. They were outside, the idea being that they would keep base camp out of the way if any violent activity occurred. The note the billionaire's son had sent with the boxes read, "Keep everything as long as you like, and good luck."

They'd spent the last hour opening up the equipment, reading instructions, and prepping for the main event. Although Ginger had experienced some paranormal activity during the daytime, all the instructions that had come with the equipment, as well as the research conducted by Chloe, said that it was better to go ghost hunting at night.

The technology wasn't revolutionary in concept, but its application bordered on genius. Traditional ghost-hunting tools included cameras, tape recorders, thermometers, and electromagnetic field, or EM, detectors. These were all used to indicate the presence of a ghost by detecting either its energy, or the way that it affected the environment around it. LuthorCorp engineers had put together tools that combined the many functions of these devices into single packages, and had linked them for better tracking abilities. The packaging was stunning, very surrealistic and futuristic, each piece emblazoned with the LuthorCorp logo.

First, there were the sensor packs. These were little egg-shaped devices that acted as multirange sensors for heat, motion, electromagnetic fields, audio, and video. A laptop base station collected all their information via a wireless radio network. The date was then processed through a specialized rendering software to create a three-dimensional grid based on the GPS positions of the remote units for tracking any paranormal activity. The software could be set to show any of the sensor ranges, and the entire system could run for twelve hours without recharging.

In addition to the base and sensor packs, there were two portable locator units. These had small flatscreens that mirrored the readout from the laptop, so a ghost hunter could track his position relative to the other data sources. Besides duplicating all the functions of the sensor packs, they featured ultrasensitive EM detectors capable of detecting electric fields as low as three volts per meter—enough to detect most living creatures through a wall. Two-way radios connected the base station with the locator operators and each other.

Clark and Pete tried it out. Clark stayed outside, with the others, while Pete bravely went inside.

Of course, since he wasn't here for the previous "excitement," he has no basis for bald terror.

Unlike the rest of us.

"It's working," Clark announced. He spotted Pete through the wall several times.

But when it was Clark's turn. He went inside, not quite as bravely. Pete couldn't locate him, which privately made Clark nervous about being scrutinized by scientific equipment. Pete didn't seem to notice his uneasiness; he was too busy reading the tech manuals to figure out what was wrong.

"It says here, that sometimes a person will carry no electric charge," Pete announced, turning a page. "Go rub your shoes on the carpet or something, Clark."

The static electricity had done the trick.

"Cool! It's like I can see through the wall!"

Clark smiled faintly to himself.

If you only knew, Pete.

The principle behind using the EM detectors was that every detectable physical manifestation required energy— even just the movement of air. The EM detectors could sense it and track it, even when it became unnoticeable to the human eye.

The portable locator units had been designed to track in areas without sensor packs. Two hunters carrying them could spread out from the base station, and they could triangulate the energy reading if a ghost left the scanned area.

The units were long wands of brushed chrome with pistol grips that were attached to backpacks with black umbilical cords. The backpack carried the batteries, wireless transmitters, and a telescoping arm that held the flatscreen readout on it. The arm was angled forward so users could read the data as they walked. Somewhat ominously, the locator units were also equipped to detect ionizing radiation.

In addition to the ghostbusting equipment, Lex had sent over an assortment of flashlights and extra walkie-talkies so everyone could stay in touch.

Chloe had suggested that LuthorCorp created the devices for tracking ghosts in atomic power plants. "Why else would it have a built-in Geiger counter?" she'd quipped, head turning, flipping her hair slightly.

"Well, whatever the reason they made them, it was nice of Lex to lend them to us," Clark had replied, as he milled in the front yard with the others.

Pete rolled his eyes. "Keep looking on the bright side of the Luthors, Clark. Pretty soon you'll just go blind." Then his mood brightened as he took in the array. "Hey, you guys, I can't deny this is cool. We're *ghostbusters*! 'Don't cross the streams!' "

Pete was right. The devices looked like streamlined versions of the equipment from the old movie. Clark had watched it years ago with Pete once when he spent the night at his friend's place. He and Pete had played for hours, chasing pretend ghosts. They'd gotten themselves all worked up and had been afraid to go to sleep. It had taken Pete's mom and a call from his own mother to settle them down.

"There are no such things as ghosts, Clark," his mother had advised him. "Now go to sleep."

After the previous evening, Clark had cause to believe otherwise—at least *here* at the Welles house.

Then Chloe drove up, and Clark was surprised to see Ginger and Joel with her.

The three climbed out, and Chloe said apologetically, "I picked up a couple of hitchhikers. Literally."

"Chloe told us what you guys are doing," Joel said. "We're both in."

Clark shook his head. "I promised Lex—"

Lana came over to them. "It's starting to get a little chilly. I brought some coffee from the Talon. Would you care for some?"

"That's so thoughtful," Ginger said. "I would."

"I have scones. Maple, oatmeal, and blueberry. And corn muffins," Lana continued, dimpling. "Of course we have to have corn *something*. This is corn country, after all."

Ginger and Joel shared a look that Clark couldn't decipher. He tried to concentrate on learning how to use the pack, but he couldn't stop watching Lana's graceful movements as she served Ginger her coffee and pastries from a coffee pump and a basket she had brought from her coffeehouse.

The team made their final preparations, activating sensors and putting on backpacks. Clark and Pete had been assigned the job of lugging around the heavier locator units, while Chloe had automatically taken over the base station.

"Computers are my tool of choice," she said.

Lana, Ginger, and Joel were the support team. If anything went seriously wrong, one of them would call for help. They'd also go running to help anyone who got lost or injured. The sensor packs, the two-way radios, and the built in GPS transponders in the locators meant that no one should suddenly go missing.

Whitney had wanted to come help, but he was stuck doing an inventory at his dad's store.

The lassitude that had plagued Clark since the accident was still with him. To top it off, he had developed what looked to be a sunburn. That had really alarmed his mother, who had begun researching common forms of radiation sickness on the web. He still had full use of his X-ray vision, and his perception was still superfast, but his speed was still virtually gone, and his strength was remained half what it normally was.

"Yo, Kent, snap to," Chloe commanded from base camp.

Lost in his thoughts, Clark hadn't noticed the last fading glimmers of the sun retreat across the cornfields.

It was time to go ghost hunting.

Two hours later, nothing was happening.

Clark and Pete were walking around the house playing with the LED flashlights Lex had lent them. The Luxeon Star II LEDs were still bright, and the two boys were having fun shining them all around the house.

In their headsets, Chloe kept going over the same old information.

"Temperature readings on units one and two normal, within household variations, no movement detected, aural sensors register nothing."

A big fat zero.

Chloe stopped the recitation. "Clark, tell me I'm not crazy, We *did* see what we saw, didn't we?"

Lana and Ginger cut in.

"You saw it. So did I," Ginger asserted.

"No question," Lana agreed.

Clark managed to cut in. "If you're crazy, Chloe, we all are. I saw it, too."

Joel added, "Well, after what I went through in the cornfield, I'd believe anything. Even if I saw a UFO."

Through a window, Clark aimed the LED light up at the stars, watching the bluish beam cut through the night sky. After learning that he'd been found in a *spaceship* by his parents, he didn't have much trouble believing the unbelievable, either.

He wondered if he'd ever be able to translate the writing

on the tiny ship in the farm's storm cellar and learn a little about which star he'd come from.

And why.

Then Chloe came on again after a short pause. "Looks like Lex might have skimped on the gear, guys. I'm showing a sensor pack down. Could it be the batteries?"

Clark was confused. The high-capacity nickel-metal hydride batteries had all been charged that afternoon in an ultrafast charger prior to setting the units up. Clark ought to know—it had been his job.

He came out and glanced over her shoulder. "Which unit is it?"

She pointed to the screen. "Number seven."

Clark looked at the flatscreen readout and identified the missing spot in the grid. Number seven was in the attic, on the third floor. He looked up at the house and unfocused his eyes slightly, *shifting* in a way that he couldn't have explained.

His X-ray vision showed the sensor pack sitting there on the third floor, just as he'd left it.

But the little door on the back is open, and there's no battery inside.

Uh-oh.

He took a closer look, and saw the battery lying on the floor, across the room. There was no way that that should have happened.

"I'll run up and take a look," he ventured, heading for the front door stairway.

"You okay to go up there alone, Clark?" Lana asked.

"I'm good, Lana," he replied. "Thanks."

"I'll come with you," Joel said.

Brave guy, Clark thought. *After what he's been through, I'm amazed he agreed to do this. But to go upstairs with me . . .*

"It's okay," he insisted. Then, "Stay with Ginger and Lana, okay?"

Clark walked up the staircase, his senses tuned to full. He checked the readouts on the flatscreen, waving the detection wand around as he walked.

Nothing, and nothing is still nothing.

But *something* had taken the battery out.

He scanned upward with his X-ray vision again. No sign of the green things he'd seen before.

Good.

The stairs creaked as he moved up past the second floor. The house was less well kept here, and the old wood looked its age, reminding him of something out of a monster flick.

Not good thoughts to be having here, Clark.

He probably wouldn't have been so concerned if he hadn't been weakened from the lab radiation.

He reached the door at the top of the attic stairs and turned the handle.

Suddenly, he felt himself *pulled* into the room, and the door slammed shut. He heard the lock click over. Fear jolted through him like an electric current.

Chloe picked up the readings from his locator.

"Clark, it looks like there's something in there with you! Are you okay?"

He was pinned . . . or else he had just lost some more strength. As he fought down his fear, time slowed down as it usually did, but this time he slowed down with it. He felt as if he were trapped in molasses, every movement thick and slow.

"Clark? Clark?" It was Lana or Ginger, he couldn't be sure. An icy fear gripped his limbs, and he couldn't speak for a second.

"The readings are off the scale," Chloe shouted. "Pete, better get up there!"

"I'm going, too!" It was Joel.

Is it a ghost?

Whatever it was, it had the same feel to it as the meteor rocks. Clark felt weaker and weaker; pain jittered through him, and he broke out in a sweat.

Then something grabbed him in a bear hug and threw him against the wall.

Ironically, he immediately felt better.

It's gone. Whatever was in here, has vanished. Or faded away.

Finding himself relatively unhurt, he finally managed to say something. "There was something here. But I think I'm okay now."

Chloe answered. "It's not there now, because it's coming down the stairs. It just passed six and five."

"Look out Pete! Aaaaah!"

That was Lana.

Clark cursed the fact that his speed was gone and tried the door. Instantly his hand pulled back from it. The apparition—the energy?—had left behind some residue on the doorknob. It was slimy, and it burned like meteor rock when he touched it. He wiped it on the wall, and looked for another way out. He didn't have the *time*!

"It just pushed me across the floor!" Pete shouted.

Clark ran to the dormer window on the side of the house and yanked it open, the old wood scraping a loud protest as it was moved for the first time in the new century.

He looked out the window and spared a second to shut off the video feed on his locator before jumping. The landing was hard, but even at only half strength he could have taken a lot worse.

"Clark?" It was Chloe. "According to the GPS sensors, you just jumped out of the third-floor window. Tell me that's not true."

"I'm just downstairs, Chloe," Clark said. "Must be a bug."

He dashed inside the house and ran up the stairs. At normal speed it felt like it was taking years.

When he got there, he saw Pete on the floor, with Ginger and Lana over him.

"You guys okay?" he said.

And there was a scream over the headsets.

"It's got me!"

Joel, Clark thought.

"Out here!" Chloe shouted.

Clark dashed outside, to find Chloe on her feet. Chloe was waving her hands and pointing in the direction of Waitley Lane, where Joel had just bolted.

Then Ginger emerged from the house, shouting for Joel. As she raced past Chloe, Chloe tried to grab her arm, and failed.

"Ginger, no!" she cried.

Clark doubled over, amazed. *I'm out of breath.* He said to Chloe, "Car!"

Chloe nodded and headed with him for her car. She slid behind the wheel as he tumbled into the passenger seat, still encumbered by all the heavy equipment on his back. He leaned forward on the dash, gesturing for her to go.

Ginger dashed toward them, waving her hands for them to stop for her.

"Stay there!" Chloe ordered through the closed window. Clark knew Ginger couldn't hear her, but Chloe seemed too panicked to think of that. Her hands were shaking, and she put the key in the ignition.

Then she turned on the car and put the pedal to the metal . . . forgetting in her upset that the car was in reverse.

It shot across the front yard and slammed into a ditch, the

back wheels careening down the slope while the front end planted itself in the rise above it.

Ginger dashed past, followed by Lana.

Chloe said nothing, only slammed out of the car and hurried down the slope to the rear. She threw herself against it and began to push. It was a futile maneuver.

Clark joined her, frustrated beyond the telling by his weakness. There was no way they were going to dislodge the car . . . at least, not in time to do any good.

So he ran.

Despite the pain in his side and the hot, stinging dryness in his throat, he ran as fast as he could.

Ahead, Chloe stopped, her hands on her thighs as she sucked in oxygen and gestured for him to pass her by.

He did. He didn't know how he managed to keep running, but he did.

Beneath the moon, the cornfield spilled across a quadrant of land. As Clark raced toward it, Joel reached its outskirts. Ginger was close behind him.

"No!" Clark shouted, but the word came out as a raspy whisper.

With his acute vision, he could see that Joel and Ginger were running straight toward a huge conglomeration of the green beams he'd seen during the séance. The green things fanned out from a centralized location, seeming to make a huge circle, like something the football team would run through at homecoming.

Like a gate.

He pushed himself harder, wishing it had been some other ability that he'd lost temporarily instead of his speed. Desperately he looked with his X-ray vision, trying to see if there was anything he could do to stop the pair from running any farther.

Joel and Ginger were almost at it now, the transparent

outlines of their bodies underlaid with the hard edges of their bones as they neared the ringed gate.

And then he noticed a thin streamer, a tendril of green that stretched from the gateway backward.

To the house.

Clark looked to his right and saw the nearest point at which the streamer crossed his path.

There!

He dived for it, but his hands sailed through it to no effect. What would affect it? What did he have . . . ?

He turned on the Geiger counter, turned on the EM detector, and even pointed his flashlight at it. Some combination of the three must have worked, because as he watched, the green string seemed to break, and he heard Joel cry out.

Joel and Ginger finally stopped running.

The glowing green ring that had nearly captured Joel and Ginger faded almost at the same time.

Clark finally caught up with them both. Joel was leaning against Ginger, and her arms were around him.

"Glad to see that you're all right," Clark said.

And then he passed out.

When he woke up, he felt weaker than before.

Lana was kneeling over him as well.

"Clark?" she said.

"Yeah?" he muttered, still groggy. "Lana, what happened?" They were still in the cornfield.

"Clark, can you sit you up?" she asked.

"Yeah." He laughed shakily to cover his discomfort. *There's a meteor in the cornfield. And I got too close to it.*

Then Chloe came loping over. "Clark, God! Are you okay?"

"Yeah. I stumbled on something and went down a little hard," he fibbed. "I'm fine, though. Really."

"You really smacked the ground," she said. "It would have been a great play if you'd been tackling a rival quarterback. With a helmet on," she added pointedly.

"Well, my head's pretty hard," he told her.

"I've noticed that upon occasion." She gave him a huge smile. "Guess what."

He said, "You've got that look. Like when you have a scoop."

Her eyes glittered. "Oh, *yeah*. I do, Clark. It's Wall of Weird time! We found a huge meteorite right near where you did the face plant. It's almost completely buried, and it's the largest one I've ever seen."

Thought so. Knew so, Clark thought. And then he had a chilling thought—*Have we been interacting with actual ghosts that have somehow been permeated with meteor radiation? Is that why I see the trails, and why the green glow seems to move through the house and then back out here?*

"So you're thinking what's happening is a result of that?" he asked her as he slowly got to his feet, his mind reeling.

"Looks like." She looked over her shoulder as the others joined them. "Pete isn't happy about discovering the meteorite. Doesn't think it'll help the governor's campaign."

"It probably won't help with our economy, either," Pete said, crossing his arms over his chest. "How many people do you think want to eat corn growing next to big glowing boulders?"

"Are you suggesting we suppress this information?" Chloe accused, her eyes narrowing.

Pete lifted his chin. "I'm just suggesting that the farmers around here have enough to worry about without some bad press."

A wave of dizziness washed over Clark, followed by chills and nausea, and he realized that he was feeling the effects of meteor radiation. *Its influence shifts around in here. Or is a radiation-soaked ghost coming near us?*

The hair on the back of his neck stood up at the thought.

"Guys," he said, as Lana reached out a hand, her face shadowed with concern.

"You okay?" she asked him.

He nodded, liking her attention. *Liking it very much.*

"I'm fine—just a little shaky." *And eager to put as much distance between that meteor and myself as quickly as possible.*

She bit her lower lip. "You fainted, Clark. And you don't look fine. Maybe you should see a doctor."

"I'll be fine. I just . . . I haven't been sleeping well. I'm really tired." That seemed to alarm Lana even more, so he amended. "I was winded, that's all. I'm fine." He gestured in the direction of the meteorite, and said, "I think we should get out of here. It's dark and a lot of very strange stuff has happened tonight."

The others nodded somberly and Clark took the lead, walking away from the ghost or the radiation or whatever was affecting him as fast as he could.

"We'll make sure Lex's equipment is safe for tonight and repack it in the morning," he continued, pointing in the direction of the farmhouse. "I'll volunteer to do that."

"I'll help," Pete offered.

Joel put his arm around Ginger, and said, "I should get her back to her mom. We'll need a ride back to town. And I . . . I'm going to stay at Holly's house." He set his jaw, his mouth pursed into a tight, angry line. "I'm not going back to my parents, at least not tonight."

"Sure thing," Chloe said. "I can do that."

"Thank you, Chloe," Ginger said, snuggling against Joel.

Then, as the two walked away, Chloe wheeled around and mouthed to Clark, *You blew it.*

Clark shrugged.

Maybe, he thought, *but I'm standing next to Lana.*

She glanced at him as if she could read his thoughts. He smiled at her innocently.

"Let's get the equipment stashed," Pete said. "This place is freaking me out."

"Me too," Clark replied. His vertigo and nausea were subsiding.

Because I'm farther away from the meteorite, or because whatever was coming near us has moved away? he wondered.

Are we being haunted?

And somewhere else . . . sometime else . . . Holly Pickering ran screaming—over a floor of brick and a field of corn—

—screaming, as the drunken man shouted to the boy, "Shoot to kill!"

—and though she was filled with terror, rage flew around and through her like a hot, cutting wind—

—so much rage, at the evil and the horror and the murder . . .

Holly ran for her life . . .

. . . which, it appeared, she was very shortly going to lose.

CHAPTER ELEVEN

Clark was spared from talking about what had gone on at the farmhouse and in the cornfield when he got home because his parents had gone to a meeting at the grange about Governor Welles's reelection campaign. And in the morning he overslept, and his dad helped him out with his chores again . . . and he just never found a good moment to bring it up.

He felt bad. It wasn't like him to keep things from Jonathan and Martha.

When I get home, I'll talk to them about it, he decided.

His mom gave him a nice basket of produce for the Bruckers—"since I haven't had a chance to welcome them yet"—and Clark realized she didn't know that Ginger and her mother were staying at the Smallville Hotel. That was another thing he'd have to fill her in on.

Lana picked him up, and they drove to the farmhouse to repack the equipment before school. He smiled shyly as he climbed into her truck. She was dressed in a turquoise top and a long, flowing turquoise-and-lavender skirt, and she looked beautiful.

"Hi. How are you?" she asked.

"Fine. Spooked," he admitted.

She breathed out. "Me too. I don't know what to make of all this, Clark. I keep wondering how much of it is has to do with ghosts, you know? Or are we being affected by the meteorite, having some kind of shared delusion?"

He shook his head. "No way to tell."

"Because, if it is ghosts . . ." She smiled sadly. "Well, you know what I'm thinking."

"About your own parents."

"Yes," she replied in a half whisper.

She glanced in the side mirror and drove onto the main road. It was a beautiful Smallville day, the sky a glorious, uncomplicated blue. Sunflowers grew along the roads and beyond them.

They drove in silence. Then Lana signaled and braked for the left turn to Waitely Lane. The truck slowed, brakes squealing.

Sounds like the left rear brake's lining is about to go.

He took a quick look back with his X-ray vision. Layer after layer of the truck's structure revealed itself: He saw the floor of the cab, the underlying frame, brake lines running to the back of the vehicle. He traced one of these before delving deeper, past the tire, the rim, and the hub. Within he could see the surface of the brake shoe.

As he had suspected, the lining was about gone.

I'll have to figure out a way to let her know.

He rolled his shoulders. He still felt so weak. It was strange, being so slow as he worked on his chores. He didn't usually give it much thought, but the fact that he could suddenly shift time frames—make falling objects seem suspended in midair, like some kind of Hollywood special effect—was something that had become so much a part of his life that he hardly noticed it, until it was gone.

What was stranger was that he could still *see* things at zerotime, he just couldn't *move* at that speed. He tried it, making the perceptual shift, looking out over the green fields of wheat, each stalk suddenly frozen in the morning's slight breeze. His truck was still, too, and him in it, staring at the yellow morning sun, birds frozen in flight overhead casting sharp shadows on the hood of the truck.

But like last night in the attic, he, too, was frozen. He could look, but not move.

Freaky.

Clark shifted back into real time, as they drew closer to the Welles house. He used his X-ray vision to look for the huge meteor rock that had knocked him out in the cornfield.

There.

It glowed near the center of the field.

It is a big one, all right.

He skimmed the soil around the house in all directions, looking for more large rocks. After last night, he didn't want to take any chances. Since the Kansas dirt was almost rock-free, he figured if he saw anything at all, it could be worth worrying about.

In the few months since he'd learned how the rocks affected him, he'd done the same thing on the Kent farm, working to eliminate the danger from his immediate environment. It was funny how he'd never put it together earlier in his life—but then again, as his powers got stronger, the rocks seemed to have a stronger effect, which made it easier to make the connection.

He didn't see anything near the house other than the usual objects buried around farms—old tools, coins, and the like. He started to look toward the right side of the house, and as he did so, his gaze passed over it, at basement level.

He didn't figure that there'd be many rocks down there, since the house had probably been built about a hundred years ago, but he looked anyway.

There was a large furnace at the center of the basement, old boxes, filled with who knows what. As his eyes passed over the boxes, toward one of the walls where it looked like there had been a firewood stack, he saw it.

Oh, my God.

A skeleton.

It was human, and buried in the floor, in a section of the basement that wasn't set with bricks.

Could that be our ghost?

His mind spun. He looked at Lana, on the verge of blurting out what he'd just seen, when he realized that he had no way to explain how he knew it was there. It was just like her brake shoe lining—how to let her know?

It was one of the drawbacks to having that gift. No one would believe that he'd just looked through the floor into a basement and found a skeleton—they'd lock him up in a rubber room by the time the words left his mouth.

Worse, if he *was* believed, the government might come collect him. He'd seen *Firestarter*—it did not appeal.

A couple of times since he'd learned how to use his talent, he'd cloaked his knowledge with hunches. The fact that he was frequently right gave his friends a respect for his intuition—not a fear of his freakish skills.

The funny part was that whenever anyone else had a hunch and turned out to be right, he always wondered—was it *really* a hunch, or were there others like him, all hiding their abilities?

Yeah, sure.

Lana parked the truck, brakes grating to a stop, and got out.

"I think you'd better have those looked at," he told her.

"Yeah. I know. My aunt's taking the truck in this afternoon," Lana said. Then she gave a wave out the window. "Look. Ginger's here. You can give her your mom's goodie basket."

Ginger was dressed for warm weather in a little T, jeans, and black platforms. She looked very cute.

She, Joel, and Pete were putting the sensor packs back into matte gray containers marked LuthorCorp on the side. Ginger waved and Lana waved back as Clark picked the produce basket off the floor. A small tag with the Kent Organic Farm logo on it was tied to the handle with a pink ribbon. On the back of the tag, Clark's mom had written, *"Welcome to Smallville! —Martha Kent."*

The basket was filled with a cornucopia of goodies: Apples from their orchard, tomatoes, squash, and, of course, corn. All organic, all grown on the family farm.

"Hi, guys," Pete said by way of greeting as Clark and Lana walked over. "What's this?"

Clark held the basket out to Ginger. "From my mom," he told her.

She rushed forward and took the basket from him. "Wow, corn—my favorite! Imagine getting some corn here in Smallville. There must be a bushel of it in here." She laughed softly.

"Old family joke. You kind of had to be there—my dad got some corn one time from a roadside stand and told the guy he wanted a bushel before he knew how much it really was. The guy was so happy that dad didn't want to disappoint him, and we ate corn for weeks."

Clark laughed, too. A bushel of corn was equal to about fifty-six pounds—far more than anyone would want to eat in several months, much less weeks.

She set the heavy basket down. "That was really nice of your mom. She went to a lot of trouble."

"She's like that," Clark replied. "How's it going?"

How can I tell you guys that there's a body buried in the basement?

"Well, I don't care if it's midnight or the middle of the day here," Ginger said. "I don't like being here."

"I second that," Joel said. He looked tired and ragged. "Holly's mom and I convinced the sheriff's department to start looking for Holly today. And she and I made a flyer."

He crossed to his backpack, squatted, and pulled out a sheaf of printed paper. He handed one to Clark and Lana each. Across the top, in a huge-point font, were the words

"HOLLY IS MISSING." Directly beneath it, a photograph of a girl had been scanned in black and white. She was seriously goth.

Clark's heart skipped a beat. *What if the skeleton is Holly?*

While the others were examining the flyer, he focused his X-ray vision through the wall of the house and down into the basement. The skeleton was small. *It belonged to a child,* he realized uncomfortably.

"We'll find her," Ginger said to Joel.

There was a moment when no one spoke. Then Pete set down the flyer and picked up a couple of walkie-talkies. "Chloe called this morning and said she had a paper deadline so I told her she didn't need to come help us." He looked uncomfortable. "I hope she's not writing some big exposé about what happened last night," he muttered half to himself.

Lana surveyed the boxes.

"There's not much to do," she ventured. "Whitney's going to be on the practice field this morning. If you guys don't need me . . ."

"We're fine," Pete assured her.

Lana brightened. She said to Clark, "I can drive you to school with me."

"No, that's okay. I'll finish up." He picked up one of the chrome wands and wrapped the cords around it.

"I'll give him a ride," Pete said to Lana.

"Okay. Great." She smiled at the four and turned on her heel, walking briskly back to her car.

Joel and Ginger moved off to put one of the boxes in a stack with the others, their gazes on each other.

That's nice, Clark thought wistfully.

"You could've had her," Pete said, as if he were reading

Clark's mind. "I mean, Ginger was interested in you first. But I think she knew there was unbeatable competition."

"Yeah, right," Clark said, but he knew Pete was right. He was glad Ginger and Joel had hooked up. He wouldn't have wanted to hurt Ginger's feelings. She was cute and all, but she wasn't Lana.

So it's a good thing.

Joel said something to Ginger, and she laughed . . . actually laughed, in the shadow of the farmhouse. *A good thing that . . . I . . . still don't have a girlfriend.*

They got to school on time, and Clark went through the motions of being a student. But the discovery of the skeleton had unnerved him, and he didn't know what to do about it.

He was so distracted that he almost drifted past Pete and Chloe, arguing in the hallway.

"I'm telling you to leave it!" Pete was almost yelling.

Chloe stood her ground, head held high, shoulders back. She was being indomitable Chloe. "No way, Pete! This is *news*!"

"Guys, what's the matter?"

Pete frowned at Chloe. "Well, of course it's what I was talking about this moment." He spread his hands as if reading a headline. " 'Governor's Boyhood Home is Spook Central!' "

Chloe looked over at Clark and smiled. "Surely *you* can see the implications of having the possible future president of the nation grow up in a haunted house?"

He was wary. "What implications?"

"Well, Clark, the implication is that we need to know his *position* on ghosts! If he says there aren't any, then what kind of politician does that make him? *We* know there are."

"And . . . ?" Clark said leadingly.

Whatever it was that Chloe wanted to say had to wait. The

bell sounded, signaling the start of next period. The three split up, Clark and Pete going into the guys' locker room, and Chloe the women's.

The musty smell of old gym shorts and T-shirts was only slightly overpowered by the scent of deodorant from the previous class. Pete and Clark made their way to two of the lockers near the center of the room and unlocked them, getting out their gym clothes. Clark kicked off his shoes as Pete talked.

"Am I right Clark, or am I right? Chloe always has to have the last word."

"Well, she is right a lot of the time," Clark said reasonably.

"That's true, but it doesn't make her right now."

"Why so intense?" Clark pulled on his gym shorts, racing to get dressed. The coach didn't like stragglers—ten times around the gym wouldn't hurt him, but it would be embarrassing.

"I know I shouldn't get so worked up, but there's something about the fact that the governor came from Smallville that makes me feel good."

Pete pulled on his shorts, and Clark took off his shirt, wincing slightly as it scraped over his neck, where the burn was particularly sensitive.

Pete's eyes widened. "Whoa, Clark! What'd you do, wrestle an iron?"

"It's just a sunburn," Clark said, pulling on his "Property of Smallville High School" shirt.

"Sure, like from an oven!"

Or a radiation leak. "I'm fine, Pete," he assured him. "Don't try to change the subject."

Pete shook his head. "It's like we live in this tiny town, that's hardly known for anything—creamed corn? Meteors? Come *on.*"

The two guys laced up their shoes and headed for the gym. They weren't going to be the last out, but close.

"And the idea that one of us—someone from Smallville—is out there doing great things, running the state, and maybe even the *country,* makes me kind of proud."

They walked through the locker room, hurrying for the entrance.

"It sets an example that I guess I want to follow." Pete looked at him as if he wanted some kind of response.

Clark nodded. "That's not a bad thing," he said.

They reached the basketball court, and the coach had already started talking. Quietly they slipped behind a group of boys, trying not to be noticed.

"Come on, boys, we've got muscles to build!" he shouted, "You! Perry and Comb! Ten laps!"

Behind him the assistant coach, Mr. Caton, who doubled as the shop teacher and was missing several fingers from his left hand, came in rolling a huge bin of red rubber balls.

Pete looked over at Clark and nodded. They knew what that meant.

Bombardment.

Instantly they separated, getting on either side of another boy, a guy named A.J. He eyed them cautiously, not sure what they were up to. When the coach told them to count off by twos, he relaxed. It was an old gambit, to make sure that they were on the same team.

It was a trick. One that most of the football team knew as well, which Pete and Clark found out when the two groups split up. Somehow, yet again, it was going to be the jocks versus the brains.

The coach knew it, too, and grinned. He followed the old, old school of coaching—if it didn't kill you, it made you stronger. And if it didn't hurt, it wasn't good for *anything*. He figured he was going to be doing the weaker kids a favor.

"Let's see how long you last," he growled, looking at Pete and Clark's team.

Great.

The game began.

It was simple—the red, hollow rubber balls were used as ammo against the other team. The two teams were separated by the half court line on the basketball court, and no one could cross it. If you were hit by the ball, you were 'out' and went to 'jail,' an area at the back of the wall behind the court. If someone on your team caught a ball, one person could come out of jail.

The ball throwing went back and forth until one team was wiped out.

It wasn't a politically correct game, but that was the way the coach liked it. He usually used it for warm-ups before getting into the serious exercises, but sometimes the entire class period would be spent "preparing you for life's war," as he put it.

Over the years, Clark had developed a knack for playing the game well without looking too good at it. His father's admonitions to be careful when playing with other kids meant that he chose only to play defensively, catching balls and getting his team out of jail.

But he had to pretend to be bad at even that role some-times, lest he be spotted as having too much talent catching and be asked to play on a team.

Today, his coordination was off, and he very nearly couldn't catch the first ball that came his way.

"Nearly got you, Kent!"

"Come on, Clark!"

Balls were whizzing right and left. The normally easy game had become treacherously complicated.

It's my speed. Without it, I'm having trouble coordinating.

It was true. Clark was spending a lot more time dodging than he wanted to—and less time catching.

"Give me some ammo, Clark!" Pete shouted.

The jocks had intercepted most of the rubber balls and were waiting to launch a major offensive. They'd approach in a rush and take out more people with a volley than they could with single shots.

Usually Clark handed off his catches to Pete, but today he was having trouble getting them.

Here came a low one. He managed to snatch it out of the air before it hit him, getting Andrew Alvsted—"Double A"—to those who teased him for his high grades—out of jail.

"Nice one, Clark!" It was Chloe from across the gym. The girls were playing volleyball, and she had seen the catch.

Mike Harrop and Doug Tomko, both football players, took advantage of his lapse to throw two balls at him from about thirty degrees out each.

He managed to catch the first one, and nearly blocked the second, but it pegged him in the head, hitting hard enough to knock him over.

"Oooh, Kent!" said the coach. "That's got to hurt. Better get some ice on that after class."

Clark rolled to his feet and got pegged twice more by balls. He walked back to the jail. Without him, the team didn't last very much longer. There were some good plays made by a few of his teammates—Pete managed to take out three of the basketball team—but the outcome was never really in question.

After the game it was laps around the building for a while, and then the obstacle course. Clark found himself feeling more tired than usual, and again he wondered what the cumulative effect of the radiation from the meteorites was doing to him.

It wasn't until they were getting dressed back in the locker room that Clark could talk to Pete about the governor again.

"So why are you worried about Chloe? She's just one person."

"Yeah, but if she gets the media after him, it could hurt." Pete looked at him, serious. "If he gets pulled down for a ghost story, it will hurt everyone in Smallville."

"Take it easy, Pete," Clark said, "One high school reporter won't ruin an election. But," he continued, "I do have a question for you."

Pete looked over, made a go ahead gesture with his head.

"What if—what if this *did* open something up that made the governor look bad?"

"You're talking about beyond the humiliation of a ghost-busters' story," Pete said slowly. He looked wary. "Like what?"

Clark shrugged. "I'm not saying that he did, Pete. All I'm asking is if he *is* involved in something shady, would you still want him to represent Smallville to the world?"

Pete was silent for a long second.

"Of course not, man. If he *did* do anything wrong, which I'm not agreeing to in any way."

Clark nodded. "So shouldn't someone be checking on things like that? That's the role of the press, isn't it?"

Pete threw his hands up.

"Ooof! You got me, Clark! Wiped me out with your clever Socratic reasoning." He paused for a second. "But don't tell Chloe."

They headed for the next class.

Lana hurried into the Talon. She'd arranged her class schedule so that she had a free period for her last class and had permission to leave school early so she could get to the restaurant early enough to help the day shift prep for the after-school rush.

The darkened interior of the theater-turned–coffee bar was full of decorated columns: Gold stars, moons, and planets adorned some, and an art deco rendering of acanthus leaves garnished the pair by the stairs.

Red tablecloths covered the small round tables at which sat a few afternoon customers. Mr. Eckerman, the mailman, and Mr. Chirrick, one of the sheriff's deputies, sat at two of them.

Lana had the same feeling of pleasure she always did when she entered the building. She'd felt it even more strongly since she took active steps to save the old theater. Her original motivation was simply to see that it remained standing to preserve the place where her parents met, but the rewards had grown beyond that.

The feeling of accomplishment she had gained after selling her business plan to Lex was one of the extras she hadn't anticipated. Selling the jaded businessman on her own merits—Lex had made it clear it was her pitch that made him go for the renovation and not his friendship with Clark— boosted her ego and gained her some respect from Aunt Nell.

The first week she saw the project make a profit was another benefit. After she counted the money, told Nell, and reported it to Lex—she'd felt on top of the world.

She didn't know who to thank more—Clark or Lex. Clark had encouraged her, given her the support she needed to try for her dreams, and had helped her with the business plan. But Lex had given her the backing—felt that the idea was good enough to spend money on.

Funny how the two people instrumental in making this dream come true are both not Whitney.

Of course there were prices to be paid for the success as well.

She had less time to spend on schoolwork, less time with Whitney or her friends. If she hadn't quit the cheerleading squad before the Talon, she would have had to when she'd started working at it.

As the Talon blossomed, her old hangout, the Beanery, lost business, forcing staff cutbacks. In one such layoff, she hired her old boss from the Beanery—the one who had fired her for not doing a good job.

That had been a reversal.

She'd told Lex about how she felt once, and he'd smiled. "Economic Darwinism, Lana. Only the strong survive."

A little hard, Lex's view, but she supposed someone who had grown up in business the way he had *would* have a different point of view.

She checked the supplies of milk and coffee and made sure all the machines were warmed up.

Scones, check. Biscotti, check. Chocolate espresso beans, double check.

Everything was okay. Maybe Lex was right—she *did* have the best-stocked coffeehouse in Smallville, maybe in Lowell County, *and* management who really *listened* to her customers. She grinned.

And maybe an ego the size of Texas.

She wished her parents could see. Lana recalled her mom's valedictorian speech from 1977, back when *she* had been in high school. The line, "I never made much of a difference here, but maybe my children will," stood out in her memory.

Well, Mom, I've saved a landmark and managed to start the best coffeehouse in Smallville.

It was something.

Lana completed the checks, making sure the staff was

ready, and stopped for a second, thinking about what had
happened at the Welles place.

It had been both frightening and exciting at the same time.
The chasing ghosts part had been frightening in a *major*
way, but the underlying idea—that there *were* actually
ghosts, and that people didn't just die and disappear was
kind of comforting.

And now they had *evidence* of it. Enough so that maybe
Dr. Brucker would follow up on it and do something.

Not that Lana thought Janice or Ginger would ever set
foot inside the house again. She sure didn't plan to.

But still, if there was one spirit . . .

Are you watching me now, Mom? Dad?

The sound of laughter alerted her to the fact that the first
students had arrived. The few adults left from the day crowd
sensed that their time had passed and retreated; they'd be
back in the evening, or maybe tomorrow. It was the ebb and
flow of the business, a quiet tide of housewives and trades-
people during the day, swept out with waves of high school-
ers in the late afternoon.

There were Chloe, Clark, Pete, and the other ghost-
busters. Lana noticed that Ginger and Joel were walking
with hands around each other's waists and was surprised to
feel a sense of relief. Ginger wouldn't be chasing Clark anymore.

Now, Lana, why does that *matter?*

Pushing the uncomfortable question from her head, Lana
went to see her friends.

"Hi, guys! What's up?"

Veronica, one of the day shift waitresses, trotted over at
Lana's signal.

"Get them the usual?" she said. Everyone nodded.

*There are definite advantages to being the manager. See-
ing that your friends are well treated is one of them.*

"It all fits. Ghost. Big meteor rock. Do I need to spell it out? The end result and the catalyst. All we need is the beginning, and the story is *there*."

"The Wall of Weird," Ginger said.

"So what we need to find is the body," said Chloe.

They all looked at her.

"Think about it," she said, "The meteors supercharge things—there must be a body, ghost attached, near the house that's been there for years. Since the meteors hit, the spirit has been *charging*."

Lana shivered, freaked.

"We just need to start digging," the reporter finished. She raised and lowered her eyebrows. "Little joke there."

"Governor Welles wouldn't like that," said Pete.

"Hello, Pete, this is America," Chloe shot back. "I can't be stopped from researching."

"Oh. Researching." Pete looked uncomfortable. "Never mind."

Chloe scrutinized him. "Digging. You thought I meant it. That's the best idea you've had all day, Pete!"

"No way, Chloe," he said, raising his finger and pointing it at her. "We are not digging around in his house."

While all this was going on, Lana looked over at Ginger, whose eyes were welling with tears. "You okay?" she asked.

Joel, next to her, wrapped his arm around her.

Ginger answered pensively. "I guess so. I think I was just hoping . . . hoping the ghost might be . . . but if . . . it can't be with what Chloe is suggesting . . ."

She started to cry a bit more openly now.

"And the basement's way scary. Maybe um, the basement . . ."

She was losing it.

Poor Ginger, thought Lana, and then felt a wash of emotion herself. *She's been hoping all along the ghost is her fa-*

ther. Well, there's still no reason that it can't be. It's just a
theory, after all, one of Chloe's Wall of Weird things . . .

Chloe broke the awkward silence. "So Clark," she said.
"You live on a farm—have any extra shovels?"

CHAPTER TWELVE

Smallville was a small . . . ville, and word got around town quickly that Lex Luthor's newest employee and her cute daughter were living in the Smallville Hotel instead of the newly rented farmhouse that had been procured for them.

Robin's colleagues at Smallville Realty asked her a few questions about the situation. Per Lex Luthor's instructions, she had a script of prepared responses, all generally vague and all having to do with the "emotional well-being" of Ginger—for which Robin was sorry, having to pin the blame on such a young, pretty girl. So the story went around that Ginger Brucker was having trouble with her move from Metropolis, which made some kids like her more and some kids like her less.

In high school, most people have more than enough of their own stuff to handle. It's a rare creature who can honestly reach out to another young adult with a true helping hand.

The situation bothered Robin. It also bothered her that no one was telling her the real reason the Bruckers had moved out of the Welles house so hastily. She'd grown up in Smallville; she'd heard ghost stories about the Welles place ever since she was old enough to go on sleepovers. Why couldn't people just acknowledge it?

She left the office early and drove her Camry down Waitley Lane.

The way the slope-roofed farmhouse stood in the light, the way the brilliant yellow sunbeams shone made the whole scene seem cornier than Kansas in August. She appraised with a practiced eye, imagining new shutters on the windows and an extension of the porch all the way around the building, like a Southern veranda. Then some French doors. It had potential. But remodels like that didn't come cheap, and there was not exactly a run on the rental market here in town. The thundering hordes were not moving to Smallville in order to commute to Metropolis, for example. In some ways, Smallville was like the town that time forgot . . . and still hadn't remembered.

Nevertheless, she hadn't been quite satisfied with the job that had been done preparing the house for their move-in. She had really wanted to attack the third-story attic with a mop and some paint before the mother and daughter had moved in. But for some reason, she'd never quite gotten around to it.

A bird chirped. It was such a beautiful day.

She fished the keys to the house out of her purse. Despite the fact that she was out in the country, with little chance of discovery, she didn't want anyone to know that she was entering a tenant's property without permission. That was unprofessional, not to mention illegal.

Such is my curiosity, she thought, trying to defend her actions.

Her high heels clacked on the wooden porch; they were new, and the soles were slick on the painted wood. One of them scooted out from under her, and she almost slipped, but she caught on to a post just in time and caught her balance.

She was about to put the key in the lock when she thought she heard someone moving around inside.

Uh-oh. She thrust the keys back in her purse and dithered a moment. If she hadn't been seen, maybe she could quietly descend the stairs, get in her Camry, and drive away with no one the wiser. But if she had been seen, she could follow through with her charade, ring the doorbell, and have her reason for coming over ready to audition.

Snoopy real-estate ladies are par for the course, she thought. *All I have to do is tell her I wanted to make sure she's all right.*

She waited, shifting her weight as she tried to discern if someone were truly inside. Then she checked her watch. She was going to have to go soon. Another farm family was selling out, and they wanted to talk to her about how much their home was worth. Simon Jackson did the actual farm appraisals; she concentrated on the residential portion of a failed dream . . .

Failed dreams.

I didn't grow up expecting to be a divorced realtor. I wanted to go to the big city, become an actress . . .

Shaking her head at her own drama, she turned on her heel and began to go down the steps.

There was a definite thump inside the house.

"O . . . kay," she said. Her heart picked up a little speed; despite the warm day, her hands were clammy.

She grinned at herself. *I'm scared. All those old stories about this place . . . let's see, which one was my favorite? The insane wife who flung herself down the stairs?*

"Dr. Brucker?" she called loudly, punching the bell to break her reverie. "Are you home?"

As she peered through the glass in the front door, a shadow passed across the opposite wall of the foyer.

"Oh," she breathed, jerking backward.

Just then, her cell phone rang. Startled, she stumbled backward, then put the phone to her ear.

"Hello?"

"It's Janice Brucker," said the caller. "I was wondering if the locks on the farmhouse had been recently installed. If anyone else might have keys."

Inside the house, the shadow was moving.

"Oh!" Robin said again, then shook her head to clear it. "I'm sorry. The locks are new, Dr. Brucker. Per Mr. Luthor's request."

The shadow was joined by a second shadow.

"Is your daughter with you?" she asked shrilly into the phone. *Maybe it's some kids, pulling a prank . . .*

"I beg your pardon?" Janice Brucker asked.

"I mean . . ." Robin took a deep breath. "There should be no other people with access. Except me," she added faintly.

"Because our things are in there, you understand," Dr. Brucker continued.

"Of course. Tell you what . . ." The larger shadow was stalking the smaller shadow . . . they were clearly human figures . . . Focusing as best she could, she said, "I'll run over there and make sure everything is secure."

"I'd appreciate that," Janice told her.

"May I . . . is there anything else I might do for you?" Robin rattled on by rote.

"No, that will do it for now. Thanks so much, Robin."

"You're very welcome, Dr. Brucker."

The larger shadow doubled up its fists as the little shadow staggered backward, arms outstretched. The large shadow advanced.

Robin couldn't stop watching. She was riveted to the spot, unable to tear her gaze away. Her heart was bruising her ribs, it was pounding so hard. Her hands were wrapped around each other, and her nails were digging into her flesh.

Oh, my God, he's going to hit the little one . . .

Without looking away, she opened her purse again and felt for the keys to the Welles house. She had to stop this, whatever it was . . .

The double keys were on a small plastic chain; she stabbed at the lock and turned the key, threw open the door and ran into the foyer . . . just as the smaller shadow collapsed in a heap.

"No!" she cried, stretching out both hands as the lack of traction of her new shoes and her forward momentum made her skitter toward the wall.

The large shadow loomed over her, gazing down as if it could see her, and raised its fists again . . .

Chloe had forced Clark to come with her to Mr. Cox's office and he stood abashed in front of the teacher's desk. He didn't like failing history, but he liked begging for grades even less. Despite Chloe's breezy assurances that she was going to "make it all better," he doubted Mr. Cox was going to give him another chance to do a paper since he had blown the last deadline so badly.

But Chloe was on a mission . . . *which is a good thing*, Clark thought anxiously. *Usually*.

"Mr. Cox," she said brightly, "I have a proposal for you." She leaned toward him and smiled. "It seems we have a mystery in Smallville. Yet again." She looked at him hard, as if she were holding a magnifying lens to her eye and staring at him through it.

"Chloe, this is . . . this isn't going to work," Clark murmured under his breath.

Of course Mr. Cox heard it. He was a teacher. Teachers always heard things you didn't want them to hear.

"Let me be the judge of that, Mr. Kent," Mr. Cox retorted. He sat back and folded his hands over his chest, and for a moment Clark thought he looked like a corpse nicely laid out for a funeral.

And I'm not being morbid or anything, he told himself.

Chloe said, "There's a body buried somewhere on the property at the Welles place."

Clark half expected the teacher's eyes to widen and his

mouth to drop open. But what he did was cock his head ever so slightly at Chloe, and say, "Really. And we know this because . . . ?"

"We'll tell you more details in the extra credit paper we're going to write together," she announced triumphantly.

Mr. Cox slid a lazy gaze at Clark, who reddened slightly but kept his eyes open wide and his expression innocent. "You don't need any extra credit, Chloe," he said. "In fact, you've already done so much extra credit that you've got an A-plus no matter what you do in the rest of the semester."

She preened.

"Mr. Kent is another story." He tsk-tsked. "And that's a mystery as well, because you started out so strong this semester, Clark. What happened?"

Clark thought about the irony of the teacher's words. He had started out stronger in the semester . . . *and now I'm weaker than a lot of the guys I know in gym class.*

"You'll do it anyway," the teacher pointed out. "For the sake of the story." He grinned at Chloe and added, "Our intrepid girl reporter."

"That's sexist, Mr. Cox." Chloe huffed. "C'mon. Clark has extenuating circumstances. That new girl, Ginger, she was—"

"Avoid the women, Clark," Mr. Cox said, wagging a finger at Clark. "They'll get you in trouble every time. Except perhaps this time." He sighed and shook his head, admitting defeat. "You come to me with good historical research, you discover something significant in Smallville history, and I will give Mr. Kent the equivalent of a B on his missing paper."

Clark heaved a sigh of his own.

"But . . . no good research, no B," the teacher added. "We on the same wavelength?"

"It's as if we were psychic," Chloe teased. "Right, Clark?"

Clark nodded. "Thanks, Mr. Cox."

The teacher went back to leaning in his chair and folding his hands over his chest. "Just avoid the women, Clark. They'll be the ruin of you."

After spending the afternoon posting flyers all over Smallville, Joel and Ginger sat side by side on an over-stuffed sofa upholstered in chintz in the lobby of the Small-ville Hotel. As usual, her mother was working late.

A lace-curtained window was open behind them. The weather had sizzled into summer at last; the warm summer air buzzed with katydids and crickets.

Joel was sipping iced tea; Ginger had a lemonade. She had told Joel to order whatever he wanted.

"Lex Luthor's paying for all of this."

Joel took another sip. "He must really like your mom."

"He likes my mom's work," she countered. "My parents are . . . my dad was a world-renowned scientist, and my mom still is one." She winced. "That sounds so awkward."

"You miss him." Joel touched her cheek. "A lot."

And that was all it took. Ginger put down her lemonade and sank into his arms. Her sobs were heavy, her tears, very bitter.

Joel held her, and rocked her, and she felt his lips skim the crown of her head. She was so sad, so very, very sad.

"You can't imagine how much I miss him. I can't stop missing him. And I never will, because . . . because then he would be . . ." She trailed off.

"Gone," Joel finished for her. "You don't want him to be gone."

He put his arms around her and rocked her. After a time he said, "He won't be, as long as you have your memories of him. Those will keep him alive, Ginger, more than the grief will."

"But what if I start forgetting?" she said hoarsely. "What if I let go of him if I feel better?"

"I won't let you forget. Tell me."

There was a beat. She raised her head. "I don't understand."

"A memory. Tell me a memory." He smiled gently at her. "Tell me a true story about him."

She looked truly moved. She gazed at him, and said, "He loved explaining scientific things in fanciful ways. He told me that lightbulbs glowed because fairies lived in them."

"And when they burned out?" he prompted.

"The fairy had left the bulb and gone back to fairyland." She smiled at the memory. "There were no deaths in fairyland. Everyone lived forever."

There was a moment of silence, as if to honor the story; then Joel said, "Thank you for telling me that."

She sniffled. "Thank you for listening."

They smiled wanly at each other. Then Joel said, "Tell me another story."

She thought for a moment, then said, "Butterscotch. My father loved butterscotch . . ."

Janice hurried into the lobby, a bit guilty that she had stayed at the lab so late. Tonight, however, she had had good cause.

Lex had brought a laptop to her and asked her to analyze some data. It had taken her only seconds to realize that what she was seeing was some kind of meteorite activity . . . and further, that the emissions were manifesting in very peculiar ways.

"Does it seem like a ghost to you?" he had asked her boldly.

"You sound like my daughter," she had retorted.

"Do you think you can replicate this sort of activity?" he asked her, sounding enthusiastic.

"That's the question, isn't it," she replied, watching the sine and cosine waves intermingle at the bottom of the screen. "It has such an unusual pattern . . . like nothing I've seen before. It's otherworldly."

"Well, that makes sense, since it is. From another world." He smiled at her.

"Yes, but which one?" she asked, studying the readouts again. As she watched the rhythmic waves, she murmured, "I guess that's why you pay me the big bucks."

"That's why indeed," he answered.

"Where did you find these patterns?" Janice said, her eyes still glued to the screen.

"From the Welles house." And Lex watched her eyes grow wide with shock.

For hours she had stared at those patterns, and now . . .

. . . Now her daughter was sitting on the sofa of a quaint hotel with a boy, and Janice realized with a startled pang that she had missed most of her daughter's young life. George had bridged the worlds of the little girl and the overextended mother, and with him gone . . . there was no bridge.

Oh, honey, I'm so sorry, Janice thought, hurrying to her. *I'll do better.*

But when her daughter spotted her in the lobby, there was no happiness on her face, only relief.

Maybe that's all I have a right to ask for.

The boy shyly moved away from Ginger. There was such an air of sadness about him, a bit of the wounded bird.

"Hi," Ginger said, as if reminding her that she and the boy were there. "Long day at the office."

"Yeah." She smiled uncomfortably. "Lots to discover."

"This is Joel," Ginger said.

"How do you do?" he asked politely.

"I'm fine, thank you."

"Well." Perhaps reading her curtness for dismissal, he put down his tea and rose. "I should go home. Or to the Pickerings', anyway."

Janice followed none of this, but she said, "Good night, Joel."

She wasn't sure he heard her. He was gazing at her daughter like a puppy.

Blushing, Ginger half glanced at her mother, then said, "I'll walk you to your car."

They're so young, and in those first throes of love . . .

Surprising herself, Janice said, "On warm nights like this back in Indiana, when we were in grad school, your father loved to go out for lemon meringue pie."

Ginger looked both startled and captivated. "I didn't know that."

"A memory," Joel said. He traded a look with Ginger; she smiled.

The three shared an unspoken moment, like a collective sigh for other days tinged with the bittersweet pleasure that nostalgia brought. After it was over, the boy inclined his head in Janice's direction. The two kids crossed the lobby and went out the front door.

Her mood lightened, Janice watched them through the window, walking hand in hand. She could almost see George and herself walking along with them, ghosts of the young lovers they themselves had once been.

With a deep sigh for all that had been lost, she walked to the reception desk and asked, "Is room service still open? I'd like to order two pieces of lemon meringue pie." *He loved it with iced tea.* "And two glasses of iced tea."

I'll tell her about the time we went fishing, and he felt sorry for the fish and threw them all back, she decided. *Oh, and how he worked at the university bookstore one summer, and he got caught giving some used textbooks to that poor student from Nicaragua. The manager tried to fire him and the other store clerks threatened to quit if he did.*

George was the artist in the family, but I'll paint pictures of him for her . . . with stories.

They stayed up all night, mother and daughter, reminiscing about the husband and father they missed so much. Janice regaled Ginger with story and story about her father, and Ginger reacted as if Janice had gifted her with something unbelievably precious and wonderful.

In the dawn's misty, rosy light, Ginger dozed off with a smile on her face. Janice sat by her bedside, stroking her hair, her cheek, and let the tears come.

She let the grief overtake her that she had always saved for sleep. She mourned for George as she had never really allowed herself to mourn before.

And that night . . . she slept.

Run, Robin, run.

The realtor had run, from the shadows on the wall and the thumping in the basement; from the menacing figure that swirled with green . . .

. . . run down Waitley Lane and into the cornfield, and now she couldn't stop . . .

. . . running.

She was trapped in a field of gray that sounded like something breathing, each breath labored and wheezing. It was very high-pitched, each breath a terrible effort. Her ears ricocheted with the shrill sound, bulleting and reverberating around her. It was like the overamplified sound of someone who had a lot of trouble breathing. Like someone who had . . .

" . . . asthma," Chloe finished triumphantly, as she pointed to the scanned-in copy of the *Smallville Ledger*. It was over sixty years old, but the weathered papers had been cleaned up digitally after they had been scanned in.

Another thing this town owes Lex for, Clark thought, *but they'll probably never know that he sprang for the entire graphics system.*

They were in the Smallville Public Library. If Mr. Cox could see his F student in the library, bright and early, he might have had trouble breathing as well.

"The governor had asthma." She scanned the story. "Until he was seven or eight. Then he got better. Oooh. Listen to this. A farmer died just about the time little Governor Welles's health improved. Here's a picture of him."

She gave Clark one of her patented, *Isn't that weird?* looks, and waited for his reaction.

"Okay," Clark said gently. "A man died and the governor's asthma cleared up."

"Right." Her smile grew. She had dazzling white teeth.

"Chloe, that's a coincidence. And even if it isn't, we have to *prove* they're linked. If they are," Clark added, for emphasis.

"I'm sure they are." Chloe returned her hands to the keyboard and started typing and clicking.

Friday was a half day at school for Ginger. Janice had planned to put in some long hours at the lab—but instead she impulsively asked Ginger if she'd like to go to Metropolis after school let out.

There was someone there she needed to talk to, face to face.

"I need to do some things at the university," Janice said.

She had a faculty appointment there, but she'd taken a sabbatical after George's death. She still had many friends and colleagues who knew and missed her. "You can invite Joel if you want, show him around the school," she added.

Ginger sprang at the offer, and as soon as they rounded up Joel, they drove north to the sprawling big city.

Ginger sat in back with Joel, and the two talked nonstop the entire drive. Janice was wistful but philosophical about being ignored . . . *my baby grew up when I wasn't looking . . . and it's a good thing that she wants to spend more time with her peers. It's the right thing.*

Janice took them to the faculty dining room for a late-afternoon snack. It was a wonderful wood-paneled room with a great menu, very Ivy League, with suits of armor and paintings of former university presidents and alumni on the walls. The Luthors were pictured there, of course.

"I wish I could go to a place like this," Joel said, and Janice was surprised to realize that he assumed such a place was beyond his reach.

"What's your GPA?" she asked, and when he said it was a 3.89, she asked about SAT scores. They were excellent, too.

"There's no reason why you can't go here," she said, "or at least apply."

"Money," he murmured.

"Scholarship," she replied.

He looked intrigued. She leaned forward on her elbows, and said, "What would you do with a college education?"

Without missing a beat, he said, "Help."

"Help." She smiled faintly. "Help whom?"

"Not sure where to begin," he admitted. "But I would try to make a difference."

Ginger brushed his hand with hers, and said, "You already have."

Janice thought for a moment. They were seniors, and it was already way too late in the school year for applications for fall. As the daughter of a faculty member, Ginger had been given priority and she would be coming here in the fall. But Janice did have a lot of friends in high places . . .

"If you get an application package together, I'll walk it through for you," she said on impulse. "You might have to wait until spring, but we'll see. And I'll help you get some money. You'll probably have to get a work-study job, though. Something. And it would be tight."

"Oh, Mom," Ginger said excitedly. "Mom, that would be so cool!"

Joel looked stunned. Then he lowered his gaze to his plate and said, "I . . . thank you, Dr. Brucker."

She was surprised at herself. Gestures such as this had been George's provenance, not hers.

Then I'll have to carry on the family tradition, she thought.

After they finished eating, Ginger offered to show Joel the social work, education, and psychology departments, "for ideas about your major," and Janice arranged to meet them in a couple of hours.

Feeling upbeat, she crossed the quad, past the Gothic-style halls of the venerable old university, strolling past the Luthor Building—which housed the business department, of course—until she reached a far older section of the university, well away from the main buildings of the esteemed institution.

It was home of the philosophy department, headed by an old friend of hers and George's, one Rafael Alcina. He had also spent many an evening in their apartment musing about cabbages, kings, and the interior life of the individual. But one conversation—over some of George's excellent cooking—had brought her from Smallville to talk to him now.

He had been chatting about *The Fly*—which had treated the notion that if one took a person apart and transported him or her to another location, it would still be the same person.

"What if that's what occurs in nature?" he'd asked the couple. "If, even though our bodies disintegrate, our . . . let's call them spiritual molecules . . . re-form in a different place?"

"Like a ghost," George had said enthusiastically.

"Yes, like a ghost," Rafael had replied. "Or a soul released into paradise."

"How do you account for the transportation of consciousness?" Janice chimed in.

"We now know that most of what we pass off as conscious deliberation is just hard wiring," Rafael had argued. "We are far more 'sequential' than we are holistic or organic. So, if you could essentially recombine a person's essence after death, why not his consciousness?"

Why not, indeed? And what about adding some kind of energy boost to make it more apparent to those still "alive"?

Such as the Smallville meteorites?

Rafael's office door stood before her now, dark wood panels with a bronze door knocker set into their center. The knocker was the face of a harlequin, and she had always thought it a bit sinister-looking. Now it seemed to stare at her as she rapped on the wood, ordering her to leave well enough alone and go away.

From inside, Rafael's familiar voice sang out, "Come in."

She did, and he sprang to his feet and gave her a hug. "Janice! Welcome home." He pushed her away and studied her face. "That's why you're here, isn't it? To come back to work?"

The hug felt good. She'd forgotten how much she missed simply being touched. *I must hug Ginger more. If she'll let me.*

"Sadly, no," she said, as he let her go.

"Alas," he said rather theatrically. "Then it's simply that you missed me with all your heart . . ."

She took a deep breath. "Rafael, my employer wants me to analyze some data from what I gather is visual evidence of some kind of paranormal manifestation." She trailed off, grimacing with embarrassment. "And I remembered a conversation we had a long time ago."

"Paranormal manifestation," he repeated slowly.

She blanched. "He asked me if I thought it was a ghost."

"Yes," he said. "Lex Luthor. He called me this morning. Tell me, does he know that we're colleagues?"

She raised her brows. "I would assume so. He's a thorough businessman."

"Then you know he's calling this paranormal manifestation 'the ghost of Smallville.' "

Her lips parted in surprise. He didn't appear to notice her agitation as he blithely continued.

"Apparently some local students have been conducting a ghost hunt. In some old farmhouse. I asked him to let me play, too. I want to try to channel this manifestation."

Janice's stomach did a flip.

"What students?" she asked.

After she left Rafael's office, she went in search of Ginger and her boyfriend. She stomped across the quad—they were waiting precisely where they were supposed to—and she jerked to a stop.

For a moment she was so angry she couldn't speak. Then she said, "What's been going on, Ginger? What have you and those kids been doing at the farmhouse?"

Ginger said nothing, only looked frightened and guilty, and the boy beside her cast anxious glances from daughter to mother and back again.

"How could you do this without telling me about it? Do all this . . . dangerous research without consulting me?"

Ginger straightened her shoulders and lifted her chin. "When do I ever get to talk to you about anything?" she flung at her.

"We talked last night!" Janice yelled. "And all that time, you had done this, and never once let me know—"

"Dr. Brucker," the boy began, but Ginger laid a hand on his forearm and took a step toward her mother.

"I was protecting you!" she blurted.

Janice stared at her. "Protecting *me*? From the fact that you were engaging in bizarre experiments that could have gotten you hurt?"

"Yes!" Ginger shouted. "Because you did it, too, Mom. You engaged in bizarre experiments that hurt me! They got Daddy killed. And now . . . now . . ."

Tears streamed down her face. "You're always saying in your sleep, 'I killed you, George.' And Joel"—she pointed at him—"Joel started making contact with this ghost or whatever six months ago, Mom. When Daddy died!"

Janice was so astonished that she took a step backward. "You think this manifestation is your *father*?"

"I don't know!" Ginger cried. She was sobbing. "Mom, I don't know, but it's something! Something is happening! And you're haunted, Mom. When's the last time you had a good night's sleep?"

Joel stepped forward, his arms held out as if he were handing Janice a peace offering.

"Dr. Brucker, this is my fault," he said. "I . . . I've been messing with stuff I shouldn't. I made some kind of contact." He touched his forehead. "I don't know how to explain it. I don't even know how to tell you about it."

"There's a big meteorite in the cornfield," Ginger cut in.

Janice stared at the two of them.

"I think," she said slowly, "that you both had better start at the beginning."

CHAPTER THIRTEEN

Chloe finished tweaking the layout on her story about ghosts and sent the proof to the printer. The G3 processor in the school newspaper's iMac was powerful, if a little behind the times, and quickly generated the postscript file needed for the printout. Of course the old software the school was running—a copy of Pagemaker 4 purchased back in the dark ages—didn't tax the more modern computer much.

It was late at Smallville High—even the jocks had all gone home—and the building was silent. But in the *Torch* office, the flame of journalism burned bright.

"Clark, there's page four. Go ahead and proof it, and we'll prep it for duplication on Monday."

Clark sat over in the corner, several pages of carefully created *Torch* proofs on the desk next to him, alongside the books she'd picked up for his history paper. On top sat a self-published pamphlet by Betty-Ann Carson titled *Smallville Farming: A Complete History*. He was proofreading the finished story layouts. On Monday Chloe would take them to the media center and have them copied onto eleven-by-seventeen newsprint.

In between proofing the newspaper he had been thumbing through the pamphlet, looking for historical information about the Welles place. Now that Chloe had finished the last story, she was going to do some digging herself.

I'd rather use an iMac than a shovel anyway. Although if her theory—and his X-ray vision—were right, sooner or later, bodies were going to start coming up.

And how do I "discover" the one in the basement for her?

Chloe switched on the Internet connection, a hard-won

concession that she did *not* take for granted, gained when she took over the editor's job at the paper. After much arguing she'd compromised with Principal Kwan's predecessor: A censorship program would block access to "questionable" sites and she could have the access.

One of Pete's friends in the computer club had disabled that safety in about five minutes.

The fourth estate will not be hampered in its research.

The idea that she could be a crusader for truth, a champion for people's rights, was exciting to Chloe. No—more than that—a *mission*. The fact that she might eventually get paid for it was even better. She'd always been smart, and it was both her blessing and curse, because it meant that anything she did had to *mean* something. Reporting was a way to use her brains well and without compromise.

Chloe had spent the previous summer in Metropolis, where she came up with an idea for a freelance story about underage drinking. She had gone all over Metropolis trying to sneak into various nightclubs and bars so that she could expose the ease with which teenagers could drink illegally. As it turned out, no one would serve her, so she had thrown in the towel. While she wasn't one to let the facts get in the way of a good story, there had to be *some* facts.

When she'd returned to Smallville, she'd been surprised that it had been so easy to get the job of editor on the *Torch* —there'd been no one who wanted to compete with her for the job. Amazing. And her a *freshman*!

Or just apathy, if you want to look at it that way.

Worrying to think that most people didn't *care* about uncovering the truth, and all the more reason for her to tear down the facades of the world and reveal the inner workings. She sometimes felt like a modern-day Paul Revere, trying to rouse a sleeping countryside. Many who heard her warnings just turned over and went back to sleep. Others didn't want the disruption.

Principal Kwan, for instance, had tried to control the direction of the paper since he'd arrived. They'd come to an understanding—no more woo-woo stuff. Chloe didn't write anything that wasn't related to the school unless it was for entertainment purposes. And she kept her end of the bargain—sort of.

The ghost story for instance, was disguised as trivia. Naturally Chloe had managed to slip in *some* intimations. She'd introduced the piece with "Fun facts to know in keeping with the current fascination with spirits," alluding to the rumors about Joel. The interview with him had managed to sneak in as well.

She'd learned that Principal Kwan only checked his "in" basket once a day, first thing in the morning. If she dropped a copy of the proofs off at just after, she could get it printed before he had a chance to suggest corrections.

Gosh, Principal Kwan, I did drop off a copy before school, well *before taking it to the printers.*

She glanced around the cluttered workroom. Back in the days before desktop publishing, they'd needed lots more space for all the layout and paste-ups. No one in the administration had figured this change out yet, and Chloe wasn't about to enlighten them. She planned on having more reporters if she could find them—or at least more reporters than she, Pete, and Clark. Lana wrote a few things from time to time, but the majority of the work fell on the three of them. Chloe had three more years to go; by then, she figured she'd be giving the *Smallville Ledger* a run for its money.

Pete, who'd usually be here knocking out a last-minute story, was over working on the campaign for the subject of her latest research hunt.

Not that it was bad being here alone with Clark . . . *Focus, Chloe, focus!*

She really didn't know what to make of Pete's recent dedication to politics. It was a good "rock-the-vote" kind of thing, nice to see somebody doing something they believed in—but she was *sure* that Welles was up to no good, and Pete just wouldn't listen.

She'd suggested that he be the inside man on a story about the governor, but he'd balked.

"No way, Sullivan," he'd said.

"I wonder why he's so unwilling to help," she said, thinking aloud.

"Who?" asked Clark from across the room, sounding like a big owl.

"Oh—sorry Clark. Pete," she said, pressing "Enter" on a Nexus search for stories from the last two years about the governor with keywords "house" and "Smallville."

The results page from the search started downloading at a slow 56k modem speed.

Governor in the Big House.

Governor supports housing subsidies.

Smallville Governor Wins Big.

Nothing. She started searching again, focusing on the keywords "Smallville," and "Welles."

"Pete just likes the fact that the governor is from here," said Clark.

"I don't know if that's a good thing, from what I've seen," Chloe replied.

"Thanks a lot, Chloe. Most of my friends came from here," he said, emphasizing the word "most."

"Oh no! I meant that knee-jerk 'one of us' factionalisms aren't good."

Clark tapped on the pamphlet. "Look at it from his point of view. He grew up here, and Governor Welles did, too.

Seeing him leave Smallville and becoming a success and affecting the world is a big thing for him." He paused. "I mean, Chloe, did you think there was anything cool or exciting about Smallville when you first got here?"

No, she hadn't. She'd been outraged when her father accepted the job as engineer at the LuthorCorp fertilizer plant. She'd wanted to leave within seconds of seeing the never-ending flat fields that surrounded the town.

Of course, now that she'd come to realize the uniqueness of Smallville, with its weird happenings, she saw it in a different sort of light.

An opportunity.

But Clark did have a point.

"Okay, I can see the hero-as-example kind of thing, but I'd think Pete would have gone for someone better to the environment."

"Good point," said Clark.

She grinned a smile that got larger as she read the headline from the hits that flashed up on the monitor.

Welles Blamed in Shady Deal.

That was more like it!

She clicked on the hyperlink, and suddenly the browser shut down and an error message appeared on the screen.

"What!" she said, taken aback.

Connection Lost, read the message.

Clark called out, "You okay?"

"Yeah. I lost the connection."

"You want me to help you look for it?"

She threw a pad of stickies at him. Usually her aim was way off, but tonight she might have been pitching for the Dodgers.

Smack! It hit him right in the face.

"Oh, no! Sorry, Clark!"

He just laughed, and she smiled. It was good to have him

here, all to herself. And it was all the more interesting that he hadn't gone after Ginger. There was hope yet—but better not to push it.

This intrepid reporter won't be following that story just yet.

She started the Internet connection again, the pinging and bleating of the modem carrying across the room. She restarted the browser and clicked on the history tab, but nothing happened.

Darn it! The machine had lost it.

Slowly she retraced her steps, entering the same search terms and working her way through the hits generated until she came to the same one.

She clicked on it, and again, nothing happened.

This is getting really boring.

Clark heard her slap the keyboard and turned to look at her.

"Maybe it's the meteor-rock green color of the computer," he said, a smile in his tone.

"Not funny, Clark."

Still, maybe he had something there. Perhaps it would work on the other computer. Chloe turned around so she was facing the red iMac behind her desk and fired it up. The musical chime as she started it up cheered her. She was a reporter, dang it; no Internet connection monkey business was going to slow her down.

For all the convenience of computers, she envied the old-time reporters for a second—sleuthing around, digging through old files—those were the days. Woodward and Bernstein didn't have to worry about ISP troubles or lost servers.

Once the startup process was complete, Chloe again retraced her steps. This time Clark watched over her shoulder. Pete had a theory about computer bugs—the really nasty ones only worked for one person. The moment someone else was there to watch, they'd go away. Personally, she felt that this was a little superstitious, but it did seem to work.

This time the connection held.

Governor Blamed for Shady Deal, read the headline. Chloe clicked on the link and scanned the article, her heart sinking. The governor had purchased five-hundred umbrellas for an event in the capital. It hadn't rained, but they'd wound up being used for shade from the sun.

Unbelievable.

"Looks like he's interested in people's comfort, at least," Clark said.

She turned to say something mean, and suddenly there was a crash from the other side of the room.

Clark's books had just spilled off the table.

Clark turned, startled at the sound. There was nothing there—but his books were all over the floor.

Uh-oh.

"Clark . . . tell me that wasn't you?" Chloe sounded excited.

"Uh, no."

The door lock clicked.

They looked at each other.

"They're heeeeeeere," said the reporter, grinning. She reached in her purse and pulled out her digital camera. "This time, I'm getting some shots for the paper."

She stood up and looked around the room, holding the digital camera in her hand like it was a weapon. A blinking light on the back indicated that the flash was ready.

Clark looked around the room with his X-ray vision.

There.

A greenish ball of *something*, surrounded by the same kind of green feathery strands he'd seen before in the cornfield.

Whatever it was seemed to figure out that he could *see* it, and Clark watched, fascinated as the green tendrils gathered around a small bookcase—

—which it threw at him.

Clark didn't have superspeed, but he was still faster than most people. He grabbed Chloe and pushed her to the ground, taking the brunt of the bookcase on his shoulders. Her surprised "Hey!" was drowned out by the sound of the debris smashing into the floor.

Now what?

Clark turned back and saw that another group of books was going to fly their way. He dodged, pulling Chloe with him as she fired the camera. The muted beep and flash were followed by the thumping sounds of the books as they slid along the floor past the desk.

"Careful, Clark! Watch the camera!"

It's not the camera I'm worried about, Chloe.

He couldn't believe it. Here they were, trapped in a room with what was very likely a ghost, throwing heavy objects at them, and all she wanted to do was take pictures of it.

I'm not sure I'd keep at it, and I know it can't hurt me. Scratch reporting from my list of future careers.

For that matter, what were they going to do? The apparition seemed to be gaining more energy as it threw more things at them. Books, old files, the proofs for tomorrow's *Torch.*

"Hey! Those are the *proofs!* Stop that!"

Chloe's indignant yell was cut off as the green iMac started to fall off her desk.

Clark saw it moving as if in slow motion, and *pushed* himself to try and get faster. His hands extended toward the arcing computer, on its way to certain doom. The harsh fluorescent lighting of the overhead lights glinted on the green plastic and reflected slightly on the dormant screen.

There.

He'd caught it. Still not anywhere near full speed, but *better*.

"Oh, thank goodness! Clark—that has all my files."

A bigger question was occurring to Clark as they crawled under the heavy worktable that had held the computer.

How are we going to get out of here?

Chloe was fully awake, watching *everything*, had a digital camera, and was a reporter to boot. No way he was going to pull any fast ones, particularly with the superspeed gone. Talk about secrets getting out. He could see it now, a *Torch* special edition: *High School Boy Actually from Another World*.

The falling objects stopped for a moment, and then the books Clark had been reading all started to float in the air. He lapsed into X-ray vision for a second, and saw green feathery strands grabbing each of the books, holding them up in the air.

Wow.

He slid toward the door, tugging Chloe with him.

But she was having none of it. The reporter fired shot after shot at the floating books, muttering under her breath.

"I got it! Got that shot! Oh yeah, they'll never believe, now they'll have to!"

The camera let out a beep and shut off.

"I'm out of batteries! Clark! Hand me the batteries, will you?"

"Uh, Chloe, how about we just head for the door?"

"Uh-uh."

The floating books cascaded higher into the air, and then pages started flipping. Clark was frozen, unable to decide what to do. Chloe wasn't going to leave, and he'd have to drag her out at this rate.

But he needed to be sure they could escape.

He slid backward toward the door to the newspaper room, and reached behind him for the knob.

But then he paused, and looked at it.

It's been slimed.

He reached into his back pocket, where he had a rag he'd been using on one of the tractors earlier. He and his Dad had been checking the fluids of the old John Deere he'd rebuilt, and had used the rag to check the oil.

He rubbed the gunk off the knob, moving as fast as he could. He could feel the effects of the meteor rocks through the cloth, but at least this way it wouldn't *stick* to him.

There.

Clean at last, he reached up and grabbed the knob, turning it hard with his superstrength. The lock broke, the knob moving freely in his hand. Fortunately, Chloe was facing the floating books, sliding some batteries she'd found into the camera.

"Chloe, let's get out of here!"

But she didn't move. Unfortunately, the thing—the great green *thing* did.

It pushed the huge worktable at Clark, ramming into the door, and holding it closed. Clark knew he could tear the door down, smash the table into toothpicks, but again, there was Chloe.

Come on, Clark, think!

He needed more time.

And then it occurred to him—he couldn't move superfast, but he could *think* that way. He transitioned frame of reference, effectively freezing everything in the room. The books hovered in midair, the ghostly green ectoplasm holding them. Chloe was frozen, a grimace on her face as she closed the battery door in the digital camera.

He considered his options.

Okay. Grabbing Chloe and running out the door was out

unless he could somehow do it without having to show his powers. Same with jumping out the window. If he had his speed back, he could throw his jacket over her head and rush out of the room so she wouldn't see anything, but he didn't.

As he calculated various actions, Clark looked at the green *thing* floating in the room. It resembled a giant green octopus, or squid, tendrils everywhere, grasping objects, reaching for things.

One of the tendrils was reaching for Chloe; he could see that it was almost to her leg.

What's it going to do? Throw her at me?

He couldn't afford to find out.

Then he noticed a green thread that left the room, branching off to one of the walls, piercing it, and going . . . *where*?

Clark was reminded of the thing he'd seen in the cornfield.

It's like it's reaching out . . .

For what? Something unseen? Something out away from the school?

Or maybe it's like a power cord.

Instantly he knew it was true. If he could do what he'd done in the cornfield the night Joel had almost disappeared again, he might stop it, cut off its power. It wouldn't be a supercharged spirit anymore. And it wouldn't hurt to try.

He tried to remember what he'd done than night. He'd turned on the Geiger counter, aimed a flashlight, grabbed at it with his hands . . .

He altered his frame of reference back to normal and dived forward, grabbing the camera from Chloe. The light was blinking, so the flash was ready to go. He dived toward the solitary tendril. Behind him he could hear Chloe shriek as she finally got scared. The creature had grabbed her leg and was picking her up.

He fired the flash at it, smacking with his hand, picturing the tendril severed, the power broken.

Nothing.

Chloe screamed again, and Clark could see that she *had* been lifted into the air. She was being positioned right over the books, and the pages of them were turning, flipping fast enough that they were creating a wind, fanning her hair back.

He hit the green streamer again, willing it to *break*, to separate so that he could save his friend. Suddenly it seemed to grow thinner, and then fold in on itself. Instantly the books all fell to the ground, along with Chloe, a larger thump.

"Owwww!"

"You okay Chloe?"

She nodded, rolling her shoulder, where she'd hit. Then she reached over and grabbed the camera from him.

"Nice shot, Clark, I think you got an excellent picture of the floorboards."

Outside the school, Chloe made Clark patrol while she checked out her pictures.

This is great! Attacked by a ghostly presence while in the newsroom! How many reporters can talk about a story coming to them like that? Let's see Kwan try to stop this story. It certainly relates to the school! It happened at school.

She clicked through the shots.

Hmmmm.

Some of them didn't come out so well. Picture of under the table, one of half of Clark's face, his eye filling up the little screen on the camera, that last one of the floorboards was no good . . .

But some of the others . . .

Objects milling about in the shot, books being held by

nothing and blurred motion from objects being hurled at the camera.

Great! This is great!

Chloe looked at the books that had been dumped on the floor. Why had the ghost chosen those volumes?

She squinted at the image. Three of the books had fallen and landed open, all to picture pages. Of course since they were all historical photo books about Smallville—surprising how many there were—it stood to reason they'd be open to pages with photos on them.

Wait a second.

There, in the middle of one of the pages was a farmer, glowering at the camera. He was big, with a huge head and large ears. And he looked *familiar.*

She glanced at the caption. Mattias Silver.

Clark came over and took in the viewfinder.

"That's him," he said excitedly.

"Him? Who? Clark, who?"

Clark tapped the picture of the farmer. "Remember that sketch Ginger drew? That's him."

He's right!

"Okay Governor Welles," she cried. "I have you now! You killed Mattias Silver!"

Clark shook his head. "Chloe, we've been over that—Welles was only a *boy* when the farmer died."

Maybe there are two *ghosts.*

"Clark, he's the only link—at least the only one still *living.*" She waved her arms to emphasize her point. "A neighbor dies when Welles is a boy, *right before he gets well.* Sounds pretty suspicious to me."

She was silent a moment. "And you know what? I bet he is behind *this* as well." She indicated the computers.

"Governors have a great deal of power. Maybe he's

killing any connection to the deeper stories about himself. The bad ones."

Clark looked at her as if he was trying to come to grips with what she was saying.

And to herself, *I've got to stop him.*

"In fact, I think that maybe the ghost was trying to *warn* me—like an old E.C. horror comic." She grinned. "This is so *great*! This is *big*! I'll be on the front page in Metropolis with this one!"

But even more important, she'd safeguard the public trust by helping avert a national tragedy. All by keeping the public informed!

All she needed was a few more facts. Did the governor actually kill someone? Or did he just know about it?

There was only one place to get the answers.

"When did Pete say the governor was getting to town?" she asked casually.

Clark gave her a what-now look.

She was going to pay Hiram Welles a visit, and soon.

But first she had a duty to perform. Smallville High expected a school paper tomorrow, and they would get it. Maybe no one else had wanted to be the editor, and maybe no one would believe her theories about what was going on, but she was going to be sure that they had a chance to think about them.

Chloe Sullivan, reporter, editor, and publisher picked up the proofs she'd completed earlier and tried to think about where to put the story about the ghost attack. Page one definitely. But would the picture look better higher or lower?

She walked over to the green iMac and started it up. It was time to get back to work.

In a haunted newsroom.

Clark said, "You crack me up."

She grinned, and got into the zone.

CHAPTER FOURTEEN

One of the advantages of growing up a Luthor was that Lex was rarely intimidated by anyone. The other was that he expected people who were in power to be good at being in power.

Thus, he didn't bat an eye when his personal line rang at 9 P.M. in his office in the family Scottish mansion, and it turned out to be Hiram Welles, the governor of Kansas. He didn't bother wondering how the man had gotten his private number. He expected someone in Welles's position to figure out how to get it.

"Luthor," the governor began, without bothering with the usual courtesies, which was fine with Lex. "What the hell is going on in my house?"

Ah. News of the farmhouse ghostbusting has reached the state capital. Lex's lips curved into a faint smile; he enjoyed the man's agitation. He was also intrigued by it.

"Your house, Governor?" he asked. "I'm sorry. I have no idea what's going on at the governor's mansion. Should I?"

"Don't try to be clever. You aren't. You know damn well I mean the house in Smallville. The farm."

"Oh. You mean the house on Waitley."

"Let's remember here who is running a fertilizer plant and who is running the state. Don't try to act like your father."

That hurt . . . a little. But not very much, really. Lex wouldn't be much of a Luthor if such a minor barb could cause much damage.

"Believe me, sir, sincerely. I have no wish whatsoever to act like my father."

"You are impertinent."

Where did this guy learn to talk, pompous old man school?

"No, sir. Just honest," Lex said easily, leaning back in his chair. He picked up a Mont Blanc pen and began doodling on a pad of vellum notepaper, each piece emblazoned with his initials, *LL*.

"In my day . . ." the governor began, and then he switched gears . . . as a man in his position should. There was nothing to be gained by reminding a voter that his days were past. "A man sitting in a chair I fund at the university . . . in the philosophy department . . . happened to tell a member of my office that he was going down to Smallville to channel a ghost. And he described my house."

Raphael Alcina, Lex knew. *The man's known for his interest in paranormal activity. That was why I called him.*

"Are you listening to me, Luthor?"

"Of course, Governor. Every word."

"Damn it, boy, don't patronize me."

"I wouldn't dream of it." *You huffy old egomaniac.*

The governor continued, "Dr. Alcina was told not to go. Not if he values his position at the university. Which he does. So. There will be no more table-tipping on my family's property." There was a beat. "Do we have an understanding?"

"Certainly," Lex said.

"Good."

The governor hung up. Lex kept doodling.

"We both understand that you don't want any more ghost hunting," he murmured. "But that's all we understand."

I really don't like this place, Clark thought, as he once again drove up to the farmhouse.

Concerned about his safety, his parents had initially refused to let him go when Chloe had invited him to tonight's "channeling session." Clark promised he would stay away from the cornfield—and the meteor in it—and stick to the house. That still didn't sit well with Martha and Jonathan, but Clark needed to be there. After all, Holly Pickering was still missing. And Robin, the woman who had acted as the leasing agent, had also disappeared.

The single factor that had persuaded them to let him attend was the fact that Ginger's mother, Janice Brucker, was going to be there. She had also invited a colleague of hers from the university.

"Otherwise . . ." Martha said.

He got out of the truck and took the stairs, scanning for green glows. He saw the figures of his friends gathering in the parlor. There were seven of them: Chloe, Ginger and her mother, Joel, Pete, Lana, and . . . his heart sank a little.

Whitney was there, too, and he was already holding hands with Lana.

She's his girlfriend, he reminded himself. *He should be holding her hand.*

Not wishing to disturb the preparations, he let himself in. Despite the beautiful, summerlike night air, the interior of the house was cold.

"Clark." Chloe rose from beside Lana and came to collect him. She was radiant. "Hurry. We're almost ready."

She led him into the room. The closer he got to the table, the lower the temperature.

They all looked in his direction. Lana looked beautiful, as always. Whitney's letter jacket was slung over Lana's shoulders. Pete, who said, "Hey, bro," was rubbing his bare arms.

"Hi," Clark said to everyone.

"Isn't it great? It's cold," Chloe said.

"We're sitting in the cold heart of the house," Ginger ventured. She gazed at her mother and added in a rush, "Mom's going to channel the ghost tonight."

Janice frowned and gave her head a shake. "I'm . . . now I'm not so sure this is a good idea after all. The man who was going to help me had to cancel out at the last minute."

"But he gave you some suggestions on how to do it," Chloe said.

"Yes. He was quite . . . specific," Janice said. "But he was the one with the expertise, not I. And . . ." She stopped talking, as if she was about to say something she didn't want to say. "I got the impression that he had been told not to come. Maybe by his department chair. Universities can be pretty sticky about their reputations."

"Well, you're on sabbatical, Mom. You can do what you want."

Janice Brucker's face revealed the war she was having with herself. *She wants to do it,* Clark thought. *She's just not sure how to make it okay with herself.*

"We brought reinforcements," Lana said, smiling at Whitney. He grinned back at her.

Janice clearly wasn't pleased with herself, but she said, "All right. But at the first sign of trouble . . ."

"We're outta here," Chloe said, holding up her hand. "Promise."

They settled in. Chloe sat farthest from the door. On her left was Pete, then Lana, then Whitney, and Janice Brucker. Joel sat on Janice's left, and Ginger was close beside him. She had a sketch pad in front of her and a clutch of sharpened pencils.

The only empty chair stood between Ginger and Chloe. Clark would be sitting across from Lana—and Whitney—the entire time.

As before, candles, bread, and cheese sat on the table. There were pads of unlined printer paper, too. This time there was something new . . . a Ouija board. Clark hadn't seen one in years. The board face was scratched, and the letters of the alphabet, fanned across the width of the board, were faded to an uneven pale gray. The two spaces for "YES" and "NO" were ringed as if someone had set cans of soda down on them.

Chloe saw Clark staring at it, and said, "Dr. Brucker brought that. Her friend at the university told her to use it." She placed her well-manicured fingers on it and slid it toward herself. "So I'll be the one using it."

Then she said to Janice, "Now what?"

Janice said, "Light a candle and stare into the flame. Wait. First put your fingertips lightly on the planchette . . . here . . ."

She picked up a small triangle of plastic and handed it to Chloe. Clark studied it. Set into a circular cutout was a piece of plastic from which dangled a needle.

"Like this?" She grinned as she placed her fingers on the planchette.

"I'll light the candle," Lana said, reaching forward. She flashed Clark a frightened smile and did the honors.

"Now concentrate all your energy on that candle," Janice said. "Not just your attention. Try to think of yourself as becoming one with the candle, really, truly merging with it."

Chloe moved her shoulders, and took a deep, cleansing breath. "Self-hypnosis. Got it."

"More than that. I'll guide you through it."

"We should turn off the lights," Ginger said.

"No way." Pete hunched forward in his chair. "This is scary enough."

Then Janice huffed and firmly shook her head. "Wait. I don't want you to do it. I'll do it." She reached out her hand. "Please give me back the Ouija board."

In the next instant, the room plunged into darkness, save the candle.

"That's it," Janice Brucker announced, jumping to her feet. Her chair fell backward and thumped on the hardwood floor. "We're all leaving."

Then the planchette beneath Chloe's fingertips began to move.

HIRAM.
HIRAM.
HIRAM.
WELLES.
HE KILLED ME.

And then Chloe was there . . . only she wasn't Chloe anymore, as a spirit invaded her, made her see the terrible secret of the Welles farmhouse:

I can't stop shivering; the dirt is like ice. My lungs are beginning to close up. This time it hurts so much more, so very much more. He's furious because this time, I dared to fight back. I don't know why I bothered. I never win.

"I'm fed up with you! You're such a little weasel!"

The pain from the kick . . . I can't even react. I can only lie here. I'm so cold. Everything hurts; so much is broken . . .

I can't breathe. It's happening. The asthma. Oh, God, don't let me die down here. Help me!

Stop kicking me! Stop it!

Footsteps! On the stairs!

Papa!

He's coming down! He'll save me!

He's laughing. There's a big glass in his hand, and he is swaying and pointing and throwing back his head.

"Kill him, for God's sake! He deserves it, the little weakling!"

Papa, Papa, no!

Then he yanks my head out of the dirt and grabs the cleaning pail. He's laughing, too, shouting to my father, "I'll do it! See if I don't!"

Papa's face is so red and his eyes are huge and he is pointing at the pail and screaming, "Do it!" He looks like a monster.

Oh, save me, please, please save me!

No, don't put my head in there! Stop! Stop it!

Oh, my God, it's not water. It's not water in the bucket, it's quicklime!

THE PAIN!

Chloe let out a wild banshee shriek.

"Chloe!" Clark cried, leaping to his feet.

She stirred and blinked. She was in her chair in the Welles house. The lights were on. Clark knelt on one knee beside her chair. Lana and Pete stood on the other side. Whitney loomed behind Lana with his hands on her shoulders.

"Oh, my God," she said slowly, blinking. "God." She touched her face. "I'm okay." She began to tremble hard, like a person going into shock. "I am, right?"

"Yes. You're okay," Clark soothed.

She looked at each of their faces. The Ouija board was in Janice's Brucker's arms, tightly held against her chest. Ginger and Joel stood beside her, Ginger was enfolded in Joel's embrace.

On the table, everything had disintegrated into dusty fragments, as if they had been sitting there for years. Then she looked more closely at the table itself. It was faded and distressed, as if someone had left it out in the sun for decades.

The chair she was sitting in was in just as bad condition.

She leaped out of it, ramming into Clark, who caught her and held her.

The room was a disaster. The bookcases had become weathered and splintered, many of the shelves broken into pieces and lying on top of the books below, which were coated with a nearly fluorescent patina of mold.

"What . . . what happened here?" Chloe asked, and then her knees buckled. Clark kept her standing, and, as one person, they all began filing out of the parlor.

"While you were . . . channeling, everything changed," Pete said. "Changed into old things."

She placed her hands on Clark's chest. "I saw it," she said. "I saw the murder. It happened in the basement."

"Yes, it did."

That was Ginger. She held up her sketch pad. The sketch was of a basement, and a small figure lying limp on the floor.

Clark hesitated. *The skeleton is still down there. I saw it with my own eyes. But how can I tell them that?*

Chloe raised her chin and squared her shoulders. She spoke firmly to the group at large. "We need to go down there and investigate."

"Oh, no. Not tonight," Lana said, as Whitney put his arm around her.

Chloe actually looked relieved, and Clark was glad that she wasn't going to argue.

"We need to call the sheriff," Janice announced.

Joel said, "No. Please."

Everyone looked at him.

"Holly's missing, and I'm sure this house has something to do with it. We need to follow this to the end, not turn it over now to a bunch of guys who will never believe in a million years that something supernatural is going on."

They had hurried outside, quiet and somber. Death had
become real, and no one was ready to deal with it.

They all climbed into their vehicles. Pete was the last, and
he walked up to Clark and spoke to him through the truck
window.

"I've got two thoughts," he said, sounding shaken. "One
is, if the governor decides to come to Smallville, we'd better get that place cleaned up fast. The other is . . ." He
blinked. "Is he a murderer?" Slowly he looked back at the
house. "It happened so long ago . . ."

Clark said nothing. But privately he thought, *It doesn't
matter how long ago it happened, if someone was killed.*

"We can't talk about this with other people." Pete continued. "The more people who know, the more chance we'll
screw something up, like Joel said."

*And the less anyone can protect the governor's reputa-
tion, if he did do something wrong.*

Clark didn't express that thought, either. Instead, he
started up the truck.

And drove home.

It was Saturday, and Clark's parents had left for the
farmer's market to sell some of Martha's produce. She had
made pancakes and left a heaping plate of them in the oven
for him.

He ate and did his chores, his mind spinning over last
night's episode at the house. *We're onto something very
big . . .*

He didn't know what he would say to his parents. If they
insisted on calling in the sheriff, he would feel as if he had
betrayed his friends . . . and he couldn't allow anything to
happen to Holly or Robin.

When the phone rang around ten-thirty, he wasn't at all
surprised to find Chloe on the other end.

"We're going over there," she said. "Your folks went to the market, right? Lana will come by to give you a ride."

"Wait," he said, then realized that there was no reason to wait. It was daylight, and if they were going to do this thing, there was no better moment than as soon as possible.

"Sorry, never mind," he said. "Tell Lana—"

And there Lana was, coming up the drive. He said to Chloe, "We'll be there shortly."

Then he saw his stack of books for the history paper. *Smallville Farming* lay on the top of the pile.

He opened it, and the face of Mattias Silver glared hotly up at him.

And then they were in the house, all of them, except Janice and Ginger. Lana was minus Whitney. Clark didn't know why, and Lana didn't say.

"Dr. Brucker wouldn't let Ginger come," Joel told the others, as they walked into the kitchen. "And . . . I kind of agree with that."

Chloe nodded at him. "You're a good boyfriend," she said. Then she said to the group at large, "Everybody ready?"

Clark did a rapid-fire scan of the house, searching for telltale green trails. There were none, and he nodded.

The key to the basement hung from a hook beside the door. Lana stared hard at it and licked her lips. Sending her glance toward Clark, she said, "There were these terrible thumps the first time I came over. From down there."

"Mattias's restless spirit," Chloe said.

Clark unlocked the cellar door. The black rectangle seemed to suck in the light from the kitchen, giving none back.

"There's a string pull for a lightbulb," Lana coached him.

Clark reached his hand into the darkness. When the string

gently brushed the back of his hand, he started. Then he grabbed it and yanked.

The light came on. It was very dim. He couldn't see past the third or fourth stair.

"May I have my flashlight?" he asked, holding out his hand.

They had come equipped, each person bringing one or two. To Clark's surprise, Pete was the one who thought to bring a sledgehammer and a shovel.

He flicked on the beam and began to descend. Chloe came after him, followed by Lana, then Pete, then Joel, who stopped to prop the door open with the head of the sledge-hammer.

Their lights played over brick walls and cobwebs. Something chittered, scuttling away in the shadows. There was a shelf against the wall, littered with cleaning supplies that must have been used to ready the house for Ginger and Janice. As the lights played over the cans and bottles with the familiar brand names, the half-used rolls of paper towels and a cluster of sponges, Clark felt a wave of vertigo.

I have to be careful. If we find some meteorites, I'm going to have to get out of here as fast as I can. And my strength and speed still aren't back up to normal.

"How's everyone doing?" Chloe asked.

"I'm . . . I'm scared," Lana managed. "I'm really, really scared."

A hand reached from behind him and slipped into Clark's left hand. In the darkness he couldn't see its owner, but he held it as he kept the light focused in front of him. He wondered if it was Lana's. It seemed too small . . . but he could count the times he'd held Lana's hand on one of his own hands. Too shy to give it a squeeze, he kept on.

He began to feel dizzy.

Then Chloe started moaning.

Clark turned around.

He was holding no one's hand.

No one's at all.

"What?" Lana asked. "Chloe, what?"

"So cold," Chloe muttered. Her voice was high and thin, not at all like her own. "So cold . . . such pain . . ."

She fell to the cellar floor.

"Help me. Save me. Helpmesavemehelpme . . ."

"It's there," Joel said. "The body has to be underneath the floor."

Lana and Pete crouched down and took hold of Chloe's hands. Then Lana brushed Chloe's blond bangs out of her face and looked at her steadily.

"Chloe, you're with us. It's okay, Chloe."

Chloe snapped back to herself.

She pointed to the floor.

"There," she said.

I can't believe I'm doing this, Pete thought, as he raised the sledgehammer over his head and brought it down on the floor. *I should be the one speaking up, saying we shouldn't do this . . . .*

But we should do this. Sometimes in Smallville, you can't play by the rule book. You can't think about the mundane things like this is someone's private property and what about the sheriff, and all those things.

He brought it down again. And again. And again.

Joel stepped forward next and scooped away the fragments of the floor with the shovel. His heart was pounding.

What are we going to find? he wondered. *What the hell are we going to find?*

Better question: who are we going to find?

◆◆◆

With each swing of the sledgehammer, Clark's dizziness was getting worse.

Whose hand was I holding? he wondered. *The ghost's?*

He opened his mouth to tell the others, when an eerie, high-pitched wail penetrated the sound of the shoveling. Joel froze. Everyone did.

It was like the squeal of a sick infant, or the panting disbelief of someone so terrified he was unable to breathe.

"Guys?" Lana said.

"Asthma," Pete told the others. "My cousin has it. That's the exact sound."

"Um, oh, wow," Chloe said, gulping. "If I go all Exorcist again, haul me out of here, okay?"

Then footsteps, distant and echoic, joined the cacophony.

"Someone's on the stairs," Joel said.

Clark swept the portion of the stairway that could be seen from their position with his flashlight. There was no one there.

Then a low keening rose up from the floor like a mist. It was ineffably sad, beyond heartbroken . . . it was the misery of someone broken and crushed and abandoned . . . all love denied . . .

It was hopelessness given a voice.

"Oh, my God," Lana breathed. "What's happening?"

Chloe cleared her throat. "Mattias? We're here to help you. We want to help you," she called out.

Again, Clark sensed the pressure of a small hand slipping into his grasp. He was already dizzy; now the invisible hand tugged on his arm and he sank to the floor.

There's meteor rock under there, he thought anxiously. *I'm in trouble.*

The hand urged him toward the hole in the floor . . . and in the direct line of influence of the poisonous emanations. Weakened and in pain, Clark tried to pull back, but his body wouldn't respond. He hunched helpless over the hole, and focused his acute vision to see what he could detect. It was no good; his eyes were tearing up. Sweat beaded on his forehead, and he gasped aloud.

Miraculously, Lana heard him.

"Clark?" she queried, pushing past Joel to crouch beside him. "Clark, what's happening to you?"

"I feel so sick," he said to her. Even in his heightened state of discomfort, he knew he couldn't tell her everything. "Somebody's hand tugged on me, got me to sit down. And now . . ." He gestured limply at the hole. "I'm sick . . ."

Lana concentrated her flashlight beam on the hole.

In the yellow light, a fine, green mist rose among the chunks of concrete. As the others watched transfixed, it began to undulate, then to rise. Lana kept her vigil beside Clark, and he was grateful.

The wavy forms began to collect into a mass, creating a shape that stretched vertically. Then the lower half sank back down toward the floor.

It was becoming a human figure.

The keening intensified, bouncing off the brick walls.

"It's crying," Chloe said.

Clark's head drooped forward. The shape was a drifting mass of meteor radiation, and he was too weak to get away from it.

"Clark's in trouble," Lana said, raising her voice to be heard above the chaos. "We have to get him out of here."

She wrapped her hands around his forearms, trying to hoist him to a standing position as she got to her feet and tried to straighten up.

"I'll do it," Joel offered, taking over. Lana moved aside, and Joel said, "Come on, Clark. Help me out here."

Clark was in no shape to do much. It was taking all his concentration not to collapse again. But Joel got him to his feet and began to guide him toward the stairs. Summoning all his concentration, he put one foot in front of the other. He had no idea how he was ever going to get up the stairs.

The sound of footsteps rang out again.

CHAPTER FIFTEEN

At the echo of the footsteps, everyone in the basement stopped moving again, including Joel.

There was another moment of high tension, and then Lex Luthor's expensive Bruno Magli loafers came into view.

He walked down into the flashlight beams, followed closely behind by Janice Brucker. They both peered into the brightness.

"What's going on?" Lex asked. "What's all this noise?"

At the foot of the stairs, Joel looked up at the billionaire's son, and said, "Clark's really sick."

Lex needed no more information than that to hurry downstairs and move to Clark's left side. Positioning his shoulder beneath Clark's arm, he indicated that Joel should do the same. Together, they walked him injured-player style toward the stairs as Janice Brucker hurried down them to get out of their way.

"Let me look at you," she ordered, in her best scientist voice.

"I'll be fine," Clark managed to say. "I just need some air."

Clark sounded so positive of that that Lex gave him a careful once-over. He wanted to ask, "*How do you know that*?" But he kept his silence and focused on the crisis at hand.

One mystery at a time.

Moving forward to the first step, Lex assured the woman, "I'll let you know if we need you."

Then he and Joel began the arduous task of getting Clark up the stairs.

Lex frowned, and said, "That wheezing noise. It's not you, right?"

"Ghost," Clark said hoarsely.

"Oh, my God! Look!" Chloe shouted.

"What?" Clark rasped.

"Never mind. Whatever it is, it'll wait," Lex said authoritatively. But he was dying to go back to see what Chloe had found. His father might scoff at his priorities, but Lex's first concern was Clark. Even though every instinct told him to investigate, he continued up the stairs with Joel and Clark.

He and the other guy reached the top of the stairs, then walked Clark through the kitchen. They had almost reached the foyer when Clark said, "I'm better."

"You're going outside," Lex insisted, "and sitting down."

Clark was too weak to protest. Lex took advantage of that and got him outside. Then he and Joel settled Clark on the porch. Lex hustled over to his Porsche and popped the trunk, getting out three sports bottles filled with Evian.

He handed one to Joel and one to Clark, and Clark drank his down greedily. His color was already returning; Lex turned to Joel, and said, "Go on back down there if you want."

Joel took a deep breath. "I don't want," he confessed, "but I'm going down." To Clark, he added, "Hang in there, dude."

"I'm good," Clark insisted. "I'm fine."

"Sit," Lex ordered.

Clark sat.

Lex had no idea how much time passed, but the others finally barreled out the front door. Chloe was in the lead, her eyes swollen from crying.

"We found him," she said, wiping her face.

Janice walked up to Lex. "Skeletal remains. A child."

"Oh, my God," Lex breathed, growing pale. "In the governor's boyhood home."

"I took a sample," she continued. "I suppose one could cite me for contaminating a crime scene . . ."

"We need to find Holly," Joel reminded her, his voice anxious and sharp.

"I'm going to run some tests, do a DNA scan," the scientist concluded.

As she walked past Clark to go down the porch steps, Clark turned chalk white. Lex didn't know what to make of it, but he knew he should make *something* of it.

Someday I'll figure you out, he silently promised Clark. But his friend didn't see him. His head was bowed, and he was obviously in pain again.

No one wanted to stay at the farmhouse; the ghost hunters scattered to their cars almost as soon as they had emerged from the basement. Chloe trailed after Clark and Lex, and as Clark wearily climbed into Lana's truck, she leaned in through the rolled-down window.

"Big day," she murmured. "But confusing. Mattias was a grown man. This is a little kid. I'm thinking twins. A weak one, and a strong one." She smiled wanly. "We're going to have a great history paper, Clark. Not to mention the biggest scoop in the history of Smallville."

In the driver's seat, Lana said, "I wonder what it means. We keep seeing a farmer, but this family didn't farm. And that skeleton . . . what you saw, Chloe. It was a child." She looked as if she were going to be sick.

"I'm going over to the historical society," Chloe told them both. "They're open until three today. See if I can make any connections with what we have so far."

"I should go, too," Clark said. He smiled wanly, trying to

go for the joke. "After all, I'm the one who needs the extra credit."

"Just go home. Get well." Chloe smiled again, and this time it was not so forced and frightened-looking. "You'll need your strength to type up our findings. We'll have a lot to report."

"Okay." He tried to match her bright smile, and came far short. "Thanks, Chloe."

Her gaze was more than fond. "Sure."

Lana put the car in reverse, and they took off.

Despite everything that had happened that day—*or maybe because of it, maybe I'm that punchy*—Chloe had a very, very hard time not making with the happy feet when Daphne, her friend who worked at the Smallville Historical Society on weekends, showed her a new exhibit. It was of mourning jewelry and mourning customs.

"People made rings and brooches out of the hair of the deceased," Daphne told her. "Check it out."

Sure enough, rings, pins, and armbands woven from human hair were lovingly displayed in a glass case near the stuffed animals.

"See that one?" Daphne continued, pointing to a small ring. "That's made from the hair of Governor Welles's father. "Did you know the governor grew up here in Small-ville?" she added proudly.

"That's his hair?" Chloe said slowly. *His hair, which contains DNA?* "Wow. I mean, eww. That's a very strange tradition. I'm glad it's died out. Ha-ha. Died, get it?"

"Miss?" someone called. "May I buy this guidebook?"

Daphne said to Chloe, "I have to go take care of that." She gestured expansively to the historical treasures of Small-ville. "Look around. Take all the time you want."

"Thanks," Chloe said innocently. Then, as soon as

Daphne's back was turned, she lifted up the glass top of the case and snagged the ring made out of Jackson Welles's hair.

She pocketed it, telling herself, *I'll put it back later*, and dawdled around for a while so she wouldn't look suspicious.

Dr. Brucker can find out if those bones have any DNA in common with this hair.

This is going to be such a great story . . .

. . . I hope . . .

Janice Brucker asked Joel to go to the hotel to check on Ginger, adding, "I'm going to my lab. I want to analyze the . . . fragments." Then she gave him a gentle look, and added, "I'm sure Ginger would love to have a visit. She's pretty angry at me for not letting her come here."

"I'm glad you didn't," he told her sincerely.

They parted, Joel climbing in with Pete, and Janice high-tailed it to Plant Number Three.

She breezed through security and took out the paper evidence bag, into which she had carefully placed an assortment of fragments. As she separated the sample into smaller samples, the mental image of their grisly discovery haunted her: the ribs broken; one leg shorter than the other due to a fracture, probably sustained in infancy. She didn't even want to think about how that might have occurred . . .

The worst had been the skull.

Portions of the face had been eaten away by some kind of chemical agent, possibly acid. The bone had dissolved in places. Deep holes and ridges striated it like the surface of the Moon.

"Quicklime," Chloe had told her in a strangled voice, and then the girl had burst into tears. "His head was forced into a bucket of quicklime."

Monstrous, Janice thought now.

She put in a call to a friend at Wayne Industries on the

East Coast, knowing that the scientist was a fellow workaholic likely to be in during the weekend.

"Hi, Al, Janice. I need a favor," she said without preamble. "DNA scan. Rush."

"Ooh, interesting, coming from you," her friend Al repeated. "May one ask?"

"One may. But I have no answers yet. Run the scan and I'll tell you when I know."

That's probably a lie, she thought, as they hung up.

Then she called S.T.A.R. Labs in Metropolis, and LuthorCorp's own lab, and secured similar agreements to work off the clock and as fast as possible.

Redundancy. The hallmark of a good scientist, she thought grimly, as she surrounded each sample with special protective sleeves made of lead, to prevent X-ray machines from harming what lay inside.

Then she called Myra Wilkinson, Lex's new security chief, and said, "I need courier service today."

Perhaps in a less well heeled facility, that would pose a problem on a weekend. But Myra simply replied, "Of course, Dr. Brucker."

The samples were sent, and that was that.

Then she went to work on the set she had saved for herself, placing them in a compositional analysis chamber on which she and George held the patent.

These remains are permeated with radiation from the meteorites, she thought excitedly, as she scanned the initial readouts. *Is that why there's all this activity?*

Eager to share her findings, she called Rafael Alcina at home.

"Hello?" he said.

"I'm sorry you missed the channeling session," she said. "It made a believer out of me. You're never going to guess what's going on down here."

To her astonishment, Rafael interrupted her, saying, "Janice, I'm sorry, but I can't talk to you right now."

Then he hung up on her.

Hung *up*.

She was stunned.

Then Chloe popped her head in the door, and said, "Hi, Dr. Brucker. I have hair!"

Lex ran errands, and then he ran home.

It was nearly three when he checked the machine on his private line.

It was the governor.

"I'm in Metropolis," he said. "I'll be taking your father and you out to dinner. Meet me at Le Corbusier at eight."

Lex took down the address, worked a while longer, then showered, changed, and got back in his Porsche.

He arrived at Le Corbusier at seven-thirty. He was recognized by the maître d', who personally escorted him through the throng of security agents and into a private dining room.

Governor Welles was there, a huge, strapping man despite his age. His hair was white, and his suit was black. His hands were huge; the highball glass he held looked like a marble in comparison.

When he saw Lex, Welles glared at him, and said, "What the hell kind of scam are you running on me?"

Lex did not reply. He turned to the maître d', who was still there, and said, "I'd like a glass of Pellegrino." He didn't ask if they would have it. A place like Le Corbusier would get it if their shelves were bare of it.

The maître d' inclined his head, said, "Certainly, sir," and gave them their privacy.

"Why the hell is Dr. Janice Brucker working for you?" Welles demanded.

"Is there a problem?"

"If you don't get rid of her immediately, I'll shut you down so fast your head will fall off."

Lex blinked, taken aback and not at all clued in to what was going down.

"How could you be so stupid?" Welles half shouted, his face turning red. Then he narrowed his eyes as he studied Lex's face. "You don't know. That's why. You don't know."

Lex knew it was time to pay good attention. "Know what?"

The governor smirked at him. "Didn't it ever occur to you to wonder why the investigations into Dr. George Brucker's death went by so fast? Why there were no fines, no concrete findings, nothing?"

Lex waited, and the governor smiled evilly.

"Your father killed George Brucker," he informed Lionel Luthor's son.

"He cut corners on their equipment," Welles told Lex as they sat in Le Corbusier. The two were seated across from each other, and Lex was afraid he was going to be sick. "I can dig it all out, let you read the real report. But your father tried to save a buck here, a buck there, and his greed led directly to George Brucker's death. I have it in black-and-white. It cost me a fortune to suppress that information."

Then he chuckled, and raised his highball glass to his lips. "More correctly, it cost your *father* a fortune to suppress that information."

"Janice Brucker doesn't know," Lex murmured. He felt nauseous. *This guy is lying to me. My father would never . . . he would never . . .*

But he would.

It was exactly what Lionel was capable of.

"And now I hear she's snooping around in that house,

which you arranged to lease for her. After years of it standing idle . . ." He glared at Lex. "What's your game, son?"

No game. The house had simply appealed to him. He could have cared less that the governor owned it. Mentally he raced backward in time, trying to remember how Janice Brucker had first come to his attention. Of course he knew her by reputation, but why had he invited her to work for him?

Was it some kind of subtle maneuvering by my father, to achieve some goal?

"Get rid of her, or I'll release that report," Welles said flatly. "It will cost your father millions. He might get even jail time."

Which he would never serve, Lex thought, but he was still shaken.

"They didn't do that séance, right?" the governor continued. "You got them to cease and desist."

Something set him off, Lex realized, *but it wasn't the discovery of the skeleton. He doesn't know a thing about it. He'd be far more upset than this. He wouldn't have let that house stand if he'd known there was a body in the basement.*

Mistaking his silence for reassurance, the governor visibly relaxed. "All right, then," he said. "She's history, and it's time to order a *real* drink for you." He was clearly turning on what passed for charm in his world.

Then he turned, and said, "Ah. Here's your father now."

Lex swallowed down his bile.

Don't ever let me become like him, he prayed to the universe.

Then he said, "Hi, Dad. Want a real drink?"

Lionel Luthor gave him a look, and said, "Hiram, so nice to see you. I hope Lex hasn't been boring you with the details of his sprawling fertilizer empire."

"Not at all," the governor said expansively. "We were just making polite conversation until you got here."

Lionel looked satisfied. Then he looked the governor coolly in the eye, and said, "I understand you'll be doing a town hall meeting in Smallville during your campaign circuit."

The governor nearly spit out his drink. *"What?"*

Lex's dad shrugged his shoulders. "It was on the wire service."

"I'm not . . . I . . ." He glared at Lex as if to say, *You did this.*

But Lex hadn't.

He doesn't want to go, but he can't back out. It would look bad if he promised to visit his home town, then reneged.

Wow, someone working on his campaign sure screwed up on this one.

And I can't wait to see what happens next.

"Okay," Pete said to Chloe as they sat side by side in the *Torch* office at school. "I have spread enough disinformation for one day." He yawned and looked very depressed. "It's much easier to do than I expected. Now the governor's going to have to come to Smallville, or he'll look bad."

"He said he wanted to," Chloe drawled, all innocence. "What date did you set for his town hall meeting at the Talon?"

"Exactly one week from tonight," he said, grinning. "At 6 P.M."

"Someone should let Lana know." She got her cell phone out of her purse. "Oh, and by the way, this room is haunted."

Pete looked less than thrilled. "Then let's get out of here."

"I have a week," Lana said nervously to Clark. It was very late. She had just received a faxed confirmation that the governor of Kansas wanted to hold a town meeting there. They both knew that Chloe and Pete had thrown down the gauntlet, faking a news report that he was finally coming to Smallville, as he had said he wanted to do so very many times. He could have backed out, claimed it was an error . . . but he didn't, and to Chloe's way of thinking, that proved that he was nervous about going home again. "It's such short notice."

"I'll help you. We all will. But I'm not sure what Chloe expects to happen. Is she going to stand up in front of everyone and accuse him of murder?"

Lana walked across the floor, glancing around as if she were taking measurements, arranging seating. "We don't know that he's involved at all. His name came up. But it's that farmer's face we keep seeing." She shuddered. "Doesn't look like a nice man."

"Chloe will do anything for extra credit," Clark said, smiling faintly. "I think she wants to break this thing open. But we still haven't found Holly Pickering and that real-estate lady."

Lana frowned, obviously troubled. "The séance didn't work, didn't draw them out of the field the way it did Joel. Now that a body's been found, we can't keep it a secret forever. Sooner or later, we do have to notify the authorities."

She moved her shoulders in that lovely way she had; he was charmed. "For all we know, Holly ran away from home and Robin embezzled all the real-estate office funds and went to Las Vegas."

"The explanations are usually not that simple in Smallville," he said.

"They never are." She looked at him steadily. "Nothing's simple. Is it, Clark?"

In that moment, they made a connection. Clark's cheeks

grew hot, and Lana's eyes shone. *Don't let this moment end*, he thought.

But of course it did.

"I have to provide blueprints of the Talon, so they can organize their security detail," she told Clark. "Luckily, I have them all."

"Blueprints," he echoed. "Blueprints." He looked at Lana. "I wonder when the cement floor was put in, in the Welles house?" When she shook her head as if she wasn't following him, he continued, "In Chloe's . . . channeling, it was a dirt floor. The boy was killed when it was a dirt floor."

She swallowed.

"I don't know, Clark. What do you think it means?"

"More research," he said wryly.

Janice Brucker got a fax, which she scanned very quickly. Once she understood the implications, she read it again very slowly.

Her lips parted, and her mind began to rearrange the pieces of the puzzle that was the haunting of the Welles house.

It was the DNA report from her friend Al at Wayne Industries.

"The skeletal remains—permeated with a strange mixture, for which I did not triturate, since you're in a hurry—are those of a male child, approximately seven years of age. The sample from the ring woven from Jackson Welles's hair indicates that the two were related.

"In a close familial relationship, such as father and son."

The body is of one of his children. But Chloe's research shows he only had one son . . . Hiram Welles, the present governor.

But if Hiram Welles's body is lying in the cellar, then . . . who is the governor?

She put the fax in her briefcase and took it back to the Smallville Hotel with her. She put it in the safe.

A day and a half later, a FedExed report arrived for her at Fertilizer Plant Number Three. It was from S.T.A.R. Labs, and their forensics expert used nearly identical language to describe his findings.

The LuthorCorp report showed two days later . . . and the findings were very different. Too different.

They ran the wrong sample, she thought, frustrated. And then she thought, *No. They ran the one they received.* But how could they be so different? It was almost as if they were purposely forged . . .

Angrily she picked up the phone and dialed Lex Luthor's cell phone. Then she paused and thought the better of it.

"What's going on?" she muttered.

She slammed down the phone and went home.

Joel and Ginger stood at the perimeter of the cornfield. She had her sketch pad, and she poised her hand over it while Joel called softly, "Holly?"

Nothing happened. The bright sun shone down on the field, which looked like . . . corn. Not ghostly hands, or skeletal arms.

Just corn.

"I'm not getting anything," Ginger said. She looked at him. "I'm sorry."

"Maybe at the house. You felt compelled to draw the wheatfield," he reminded her.

She took a breath.

"Welles will be here in two days, Ginger," he said. "It'll be all over. We can't hide a body from him in his own house."

"I hate that place," she murmured. "I never want to set foot in it again."

"I know. You wait outside, and I'll go in." He took her hand. "She's my friend."

"But you're my friend, too." She raised on tiptoe and kissed him. "I'll go."

"I'll go first, check things out," he insisted.

They walked up Waitley Lane together, hand in hand. The farmhouse stared down at them, and Ginger drew back a little.

Joel gave her a brief smile, let go of her hand, and went into the house alone.

He's so brave, she thought. *So incredibly brave.*

He came back out a few minutes later. His face was chalk white. He said, "Ginger, it's gone. It's all gone."

"What?"

He pointed at the house. "The body. The way we hacked up the floor. It's been repoured, and the cement is as hard as a rock. It doesn't even look new."

"No . . ." she breathed. "How can that be?"

They looked at each other in complete and utter confusion.

Lex looked up from his desk as Dr. Hamilton strode in, angrily waving Lex's memo. "What is this?" he shouted.

Lex put down his Mont Blanc pen and folded his hands on top of his desk. "What it says. I'm terminating the radiation replication project. I've decided that it's not a good allocation of resources."

"But that's ridiculous! We've barely gotten started!"

"There was an accident," Lex said smoothly. "We can't have that sort of thing."

"And Dr. Brucker! You can't fire her! That's absolutely—"

Lex raised his hands to his chin. "Dr. Hamilton," he cut in, without raising his voice, "there will be other projects. Projects nearly identical to this one. So like this one, in fact, it will be very difficult to distinguish them." He waited a beat, then added, "For you."

"For . . ." The scientist got it. "We'll resume."

"You'll resume. After she has left Smallville." Lex looked sad. "She was . . . indiscreet."

Hamilton sagged with relief. "It's a shame, though. She's an excellent scientist."

"And she can move on," Lex said. "The project she was supposed to be working on was so beneath her capabilities. She needs to go back to more high-level work." He leaned back in his chair. "You, on the other hand, can't do that."

"I'm stuck here, in exile," Hamilton agreed. "I have nowhere else to go." He glanced down at the paper again. "You sent this only to me. When will you tell her?"

"I'm certain she's gotten my message," Lex replied.

CHAPTER SIXTEEN

WELCOME BACK TO SMALLVILLE, GOVERNOR WELLES!

The banner was draped over the entrance to the Talon. Farmers in casual dress mingled with the more upscale folks as women opened their purses for the security personnel to check. There were metal detectors and surveillance cameras.

Lana and her aunt Nell were very, very nervous.

And Chloe was outraged.

Joel had told them all about the floor, and Dr. Brucker had shown them the results of the three forensics reports. Clark had been unable to pinpoint the date when the dirt floor had been replaced with cement, despite asking Daphne at the historical society for pointers on how to research it.

"It's Lex," Chloe had insisted, as she had pinned on her PRESS badge. "He redid the floor and he switched samples, or something. He's covering up for Welles."

"It could be someone else," Clark said, hoping against hope. "LuthorCorp is huge. The governor might have found out about it."

"Oh, Clark, give it up," Chloe snapped. They were seated about halfway back, each with their parents, though Chloe had moved so that she could be as close to one of the stand-up microphones that had been set up so people could ask the governor questions. TV crews from Metropolis, Kansas City, and other large urban areas of Kansas had set up. The publicity for Lana's coffeehouse would be excellent.

Then a woman with big hair and wearing a dark blue business suit walked up to the podium. She made sure the microphone was on and asked people to take their seats. As the audience began to settle in, Martha murmured, "I'm going to pin him down about his environmental legislation record."

Jonathan patted her knee. "He'll never know what hit him."

They held hands, and Clark smiled faintly. Then he grew serious as he watched Pete standing with other campaign volunteers from different parts of the state. Each wore a badge that read "REELECT HIRAM WELLES." Pete looked very uncomfortable, as if he just might take his badge off and walk out of the room.

Chloe perched on the edge of her chair. Joel and his father, and Janice, and Ginger sat directly in front of Clark and his parents. Joel's father was wearing a suit.

Lex was nowhere to be found.

Then Hiram Welles got up to speak. *He's old*, Clark thought with a start. *Everything happened so long ago . . .*

He droned on, giving a typical politician's speech. Clark's mind wandered; he began taking a mental survey of all the amazing things that had happened in the last few weeks . . . and then his mom got up and asked her question, which had to do with water pollution. She got a round of applause from the farmers in the room.

Welles's pat answer didn't please Martha, and Jonathan murmured under his breath, "Well, he didn't get your vote, did he, honey?"

More questions were posed, more standard, predictable answers given, then Chloe jumped up and moved to the mike, and said, "Did you have a younger brother, Governor? Who might have died young?"

The man was taken aback. He responded, "No, young lady. I was an only child."

"And yet," Chloe began.

"I'm an only child," he replied smoothly. "Next question?"

Fuming, she sat down. She sent Clark a look, and he shrugged, equally frustrated, perhaps, but far less surprised.

The evening concluded with a "meet and greet," and Clark boldly waited in line to meet the governor.

"It's so nice to see a nice turnout of young people," the man said, as he reached out his hand.

And Clark thought of the little boy who had died in terrible pain, and of the small, ghostly hand that had taken his and folded his hands in direct refusal to shake hands with this man.

Welles was offended, but said nothing. With so many TV cameras trained on him, what could he say?

Chloe got in line, too, but the governor announced that he had another pressing engagement and would have to leave a little sooner than planned.

The evening ended abruptly.

Chloe said to the others, "Well, that was a complete waste of time."

"Except for Lana," Clark said, watching her beam for the TV cameras.

The others wanted to stay behind and debrief about the evening . . . and decide what to do next. But Clark demurred, saying, "I have to go home. I'm still not feeling too well."

They were sorry, but they understood.

Then he caught up to his parents, and murmured, "I'm going to follow him, see what's up."

Both objected, both gave in, and both told him to be careful.

Then Martha handed him the cell phone, and said, "Call."

◆◆◆

Throngs gathered around the governor's limo; they were held at bay by his security team. There were three other cars in his cavalcade. For his top aides, Clark decided. Clark stood in the shadows, and when the stretch drove away, he tried to run after it at superspeed.

To his intense relief, he kept up with it.

Hey, feeling a little better, he thought. *In fact, a lot better.* He put on a fresh burst of speed.

Hiram Welles's next stop was his boyhood home.

Well out of anyone's visual range, Clark watched the man's every move with his X-ray vision. The man walked from room to room for the TV cameras. In the kitchen he pointed to the cellar door . . . but he did not go down the stairs.

Then his people trooped back into the limos and headed for town.

Clark began to run home when one of the limos—the governor's limo—wheeled back around out of the cavalcade and headed back in his direction. Clark watched, intrigued.

The car pulled over to the cornfield across the lane from Waitley Lane.

And Governor Welles got out alone.

He spoke to the driver, and the limo pulled away.

As Clark watched from afar, he moved into the cornfield as if he knew precisely where he was going, and stopped.

"Look, there's Welles," Chloe said, pointing through the windshield of her car. "In the cornfield."

They were on the main drag between town and her and Joel's houses. Chloe had asked Ginger to stay over so they could talk about what was happening. "His security detail is gone," Joel said, scrutinizing the area. "Or else they're hiding for some reason."

"Maybe he told them he wanted to be alone."

Then suddenly Ginger said hoarsely, "Paper."

Chloe glanced at Joel, who said to Ginger, "What?"

"Hiram Welles. Hiram Welles," she intoned in an eerie flat voice. Her hand began to move as if she were drawing.

Chloe said, "In my backpack. Steno pad."

Joel fished through it, found it, and slipped it under Ginger's hand.

She began to draw.

Under the moonlight, Welles stood motionless, as if communing with the corn.

Clark shivered. Some places were just plain spooky, even under the best of circumstances. The cornfield seemed to stretch forever, its endless striated rows funneling toward the horizon; it would have a creep factor of 9.9 at high noon on the Fourth of July. Tonight, with the cold moon spotlighting it, the stalks motionless in the still air, leaves drooping like the hair of dead women, a possible psychopathic killer standing in it . . . it was pretty much off the scale now.

He remembered his father telling him about an episode of *Twilight Zone* or *One Step Beyond* or one of those old shows that had been on back when Jonathan Kent was younger than Clark, about a boy who could magically send people he didn't like into the cornfield. He shivered slightly. Didn't seem like a nice way at all to go . . .

He moved cautiously down one of the rows, going slow and stepping lightly to avoid kicking up clouds of powdery dust. Somewhere off to his left was the meteorite; he could *feel* it pulsing out there. As long as he stayed this far away, he would be all right.

◆◆◆

"What's she drawing?" Chloe asked. She pulled the car over, looked around, then drove it straight into a stand of roadside foliage to conceal it.

"It's that farmer again," Joel said. "In a field of wheat." He said to Ginger, "Ginger? Are you okay?"

"Corn," Ginger snapped at him, still in the hoarse voice. "Corn, corn, corn, corn, corn."

She scribbled on, sketching quickly. Joel said, "It's the cornfield."

Chloe looked at him.

"*The* cornfield?" she asked.

"Kill. Kill," Ginger rasped. "Kill."

"Um, okay . . ." Chloe looked at Joel.

"We can walk back. We're close enough," Joel said.

Chloe nodded and unbuckled her seat belt. Joel unfastened his own, then undid Ginger's.

He tried to take the pad of paper from her, but she held on to it, drawing nonstop, scribbling and dancing all over the page. Despite the movement and his vain attempts to stop her, the picture was surprisingly well executed and clear.

"Mattias?" Chloe asked, peering at Ginger. "Is that you?"

"Kill!" Ginger shouted.

She lunged for Chloe.

Something's happening, Clark thought.

The earth beneath his feet began to shudder. The corn took up the trembling rhythm. Even the stars above his head seemed to jitter and dance.

Welles looked up, as startled as Clark. Then he saw Clark, and his eyes widened.

"What are you doing here?" he shouted.

The stalks began to undulate, waving wildly from side to side. The field tilted, as if it were part of a large board that someone was tipping . . . *or a table* . . . Clark thought . . . *like a séance table, tipping* . . .

Both he and the governor were thrown off-balance, but Clark reacted much more quickly and kept his footing, while the governor fell over. He disappeared among the stalks, and as Clark raced toward him, Welles let out a terrible scream.

With a snarl of almost animalistic rage, Ginger savagely pushed Chloe out of the way and dashed into the corn.

Chloe landed hard. The ground shook crazily, and Joel staggered toward her, bending to help her up, his eyes on the field as the stalks waved crazily. He yelled to her, "You okay?"

"I'm good! Let's go."

Together they ran into the forest of stalks, calling for Ginger.

Clouds were gathering in the sky, thin wisps at first, then coalescing and thickening and covering the stars and the moon—large and churning and green. They began to roll down toward the cornfield, like massive boulders—*like meteor rocks,* Chloe thought, a dozen of them or more brushing the silky tips of the ears as they careened out of control.

"Oh, my God," Chloe shouted. Joel grabbed her and pushed her out of the way as one of them slammed toward them, prevented from touching all the way down by the sheer numbers of corn stalks.

Then, as it rolled over them, green light shot from beneath them, from under the dirt; brilliant streams of it like searchlights at a store opening, or lasers at a light show. Despite their best efforts to stay out of the way, Chloe and Joel were bathed in it.

◆◆◆

Ginger fought her way through the corn, slashing with her pencils, her mouth pulled back in a rictus of uncontrollable fury. Only she wasn't Ginger anymore, she was—

Mattias Silver had come to visit Jackson Welles's beautiful wife. He would not overstep his bounds; he would not say a word to shame or compromise her. It was simply that he was worried about her; day by day, her brutal husband sucked the life out of her. She was getting too thin; her face was so wan. She looked so unhappy most of the time . . . except when she answered his knock.

And then she was a study in exquisite beauty.

He could sketch a little, could Mattias Silver. He was a simple, poor farmer, and she was a grand lady, but she treasured his sketches, and he knew she kept each one.

His hand was on the knocker when he heard the terrible screams. And the laughter.

Without another thought, he forced the door. In the foyer he called out her name—"Em?"—his pet name for her.

From the attic, she shouted, "Let me out!"

He began to take the stairs two at a time.

Then he heard the screams again.

They were coming from the basement.

"Hiram!" she shrieked. "My baby!"

And Mattias dashed into the kitchen.

The cellar door was ajar; he flew down the stairs. And what he saw . . . what he saw . . .

. . . his own son, Tommy, pushing Hiram Welles's head into a bucket, and Jackson Welles, drunk as usual, egging him on.

"Do it! Kill the little bastard!" Jackson sang out. Then he turned and saw Mattias, and bellowed at him, "Are you here to sneak off with my wife? Take what's mine?"

Mattias looked past him to the horror taking place.

Tommy yanked back Hiram's head from the bucket and Mattias saw, Oh, God, he saw—

—Hiram's face eaten away by the quicklime.

And on his own son's face was such a look of monstrous evil; glee that he had done the deed; triumph that it had been his own hands. Mattias had shrieked out, "Devil! You're a devil!"

Then Jackson grabbed him around the waist and threw him against the wall. He heard bones crack; his brain rattled in his skull. Dazed, he got up and staggered toward the hideous tableau, his boy examining his handiwork with not a trace of remorse . . . .

My own little boy . . .

Then Jackson raised his pistol.

He means to kill me, Mattias realized. And my boy is going to watch him.

And he ran.

Up the stairs, out of the house, and down the road, to the cornfield . . .

And it was then that Mattias realized he had left Em unprotected, in the attic . . .

Clark used Welles's screams to home in on his location. He ran at superspeed, searching, as the sky and the earth pressed into a green haze.

The meteor, he thought, as he felt a stab of pain. *I'm getting too close to it.*

The screams abruptly stopped.

Clark slowed down, then stopped.

The blow came from behind, taking Clark completely by surprise. He was hit hard, hard enough to put him on his knees. He twisted around, caught a glimpse of Governor Welles's silhouette against the moon, fist upraised for another strike. Clark lunged to one side, and the hammering blow barely missed him. He felt the ground shake from the force of the impact.

He kicked out with one leg, felt it strike flesh, heard the governor grunt in response. He scrambled to his feet and shot forward, putting ten rows between himself and his enemy in a fraction of a second.

Clark turned, intending to zoom back and strike the man before the latter knew what hit him. He focused his gaze on where Welles had been, made the subtle shift in sight, and the concealing plants faded to transparency. He started to turn, to do a visual sweep of the cornfield—

And Governor Welles exploded from the concealing corn rows to one side, tackling him. They rolled over and over amidst a chaos of choking clouds and snapping stalks and slashing leaves, coming to a stop with Welles on top, his hands groping for Clark's throat.

"Ginger!" Chloe shouted.

Then one of the green boulderlike clouds rolled over her. It enveloped her in a pulsating green field, and she saw—

The farmer, running for his life.

A boy and a man were chasing him through the cornfield, whistling and hooting like hounds after a fox. The man had a pistol in his hamhock grasp, and he periodically stopped and aimed it at the retreating figure.

And she felt the man's helpless rage, and his vow penetrated the core of her being—

I will have revenge. For me and poor little Hiram, and my Em . . . I will—

—And then the bullet struck.

And he died.

It's all part of the same haunting, Chloe realized. *The murder in the basement, then the chase . . . Governor Welles was that little boy, that terrible, horrible boy . . .*

Clark turned around to find the governor at his back. They were getting too close to the meteor; Clark was feeling the effects more and more.

Something large and vague in outline came whistling into view and impacted on the back of Welles's head. He grunted in stunned surprise, and his grip slackened momentarily. Clark pushed the man off him and saw Joel standing over him, his fists doubled.

"Figured it was time to cast my vote," he said grimly.

Clark staggered to his feet, and so did Governor Welles. All about them shadows in the mist solidified: Chloe and Ginger. Ginger was sobbing hysterically.

Suddenly a wind began to blow, seemingly out of nowhere, coming from no one direction, spinning eddies of dirt that rose up around them like grasping, ghostly fingers. Everyone reacted in surprise, looking around for the source of the air currents.

It was hard to miss.

About a hundred yards away the sky was splitting open. A green, viscous liquid poured from it; it was like the residue Clark had found on the doorknob.

Something spun in the center of the liquid, like a whirlpool, a swirling cauldron impossibly laid on its side. Within Clark could see gunmetal-colored clouds shifting and spinning—and parting intermittently to reveal glimpses of a cold, haunted landscape within.

"It's where I was," Joel cried. "It's going to try to trap us!"

Governor Welles stared at it, his face turning as ashen as the netherworldly mist boiling from the rupture. He turned and bolted, shoving Joel aside hard enough to hurl the boy off his feet and a dozen feet through the air. Clark had no choice; he flickered sideways ten feet and intercepted the other's arc, letting Joel bodyslam into him, absorbing the other's fall instead of letting him crash to the ground. Fortunately, no one else saw his action. Everybody's attention was on the bizarre vortex as it tumbled and spun.

He let Joel's stunned form drop gently to the ground, then staggered and went to one knee. The meteorite was close, too close. A shift in position as slight as one row of corn could mean the difference between life and death for him.

He rolled over, struggled to rise. He managed to get to his knees, but the world was spinning in too many directions for him to get any farther. He saw Governor Welles fleeing toward the meteorite, away from the vortex, and knew he couldn't go any farther in that direction . . . not if he wanted to live.

Lying nearby was an ear of corn that had been torn from its stalk during the melee. Clark grabbed it, drew his arm back to throw. He knew he would only have one chance—

With the last of his strength, he threw the makeshift missile. It flew straight and true, striking Welles on the back of the head. Hit for the second time in the same spot in almost as many minutes was too much even for someone as powerful as the governor. With a groan, he sprawled headlong, plowing a short furrow between the rows before coming to a stop, out cold.

Clark turned away, back toward his friends, who were still watching the vortex. He tried to crawl forward, away from the deadly radiation, but couldn't. His arms and legs were going numb. He lifted one hand, stared at his fingers. It was hard to be sure in the moon's stark radiance, but his flesh seemed to be taking on a greenish tint.

He was dying, Clark realized. The knowledge was curiously remote, as if it were happening to someone else.

He heard something: a shout that seemed to come from a great distance. He looked up.

Something was happening in the vortex.

He could see what looked like two people deep within its funicular depths, running toward the opening. A young goth girl and an older woman, the latter wearing a golden blazer that shouted "real estate." Their expressions were desperate—they were running for their lives.

Holly. Robin.

He dug his fingers into the dirt and dug into the depths of his will at the same time. He dragged himself forward, inch by excruciating inch. Trying to reach them was like trying to pull himself across the continent. But he kept going. And as he moved, he started to feel his strength returning.

Then everything happened very fast.

As Chloe and Ginger both shouted, "No!" Clark dived into the opening.

It was gray and flat, a vast plane of unending limbo.

Chloe saw a huge, gray mass advancing on Clark and the two missing women inside the portal.

And then she felt an incredible sense of rage, rage at injustice and cruelty and murder—rage that had been charged up over the years by the meteorite, until it was like a living thing.

"Mattias!" she shouted. "Mattias, stop! Clark is trying to help you! He's trying to help!"

Inside the vortex, the thing became arms, and a face, and a body . . . Mattias . . . and then he looked straight at Clark, and whispered, "Vengeance."

Like an emanation from the meteor, waves of rage and horror washed over Clark. Fury and despair gripped him, holding him tight; they were so incredibly strong that they held him in their grip like giant hands. He was rooted to the spot, paralyzed, unable to do anything but let the tide of emotion break over him.

The man said again, "Vengeance."

He's haunted by what happened, Clark realized. *He hasn't been able to let it go. He's been angry for so long, bound to the house where he had seen his child murder another child, then bounded along laughing next to the monster who had shot him dead in this very field . . . And all that pent-up emotion has been magnified by the meteor . . .*

"We know about it," Clark managed to say. "We'll do something about it."

The man shook his head and spoke again.

" 'If any harm follows, then you shall give life for life, eye for eye, tooth for tooth, hand for hand, foot for foot, burn for burn, wound for wound, stripe for stripe.' "

"He'll pay," Clark said. "I promise you."

Mattias Silver looked over his shoulder as another apparition appeared behind him. It was the ghost of a young boy, dressed in the style of the 1940s. One leg was shorter than the other.

It was Hiram Welles, the boy Mattias's son had killed.

Without hesitation it shot over Clark and his friends. All heads turned to follow the phantom's flight.

It headed toward Governor Welles, who was regaining consciousness. He staggered to his feet, then saw the boy's ghost coming for him. Stark terror filled his face, and he turned to run. But there was no escape. They all watched as the child's revenant passed *through* the governor's body. It arced up then, turning and heading back toward them.

Welles stiffened in a spasm of pain. He clasped a hand to his chest, staggered, and fell.

Clark sensed the boy's ghost hovering behind them. He turned, saw the translucent calm features looking at them all.

Then the boy slipped his small hand into Clark's and smiled at him. Without another word, he vanished.

Then Holly and Robin darted from around him, leaped through the vortex, and landed on the ground.

"Oh, my God," Joel slurred, sitting up. "Holly."

And then another apparition appeared, this one a shimmering form that stayed within the spinning opening.

"Ginger," it said.

"Daddy!" Ginger cried.

As Clark looked on, the form took on the distinctive features of a man who looked very much like Ginger herself.

He held out a hand, and Ginger rushed forward to take it. She caught her breath and bent her head to lovingly kiss each finger.

"Oh, Daddy, Daddy!"

"I can't stay, baby," he said gently. Tears streamed down his face as he stroked his daughter's hair, cupping her chin, gazing at her with complete fatherly love.

"But tell Mom this. She's so haunted. The accident wasn't her fault. Lionel Luthor covered it up. The report was a lie."

"Oh, Daddy. Daddy." She wiped her face. "Daddy, I was so afraid that she . . . that . . . ."

"Tell her," he said gently. "Guilt is haunting her . . . just like rage haunted that man."

Then the ghost of Ginger's father turned and shot into the shrinking vortex, leaving a cometary trail.

"Daddy, wait!" she wailed, racing toward him. "Come back!"

And Chloe fell into the light, and she saw—

Emily Welles watching from the attic window as her drunken husband finished digging the hole in the wheatfield. He tossed the bundle in; and she saw one foot, and one small, misshapen leg.

Her face contorted in a silent scream, she collapsed to the floor.

But she bided her time, did Emily Welles. Her only friend, Mattias Silver, was dead; her only son was dead, and Mattias's brutal, insane boy was reared in his place. She understood that the only way to survive was to never, ever tell.

So she bided her time, marking time, every morning winding the great grandfather clock in the hallway, staying alive until the day when that monster, Tommy Silver, moved away to Metropolis to begin his political aspirations.

That very night, she dug up the poor little skeleton from the wheatfield, and carried it into the house. Weeping softly for her dear child, she laid him in the cold earth of the basement . . . and then she asked Jackson, ignorant of what she had done, to pour her one of those new cement floors.

"Someday, someone will find you," she promised as the field of gray hardened and became his gravestone. "And it will all come out."

And then she took too many sleeping pills, and joined her loved ones in death.

And now, as Clark bent over the governor and confirmed that Tommy Silver's heart had stopped . . . *been stopped* . . . a white shape drifted over the cornfield. Chloe whispered, "Emily."

The ghostly woman glided past them without giving any indication that she heard or saw them, moving to a patch of field that had recently been disturbed.

Bending down, she held out her arms.

From beneath the earth, the ghost child reemerged. He sprang into her arms, and they faded from view.

"I think it's over now," Clark said.

As if on cue, the grandfather clock in the Welles house stopped. Then the sick, mad house collapsed in a groaning crash.

In front of the Smallville Hotel, Janice Brucker's car was packed with a few essential belongings. Everything else had been destroyed in the farmhouse. Ginger lingered with Joel; they would see each other soon—Janice had pulled strings, as she had promised to do, and Joel would be going to the university in the fall.

She turned and regarded Lex, who stood apart from the others and said nothing.

Then she walked up to him and said, "What did the governor have on your family?"

Lex smiled sadly. "What didn't he have?" Then he added, "I didn't know about . . . what my father did, Janice. Truly." He paused. "There's no reason to go now. Welles is dead."

She looked at him with utter contempt. "Oh, there's plenty of reason. My husband is dead, too. And as usual, the Luthors are going to get away with it."

Then Ginger swept past him to get into the car.

Lex turned to Clark, who had come with Lana, Chloe, and Pete to say good-bye.

Clark gazed at him, then walked over to him and said, "Why did you move the skeleton and repave the floor, Lex? To protect Welles? Or yourself?"

Lex looked upset. "You're assuming that I did it."

Clark raised his chin. "Didn't you?"

"Your family has its secrets, Clark, and so does mine," Lex murmured.

Clark swept past him without saying another word.

◆◆◆

Back in their Metropolis high-rise apartment, Ginger looked in on her mother, who was sleeping soundly. A faint, sweet smile wreathed Janice Brucker's face.

"Sweet dreams, Mom," Ginger whispered.

Ginger bent over her mother and planted a kiss on her forehead.

That night, as he slept, Clark dreamed of ghosts: soft hands, wrapping a blanket around him; soft lips, kissing him good-bye, forever good-bye.

He dreamed words of farewell in a language he would never hear again.

He dreamed answers to the questions that would haunt him all his life.

When he woke, they would haunt him still.

But for now, he dreamed.

ABOUT THE AUTHOR

NANCY HOLDER has written over 50 novels and 200 short stroies, essays, and articles, including many projects for *Buffy the Vampire Slayer, Angel,* and *Highlander: The TV Series.* Her books have appeared on the Los Angeles Times bestseller list, and she had received four Bram Stoker Awards for fiction from the Horror Writers Association. Her work has appeared on the lists of recommended works for the American Library Association, American Reading Association, the New York Times Library Association, and others. She lives in San Diego with her daughter, Belle, two cats, and a dog.

READ MORE

SMALLVILLE

NOVELS!

═══════════════

STRANGE VISITORS
(0-446-61213-8)
By Roger Stern

◆

WHODUNNIT
(0-446-61216-2)
By Dean Wesley Smith
AVAILABLE MARCH 2003